REPLENISHED: A NOVEL

William Michael Davidson

Copyright © 2022 William Michael Davidson

All rights reserved.

ISBN: 9798441637510

Cover and interior art by Brian Brinlee

This is a work of fiction. Unless otherwise indicated, all the names, characters, businesses, places, events and incidents in this book are either the product of the author's imagination or used in a fictitious manner. Any resemblance to actual persons, living or dead, or actual events is purely coincidental.

"If you go by a school and the kids don't whistle, back to the drawing board."
—Harley Earl, designer of the Corvette

"If everything seems under control, you're not going fast enough."
—Mario Andretti

For my dad and father-in-law (who know way more about Corvettes than I ever will).

FULL TANK

Chapter One

75.70 Liters of Fuel Remaining

1

I am doing over one hundred miles an hour on I-5 South and traveling so fast it feels like the front of my vehicle will lift off the ground.

In ten minutes I'll be in San Diego, and not long after that I'll be in Mexico. I'm sure there will be some border stop before I cross over, but maybe I can find a way around it. If they have one of those rising barriers, I'll just smash through it.

At this speed, it'll break apart into a million pieces.

I'm in my black '69 Corvette Stingray, and it's loud in here. Lots of road and wind noise.

Clutching the steering wheel with both hands, I look at the rearview mirror and see the lights flashing behind me.

There are eight police cars that I can count. Three copters in the air. It is nearing midnight, and that's a good thing. I would never be able to pick up this much speed and get this far on the freeway if this were happening during daylight hours.

The "victim" is in the passenger seat beside me, lifeless and leaning against the passenger door. Blood is everywhere. On the body of the victim and all over me. I can no longer hear the raspy breathing and the gurgling attempts to take a breath, because now I'm pretty convinced I'm chauffeuring a corpse.

My phone is on the center console to the right of the stick. I'm streaming local news, listening to the updates on my own high-speed pursuit. It is a bizarre feeling. On the small screen of my iPhone, I can see myself driving. The black Stingray rockets down Interstate 5, blanched in the white spotlights of the overhead copters.

"Authorities believe the suspect is armed and dangerous," one of the newscasters says.

I reach for my phone, pick it up, and hold it my ear. There's too much road noise in here and it's hard to hear. I leave bloodied fingerprints on the small screen.

"Authorities also believe the suspect has a victim in his car," the same newscaster says. I've heard this man before on the local news. He's a young guy with a deep voice. "The question that remains, of course, is whether or not the victim is still alive."

I look to my right and see the mangled face. The matted hair. The lifeless thing beside me.

"Looks dead to me," I mumble.

"We have some breaking news," the newscaster says. "We believe we have the identity of the suspect. Charlie Phoenix. Forty-five. A businessman, of all things. He owns a storage facility here in Long Beach."

"I own two of them," I mumble again.
Can't the news get anything right?

2

No matter how fast I drive, I can't avoid the copters' spotlights.

They might lose me for a second, but then, once again, they have me.

And that's when I think of an idea: light. I'm too easy a target.

I turn off the pop-up headlights, and the road in front of me goes black. I'm not sure it will help me, but maybe it will give me a slight edge.

Yet there are bigger problems ahead of me. There's a traffic jam on the freeway. I see the blockade of red taillights. Maybe there's been an accident. Maybe it's some kind of road construction. But if I stay this course on I-5, I'm going to have to come to a dead stop in the middle of this pursuit, and that just can't happen.

I need to get off.

I wipe sweat from my forehead. My heart is its own V8, doing 5000 RPMs in my chest.

When I buzz past a freeway overpass, I see a small crowd that has gathered because they've seen this high-speed pursuit on the news and made the trip out here to root for me. People are sick like that. A couple people are even holding a giant sign that reads: KEEP RUNNING! DOWN WITH THE POLICE!

I snicker.

They don't even know me.

There is one option. I can see an off-ramp before the traffic backup. It'll be rough, but I can make it.

I ease off the gas, downshift to third, and veer toward it. The palm of my hand is sweaty and slippery on the ball grip of the stick.

The phone goes flying off the center console.

The bloodied "victim" slides into me, but I push the body away.

3

Now I'm here.

On some street near San Diego, and I have an open road ahead of me. I floor it.

There are stoplights ahead, and I choose to fly through the first red light without stopping. I don't check the cross traffic at all, but I close my eyes as I tear right through the red and pray I don't hit anything. It works. When I open my eyes, I'm on the other side of the intersection, but now there's another problem. I see police cars ahead of me on both sides of the road. Some kind of roadblock.

My eyes flick to the rearview mirror.

They're behind me too. A swarm of emergency lights and sirens gaining on me.

I have to turn around, but I can't slow down much.

I've seen how this works.

If I slow down too much, they'll perform some kind of pit maneuver on me, intentionally clip the backside of my Stingray with their bullbars and send me spinning like a teacup.

I have to make the U-turn, but I have to do it while moving as fast as I can.

There's only one solution: a bootleg turn.

4

I slow down to about thirty miles an hour for the upcoming intersection, and with one hand on the top of the steering wheel, I reach for the emergency brake.

I turn the wheel a little to the right, and then I apply the brake while cranking the wheel sharply to the left until my hand is in the six o'clock position. Tires squeal. I smell burning rubber. For a brief moment, I wonder: Am I controlling the car, or is it controlling me? Invisible pressure pushes me deeper into my seat.

I'm traveling sideways down the street, smoke pluming from the tires.

In another car, I would worry about the tires blowing out. But I know my Stingray. They'll hold up just fine.

When I've done a full 180 and come to a near stop, I release the emergency brake, straighten the wheel, downshift into first, and accelerate. The engine rumbles like a beast. Now I'm traveling in the opposite direction, and I'm protected by the concrete median in the street. The police vehicles in pursuit buzz past me on the other side of the road, and the roadblock that was in front of me is now in my rearview mirror.

I cry out in victory. I did it!

But now there's a new problem.

Another roadblock ahead.

Several cop cars stopped in the middle of the street.

"No!" I scream and slam my hand against the steering wheel.

5

There's one way to avoid the roadblock.

There's an on-ramp to I-5 South just in front of the stopped cop cars and, having no choice, I drive onto the same freeway I just exited.

But I know where this will lead me.

As I merge onto the freeway, I can see the sea of red taillights in front of me. The same taillights I tried to avoid by getting off the freeway to begin with.

Now the copters are back.

White spotlights engulf my vehicle.

Sirens wail behind me.

I slow my vehicle and look toward the blood-soaked body in the passenger seat.

"I'm sorry," I say, reaching for the cold hand of my alleged victim. "I tried."

Chapter Two

74.16 Liters of Fuel Remaining

1

My nightmares are pretty accurate about what happened before my arrest on I-5 South—except the bootleg turn.

I was forty-five then and a businessman.

I couldn't have swung that maneuver if my life depended on it.

I may be the only person convicted of murder who blamed his car for what went down, but that's really what happened. I'm not going to fool myself: I don't expect anyone to believe me. I mean, why would they? My own family doesn't believe me and has completely disowned me, and it's not like I can really blame them all that much. If I were in their shoes, I'd probably think just like them. The prison doctor even wanted to put me on brake fluid.

That's what we call psycho meds on Death Row.

It's miserable here, but what else would one expect?

My cell in San Quentin is the size of a master closet. The walls are about eight by eight, the ceiling a little under ten feet, and there is only one small window that lets in a single, narrow shaft of light, which serves as a proverbial reminder that any hope of leaving this place and regathering what is left of the fragmented remains of my life is a pipe dream. Plain and simple, I'm stuck here until my assigned appointment with lethal injection. My lawyer told me I have the right to die by gas inhalation and the State would grant it, but I stuck with lethal injection.

It's a sad thing, really.

When I was on the outside, I used to sit around and contemplate simpler decisions. What restaurant to get takeout from? What stocks to invest in? What socks to wear today? Now, as I look back, it seems like another life.

2

At least I eat three solid meals a day in here, but the food is nothing to get excited about. No shock there. Three times a day—five in the morning, eleven o'clock, and half past four—a tray of bland, though nutritive, food is delivered to my cell, complete with a plastic spork. The spork is provided for obvious reasons. The State wants to make sure I adhere to my agreement with lethal injection and not end my time in Death Row with the help of a utensil. And if there's one thing I've learned in my fifty-three years of living, it's this: The government wants to do things its way. It wants to tax you the way it wants, and it wants to kill you the way it wants.

Really, it's the same thing, I suppose. In the end, it all kills you.

At least I get to shower. Only every other day, but it's not like I'm having to entertain guests in my cell. And this place is obsessed with counting. Every hour around the clock, I'm looked in on and counted like a piece of cattle. You'd think they'd spend their time doing something more productive. Where am I going to go? I'm in this locked cell nearly every hour of the day, and when I am taken to the showers or the exercise yard, I'm in handcuffs.

There's a little entertainment here, I suppose. I'm given snacks—Ritz Crackers are my favorite—and I have access to a radio and a small twelve-inch television positioned outside the bars of my cell. There's no cable television, unfortunately, so lately I've been watching a few daytime soaps and spending my afternoons and early evenings listening to classic rock. It's summertime and there's no air conditioning here, so watching the soaps and listening to the radio at least helps me take my mind off how stuffy and humid everything is.

We get mail too, but I don't receive much in that regard.

My son doesn't talk to me anymore.

And my ex-girlfriend—well, I'll get to that.

The clothing here is about what you'd expect. All the inmates wear blue pants and blue shirts, but the ones like me—those on Death Row—wear orange shirts. Sometimes I wonder if it's simply Fate playing a final, cruel joke on me, because I've hated the color orange since I was a kid. It never went well with me. My ex-wife thought that and so did my ex-girlfriend, so there may be some truth in it.

Maybe it's my complexion. My face, so I've been told, is always kind of flushed—like I just threw back a couple shots of whiskey. And I'm short. Just five and half feet. The thinning hair doesn't help either. I have the same chance of being called up by *GQ* for a cover shoot as I have of getting out of this hellhole.

I think in my case, when you haven't been dealt the best hand in the genetic deck of cards, it's best to stick with the darker colors like black, navy, or maybe charcoal. I think I read that once in a *Men's Journal* magazine. That's how I dressed in my old life when I was an entrepreneur and co-owner of two successful storage facilities. I did well. Very well.

And that's where the car comes in.

The '69 Corvette Stingray.

3

My lawyer is meeting with me soon, one of the very few times I'll be in a room without a guard staring me down. Sure, he'll be right outside the door and I'll be shackled up, but it's refreshing to look at another human being who isn't wearing a badge and carrying a baton at his side.

My original attorney, Hasim, who defended me during my trial, is long gone.

He cost a fortune, and I couldn't afford him anymore, especially after the civil trial.

This new attorney, Mick Nelson, has been appointed by the State and doesn't look a year over thirty. Lawyer Nelson is here for obvious reasons: a last-minute Stay of Execution. Nearly all inmates like me are given one of these, and I've already received my first. The judge issued a temporary order to stop the execution because some minor, irrelevant detail needed sorting out. Maybe there was a misspelling on one of the legal filings or someone forgot to check a box on one of the seemingly endless amounts of paperwork that goes into killing a man. Whatever it is, it was totally meaningless.

I'm hoping for a second.

But either way, I know the end is near. Even if this last-minute Stay of Execution works, I feel inevitability creeping toward me.

I might try telling Mick Nelson the truth, but I'm sure he won't believe me either. Nobody does. And that's the problem I find myself in. More than I want to live, I just want someone to believe me.

I'm not a killer.

It was the car's fault.

The '69 Stingray.

Chapter Three

72.61 Liters of Fuel Remaining

1

For everything to make sense, I must go back to my ex-wife. Her name is Mara, and we married for the worst of reasons: youthful love. The marriage lasted eighteen years, which is quite amazing, considering our dynamics. But it was a lonely, desert-like expanse of eighteen years.

I think the real problem happened when our son Seth died of SIDS at only two months old. Seth's older brother, Adam, who was only two years old when his little brother died in the nursery, kept us together for a long time out of obligation—but we never really processed the grief. I know I didn't, and it certainly fit Mara's description of me. I was, in her words, "emotionally distant" and "unavailable," and I won't argue with that.

It's hard to be "emotionally available" to a woman who salves her grief by banging another man.

2

We went in two wildly different directions.

I poured myself into commercial real estate and eventually bought two storage facilities.

She went out and found another guy.

We never really talked about the affair, but we knew it was there. I was an ostrich, and I buried my head in the sand and trucked on and minded my own business until, at last, while getting Chinese takeout one Sunday night, she told me very calmly that she thought it was best that we went in our own directions. And what was I to say? In truth, we'd been going in different directions for a long, long time. Over kung pao chicken and wontons we discussed what she wanted, and I was shocked how easy it was. She didn't want that much. Freedom, it seemed, was her main desire—that and Shane Miller, the guy she'd been sleeping with for the majority of our marriage. He had lots of money, had just recently severed ties with his own wife, and I think that finally gave them a green light.

"I'll hire an attorney," she explained cordially. "No crazy stuff. Just someone to get the ball rolling and make sure everything happens the right way. I don't want anything, Charlie. I just want us to go in our own directions and be happy."

I did get one good thing out of the marriage. I got Adam, who was a sophomore at Wilson High School when Mara decided to leave me. For the most part, Adam was a decent kid, but I think he saw the divorce long before I did and chose his side long before I knew there were sides.

He was a mama's boy, plain and simple.

More so, however, I think he was enmeshed in his relationship with Mom. They *needed* each other. They *confided* in each other. Even when it came to her affair, Adam, with all the wisdom of a sixteen-year-old, was there to listen to Mom and give her extramarital advice.

It was demented.

Connecting with him in any meaningful way was a colossal struggle.

But everything really started that day when my wife told me she was leaving me. I put away the Chinese food, cracked open a fortune cookie, pulled out the little strip of paper, and read my fortune: DON'T PURSUE HAPPINESS. CREATE IT.

I thought for a while. Maybe that was why things went south. I never really tried to work on the relationship. I just kind of stood there like some paralyzed observer and watched it crumble in front of my eyes.

Within three days, my wife packed her bags, and she and Adam moved out. I was surprised how cordial everything was. There was no argument. No raised voices. Like duteous undertakers, we dumped the marriage into a burial plot and shoveled on the dirt. When she was ready to hand over her key, we sat down at the same dining room table where we'd had our last meal and talked more specifics. She would file the paperwork very soon. Nothing would be contentious. Not at all. She only wanted things to be fair—even if fair meant she wouldn't get what she wanted—because eighteen years is a long time to spend with someone, and she wanted to honor that.

"I really do wish you the best, Charlie," she told me, standing by the front door. She bent down and kissed me on the cheek. "Sometimes things like this happen in life, and you have to understand it's not you."

"I know," I said. "I wish you the best, and we'll talk soon. Tell Adam I said hello."

"Well, of course I will, but why not just call him?"

"The kid usually doesn't call me back."

She looked at me with sad puppy eyes. "I know. He's in high school, and he's young. You know how that goes. Adam said he's really looking forward to living with me and Shane."

"He is?"

"Yes. He and Shane really do get along. You know, Shane works as an investment banker. He's thinking of taking Adam on a trip to give him the feel for things. It'd be good for him. Adam's been so indecisive about what to do with his future."

"Yeah, that probably would be good for him."

"We'll talk soon." She smiled, winked, and skittered off toward the Jaguar I'd bought her for her last birthday.

I closed the door, went back into my empty house, and stood in the living room.

Conflicting emotions assaulted me.

Was I sad? Sure, but I didn't feel sad in the way that I should.

Was I angry? Kind of, but angrier at myself more than anything.

Surprisingly, I felt a strange sense of relief wash over me.

I looked at my reflection in the mirror. There I was, all forty-five years of me, in what was supposedly my prime. But the short, balding, middle-aged guy looking back at me sure didn't look like a man in his prime—quite the contrary. I knew where this kind of thinking would lead me and the women I'd bring home, the cars I'd buy, the bars I'd visit—all in an effort to push back the cruel hands of fate. I'd known lots of people who'd taken a crazy drive down the Road of Midlife Crisis.

But if I had to go down that road, I might as well do it in style.

I grabbed the *Hemmings Classic Car Magazine* off the couch and headed to the door.

Chapter Four

71.06 Liters of Fuel Remaining

1

I had barely pulled out of the driveway when my phone rang. It was my son, Adam. I was shocked to see he was calling, so I pulled to the side of the road and took the call.

"Hey, Adam."

"Are you home right now?"

"Not at the moment. I was just going on a quick errand. What's going on? Haven't heard from you in a while."

"Yeah, I've been busy. Listen, I still have some stuff at your house."

I hated that phrase, *your house*. Not long ago it was his house too.

"I was hoping I could swing by and pick up a few last things. I've been meaning to get it."

"Are you liking living with this Shane guy?"

"Yeah, he's okay. Really nice house."

"Well, you're always welcome. You can grab what you need anytime."

"How about in a couple of hours?"

"Sure thing. I'll be here. Maybe I'll whip up a meal for us, okay?"

"We'll see," he said and hung up.

Well, at least it wasn't a *no*. Much better than the last several times I'd offered to make him a meal or take him out.

2

I pushed the cell phone back into the front pocket of my slacks and was about to pull back onto the street when my phone went off again. Now what? I retrieved my phone and looked at the incoming number: *Fergus*. I hesitated about taking the call, but it seemed as good a time as any. No matter what, this was an issue I had to deal with.

"Hello, Fergus," I said.

"I'm surprised you took my call. You've been avoiding me. I tried calling you ten times yesterday alone. Are you going to respond to my messages or make me hunt you down?"

"Fergus, I don't have much more to say to you. I think everything I've needed to say has already been said. What do you want from me?"

"You know what I want from you."

"Yes, and that's not going to happen. You've lost the job. It's over."

He didn't say anything, but I heard him breathing.

"I don't know how many times I'm going to need to tell you this, Fergus, but you're not working at my storage facility anymore. You're my nephew, and I tried to do what a good uncle does and hire you, but you can't be a relief manager and have sex with your girlfriends in the vacant storage facilities."

"It's not like they were underage or anything," he said.

"That doesn't matter, Fergus. You were on the job. And smoking bud on the job didn't exactly help the situation. How old are you?"

"Twenty-eight."

"Yeah, twenty-eight. In two years, you're going to be thirty. It's time to make some responsible decisions."

That was why I'd chosen to hire Fergus in the first place—to save him from the irresponsible decisions he'd made his whole life. Fergus, it seemed, had been gifted from the womb in making dumb choices. Dropped out of high school. Didn't get his GED. Got in trouble with the law in his early twenties. Drugs. Public intoxication. Harassment. And the list went on.

I hadn't known Fergus well during his growing-up years, but he was Mara's brother's son. It was my way of helping out family, but in the end, it was definitely a mistake.

Fortunately, Mara and her brother barely talked.

Nobody cared when I fired him.

"You said you'd help me," Fergus complained. "I've contacted a lawyer. He said you can't just fire me like you did."

"Fergus, I can't return to the world of delusion with you."

"I want my job back, or at least some kind of severance package."

"You're not getting a severance package, Fergus, and you're definitely not getting your job back. You were fired for good reason."

"My lawyer disagrees." I'd heard this complaint before, and I'd already received the letters. "You never told me I couldn't light up on my breaks and, as far as the girls, all of it was consensual. And it only happened a few times, Charlie. It's not like your storage facility fell apart. You never told me I couldn't have a quick conjugal visit on my breaks."

"It didn't just happen on your breaks. And there's some things an employer shouldn't have to tell an employee."

But Fergus clung to his truth like a drowning man clings to a life raft. He had some tacky lawyer named Buck Valentine send me letter after letter arguing that I was open to a lawsuit because his termination was illegal. Fergus didn't have proper HR training, did not know it was against company policy to smoke medical marijuana during breaks, and as far as the women were concerned, the letters argued that I had no proof that he had actually engaged in conjugal visits.

And it was true. Kind of.

I wasn't physically present, but I'd seen the security footage of Fergus standing in front of one of the units, pants down, with some bimbo on her knees in front of him.

The angle was off, and I couldn't see exactly what was happening, but it didn't take much imagination.

I highly doubted he'd dropped his jeans so she could shine his shoes.

There was other footage too. Fergus going into vacant storage units with women, coming out an hour later while zipping up his fly and tightening his belt.

Maybe Fergus missed his calling. He should have gone into the porn business or something.

Whatever the case, this Buck Valentine was a quack. I don't know how much Fergus was paying him, but it couldn't have been much. There were typos in the letters he sent, and in one of them, he didn't even spell my name correctly. He spelled Phoenix, my last name, with an S: *Phoenis.*

Sometimes I wondered if there really was a Buck Valentine. There was no return address, just a PO Box, and it wouldn't be unlike Fergus to misspell the name of his own uncle and former boss. Maybe this cheap attorney was something Fergus conjured up to rattle my cage.

Wouldn't surprise me at all.

3

But I did worry, a little. It was mentally tiring. Was it possible that Fergus had some kind of case here? One thing I've learned being a business owner is that the courts always seem to favor the little guy. Once upon a time, I think the court system actually tried to do what was right, but these days it seemed like the court just wanted to make everybody equal.

And that usually meant playing Robin Hood.

I was the Sheriff of Nottingham. Fergus was a pauper in need.

"Fergus," I said calmly, "you need to stop calling me. It's over, alright? Totally over."

"You're gonna get a way better deal if you negotiate through me. We don't want to file this complaint."

"I'm not going to negotiate through you or anyone. There's nothing to neg—"

"And I'd hate it if things got ugly."

I hung up the phone. I was done. I should never have answered in the first place.

As I pulled back onto the street, I was reminded of the problems I had with Fergus as a relief manager. On top of sexual escapades, he had a temper. A really bad one.

And sometimes, it worried me.

Chapter Five

69.52 Liters of Fuel Remaining

1

I hadn't felt like this since I was a teenager. The last time I asked a woman out, it had been my soon-to-be ex-wife, Mara, and that seemed like another life entirely. I was much younger then, much more social, and I felt suddenly clumsy and out of place considering what I was about to do. I might as well try slipping on a pair of jeans that fit me back in college. I'd probably have as much luck at that.

I took a deep breath and walked through the front doors of Eden's Garden, the small café that I frequented most Saturday mornings. As I walked inside, my hernia pain acted up, and it felt like my groin muscles were on fire. I was able to alleviate some of the pain with a rigid, peg-legged walk. I had a procedure scheduled in four months. A wire mesh would supposedly take care of the whole thing, and I would be, according to my doctor, "as good as new."

I'd intentionally pushed it way back. I didn't like the idea of surgery.

I took a table at my usual spot in the corner of the café, beside the French doors overlooking the garden, and I had hardly sat down when Kiki approached with a pot of steaming macadamia coffee in her hand. She looked her usual: cheerful, big Disney-princess eyes, flaming red hair, and a cute face specked with freckles. I had learned through brief conversations with her that she had gone through a nasty breakup several months ago, never had kids, and was—in her words—spreading her wings. She was working six days a week and considering going back to school for a teaching credential. Getting her life on track. She was only in her early thirties, and she figured if she didn't do it soon, it was never going to happen.

As usual, I felt what I can only explain as teenage butterflies as she approached my table and poured a cup of coffee.

"Glad to see you again, Charlie," she said, grinning. She had dimples and a cute elfish nose. "I was hoping I'd see you this morning."

"You were?"

"I was," she said. "After all, you are my favorite customer."

I think that was what first drew me to her. My home had been a mausoleum for years. Kiki still had life in her. She was a flame of youth. Mara, I suppose, had some of it too, but she'd ceased sharing that side of herself with me;

all of that, I suppose, went to Shane Miller. I was just the guy who paid the bills, stocked the fridge with food, and bought her the occasional car.

"Well, I'm very glad to see you. I'll do the usual."

"Alright, then. Egg whites, turkey sausage, and wheat toast—hold the butter. Living wild there, huh?"

"Someone has to."

"Is that how you stay so sexy?"

"It helps," I said, "but most of it's in the DNA."

I hoped I wasn't too forward. This flirting stuff was new territory for me.

She grabbed my menu. "Coming right up."

"When's your break today?"

She was about to leave, but my question caused her to swivel around suddenly. "What did you ask me?"

"I asked what time your break is."

She sat her pot of coffee on the table, placed both slender hands on her hips, and teasingly asked, "And why, good sir, would you want to know?"

I chose to be as blunt as possible. It seemed the best course of action, considering the circumstances. "I've been wanting to ask you for a long time if you'd like to sit down and share a meal with me. I've noticed you usually take your break right now. I would love the company."

"Hmm," she said, and she fluttered her big eyes in what appeared to be a hopeful sign. I noticed her gaze darting to my hand, which, since my wife left, no longer had a wedding ring on it. "I'm off in five. I'll give the table to Sally, and yeah, I'll be right back. I'm pretty hungry myself."

2

"Gone just like that, huh?" she asked. I'd given her the brief version of the story. In all honesty, I wasn't sure there was a long one.

"Yeah, she's gone. Left with the same guy she's been sleeping with all these years, so I guess it wasn't really a shock."

"So what do you do now?" She bit into a piece of sourdough toast, sipped her glass of ice water. "It's time to reinvent yourself, don't you think? That's what I had to do. When I broke up with Duncan, I thought my life was over. But I had to break up with him. It was terrible."

"Really?"

"Yeah, really. It was an abusive relationship. I didn't know better, but I'm glad it's in my past. Now that I'm out of that mess, I'm focusing on my future. I think I've told you before. I want to be a teacher one day."

"You have, and I think that's wonderful."

"Don't you have kids?"

"Yes, one son. Sixteen years old. Adam. His brother, Seth, died when he was just two months old."

"I'm so sorry," she said.

"That's okay. It was a long time ago."

"Well, now that you're on the market again, how are you going to reinvent yourself?"

"Well, I was hoping to start off by asking a gorgeous woman out on a date."

"Gorgeous, huh?"

"Completely."

"Describe for me."

"Beautiful face. Freckles. Hair the color of fire. A smile that feels warm, safe."

"She sounds like a total keeper." Kiki sipped her water, looked at me playfully. She leaned forward. "A girl like that can be very high maintenance. She'd probably want to go somewhere very nice and be very pampered."

"Well, I think I can manage that."

"Yeah, you are a little older." She caught herself and touched my arm. "Not in a bad way, mind you. I mean you're a little older in the sense that you're refined, have some style, some taste, and the means to pamper a woman."

"Well, I certainly try."

"What's your last name?" Kiki asked, giggling. "It just occurred to me. You've come here a thousand times, Charlie, and I don't know your last name."

"Phoenix."

"Phoenix, huh? Charlie Phoenix. Does this mean you rise from the ashes, Charlie?"

"I guess we'll find that out together."

Chapter Six

67.98 Liters of Fuel Remaining

1

I thought about the Corvette the entire drive home. I enjoyed my Lexus. It was comfortable and everything I needed, but it didn't seem to fit me anymore. Not in this new life. As I pulled into my driveway, I decided I would follow through with contacting Richard Pratt—something I'd contemplated when I first saw the ad in the back of the *Hemmings Classic Car Magazine.* I'd added his number to my phone contacts.

I was startled when I noticed that the front door of my house was ajar. Hadn't I closed and locked it?

One thought came to me: Fergus. Was it possible? Was he irate and crazy enough to have broken into my house? I tried to rethink my brief conversation with him. Did I say that I was away from home?

I wasn't entirely sure what to do. My first thought was to call the police because I would be no match for him. He was far taller, far stronger, and if something did escalate into a physical confrontation, I would clearly be the underdog.

I was reaching for my phone when I noticed by son walk out of the front door with a box in his arms.

I took a deep breath.

In my rearview mirror, I saw some high school friend of his parked several cars behind me in a Ford Ranger, waiting for him. Adam didn't have his license yet.

I should have noticed. I'd seen this friend before. Couldn't remember his name.

I got out of the car just as Adam walked out of the house, the box cradled in his hands. He looked like he hadn't been to the barber in quite some time. His hair was shaggy. I'm not sure many combs had passed through it since he hit puberty.

"Thanks a lot, Dad!" he snapped.

I paused. What did I do? "What happened?"

"You weren't here. That's what happened. Luckily, you left your back window open."

Then it hit me. I'd forgotten. I had been so consumed in my conversation with Kiki, I completely forgot about him coming over.

"I'm sorry. I was having breakfast with someone—it went way longer than I thought—and I'm totally sorry. Here, let me get that for you."

I reached for the box, but he wouldn't hand it over. Pure stubbornness. When he was a little kid, I thought it was cute and often said he'd inherited it from me. Now, as a teenager, it wasn't so cute, and I tended to blame that trait more and more on his mom. I followed him to his friend's truck, where he dropped the box into the back.

"Well, thanks Dad, good seeing you."

"Wait, I just got here. Why don't you stick around for a bit? I'm still a little hungry. We can grab a bite to eat."

"I don't think so."

"Look, Adam, it's not a big deal. This doesn't have to be a thing. It just slipped my mind."

"It happens a lot, Dad."

I'm not sure where and how my relationship with my son went off the rails, but I think it happened around the age of twelve. He became incredibly artistic, almost a recluse, and he spent most of his time debating about becoming a professional poet or rock star. Mara—who lived in La La Land herself—encouraged it while I tried to be a mild voice of reason. I didn't discourage the writing or the music, I just probed him with questions. *Do you think you're going to support a family writing poetry? Are you going to pass up college to play in a band with your friends?*

I didn't mean it to be discouraging, but that was how it came across.

Just rejection. That was all he saw in it.

And I suppose it culminated when his band, the Flying Death Ninjas, played a sold-out gig at a local joint called DiPiazza's. I think that was the nail in the coffin. I couldn't go. I had an important business meeting. That was the same night I met with Trey, my business partner, to discuss Fergus's termination.

I wished I could take it back, in more ways than one.

"How's the band going?"

He paused before getting into his friend's truck and just looked at me.

"You're still playing in the band, right? The Flying Death Ninjas?"

"Dad, that was two bands ago." He rolled his eyes with disgruntled teenage precision. "It's a new band now. We call ourselves Pure Evil."

"Pure Evil, huh?" I thought about what to say and tried to push away my innate cynicism. George, one of my best friends, had a kid who was a little older than Adam. His son just got accepted to UCLA. Trey, my business partner, had a niece who was on the path to medical school. My son looked like he hadn't groomed himself in the last week and was playing in a band called Pure Evil.

It wasn't what I envisioned for him.

"Yeah, you should come see us play sometime."

"Well, send me an invite, Adam. I'd love to."

"I did. We're playing in Hollywood."

I did remember a text, but it was a mass text advertising a band that was playing. As I stood there, I realized that probably was the name of the band. Pure Evil. But I didn't know it was *his* band. How was I supposed to know? This was the core of the problem: Adam wanted me to figure him out. Crawl into his dark, artistic cavern and understand him.

But he didn't give me much help. Very little.

"See you, Dad."

"Let me know if you want to come over for a meal. We can grab dinner. Lunch. Whatever."

"Thanks."

He climbed into the truck.

The Ford Ranger sped down the road in a blur that was reminiscent of his own childhood.

I blinked, and that little boy was gone.

2

I poured myself a cup of coffee, went out to my back patio, and took my *Hemmings Classic Car Magazine* with me.

There it was: the '69 Corvette, the one I'd dreamed of owning ever since I was a kid and my dad took me to a car auction in Scottsdale, Arizona. He'd wanted to buy it then, and strangely, on his deathbed, as the cancer took the little that was left of him, he talked about the '69 Stingray. One of his greatest regrets was not buying it.

Maybe that was why, in my middle years, it represented something else for me: defiance of age and death, perhaps.

I looked at the pictures of the sleek, black body of the Vette and the chrome-like curves. The '69 model was an improvement over the '68, most notably in the modification of the Stingray badge, but the same thing could be found beneath the hood: the L88 427 cubic-inch big-block engine, with a solid-lifter camshaft and a giant Holley four-barrel carburetor. Only 111,268 miles on the odometer. It was unclear from the ad when it had been restored and whether the miles on the odometer were post-restoration.

Per the 900 code on the Corvette's trim tag, it was still the original color: Tuxedo Black. The seller claimed no body blemishes, swirl marks, scratches, or chips in the paintwork. This must have been part of the restoration. The exterior glass was reported to be original, with no wear, and seals that were "like new." The T-tops were supposedly leak-free, and the car rolled on factory rally wheels and wore the optional bright chrome front fender louver trim.

The photos of the interior looked equally impressive. The 420-code Saddle interior looked as fresh and clean as it did the day it was first assembled. No new parts in the interior like vinyl seat covers, carpet, door panels, or other trim components—this thing was restored to look entirely original. Even the round gauges hadn't been replaced with something new. The console plaque detailing fuel specs was still there, an improvement from the '68 models. The heater and stock AM/FM radio worked perfectly, and the brown vinyl seats looked like they'd never been sat on.

The engine was reportedly authentic to factory specifications, from the chrome air clear to the Tonawanda engine plant decal on the right-hand valve cover. It ran well. The four-speed Muncie gearbox shifted normally, and the chassis and suspension were up to factory specifications, including the manual steering, the four-wheel-disc brake system, suspension components, and bushings. There were no leaks. The car drove normally.

All of this, of course, was according to the ad. I needed to see it with my own eyes.

The seller, Richard Pratt, was selling the car for $74,000.

I imagined what it would be like to crawl inside the car, start it, and listen to the loud rumbling of the V8. I hadn't driven a stick shift since I was a young man, and to be able to do it again—and in such a classic automobile—would be a dream.

Of course, there was the reality of the money. It was a lot of money, but I had it. I could easily pull it from my mutual funds. Sure, it probably wasn't the smartest thing to do, and on the eve of a divorce it was probably an even more foolish decision to make, but I could do it.

This wasn't going to be a contentious divorce. Mara wanted *out* more than she wanted money, and there was plenty to divide. She'd already left the house, and her long-time lover had enough money to buy her whatever she wanted. She had told me she didn't want to fight. She didn't need money. She didn't want the house.

I looked at the pictures of the black Corvette. It was as sexy as any women I'd ever seen, and suddenly I realized why middle-aged men—guys my age—fell in love with cars. In a world that glorified youth and vitality, if you picked the right car—and you took care of it—it would turn more heads than any of the new eco-friendly, suburban, run-of-the-mill autos assembled these days.

It was a classic.

Maybe, at the end of the day, I just related to the car.

Because that was how I felt about myself.

I'd lost sense of who I was somewhere down the road.

And there was something alluring about the car, something dangerous, and that was what I wanted. For the first time in my life, I wanted to do something that made no sense. Something reckless, even.

I grabbed my cell and dialed the number of the seller. He answered on the second ring. "Hello?"

"Hi. My name is Charlie Phoenix. I'd like to take a look at your Corvette."

As I look back, I should have seen the warning signs even then. The raspy voice. The eagerness to pick up the phone and make a sale.

But I didn't.

And it cost me everything.

3

After I got off the phone with Richard, having made arrangements to see the car, Chuck, the neighborhood cat, showed up. He was a domestic shorthair. Gray with a big patch of white across the chest.

I wasn't sure who Chuck's owner was—or if there was an owner out there—and in the last several months, I had sort of adopted him. I put out milk one day, a little bit of food, and just like that, Chuck and I were thick as thieves.

I think we had some things in common.

Chuck was a little older. A little tubby. A little grumpy.

I often imagined that Chuck, like me, was going through a bit of a midlife crisis. Maybe he had a feline-woman back home who'd walked out on him too.

Chuck and I spent many evenings on that back patio, drowning ourselves in our sorrows.

I preferred glasses of brandy. Chuck opted for bowls of milk.

"Guess what, Chuck?" I told him. "I'm getting a '69 Stingray. What do you think?"

He didn't look so impressed. Just meowed.

Then I knew why.

"Sorry, buddy," I said.

His bowl of food was empty. I went inside to dish him up a serving.

Chapter Seven

66.43 Liters of Fuel Remaining

1

I assumed Richard Pratt would give me directions to his shop to look at the car, but I was wrong. He was doing errands the following day and offered to drive the Corvette to my house. He knew his stuff, that was for sure, and he corroborated everything the article claimed about the car.

I gave him my address and spent the next day boxing up a few things Mara had forgotten to take with her. Around noon, I heard the Corvette pull up in front of my house. I couldn't believe it was here. As I walked out the front door of my home, I saw the Stingray in my own driveway and heard the loud growling of the V8. The engine powered off, and when the sleek black door swung open, a tall, angular man dressed in dark slacks and a white button-down shirt stepped out of the vehicle.

"I'm Richard Pratt," he said simply, his hand extended toward me.

It was difficult to determine his age. Fifty? Sixty? He was a lean man with bronze skin, and he wore a strange smile on his cadaverous face. During my entire conversation with him, his lips were curved into a slight grin, as if he were always on the edge of laughter. But I think that was just the way he was.

I gave him a firm handshake. His fingers were cold and bony.

"So, there she is." He glanced behind him. "You wanna take a closer look?"

"Of course."

I walked around the Vette, marveling at how beautiful she looked. I could almost see my reflection in the car's Tuxedo Black paintjob. Richard lifted the hood and let me take a look. It was as immaculate as I thought it would be. The four-barrel equipped L88 427 appeared to be the original piece this car was born with: chrome valve covers, distributor shield, and nicely preserved cast-iron exhaust manifolds. Correct belts, hoses, and clamps were used throughout. It was a beautiful, spotless engine bay. Almost too spotless. Back in the '69's prime, almost every car leaked some oil.

Next, Richard asked me to look inside. I slipped into the driver's seat and gripped the steering wheel. I couldn't believe how authentic everything appeared. As his advertisement had claimed, these were the original round gauges on the dash. I won't lie—it didn't have the comfort I'd grown accustomed to while driving my Lexus—but it didn't matter. This wasn't about the comforts middle-age had led me to feel entitled to. This was about something far more important.

We talked for nearly an hour in my driveway, and I became so engrossed in the Vette that I forgot to invite the man into my house or offer him something to drink. I was amazed at how he'd restored this to such original form. How long did it take him? How much did it cost?

2

"This is quite a restoration," I said. "Must have taken you a long time."

"Not really." He pulled out a cigarette and offered me one. I declined. "What you're looking at here is the way this baby came out of its mother's womb. This is 100% original. Just like it was when it rolled out of the factory."

I laughed at the jest.

Even if this were the original, the passing of time alone would have weathered it to something much less than this.

"Let me guess, and you're the original owner?"

His perennial grin widened. "No, I'm the second. A good car doesn't need much if she's taken care of her whole life," he said.

One thing was clear. Richard Pratt had a sense of humor.

"Why don't you take her for a spin?" he asked, pulling the key out of his pocket.

How could I say no to that offer?

I started her up. It was carbureted, so I could smell the rich fumes coming off the exhaust. The engine loped while it idled from the large cam. Blue smoke plumed out of the dual chrome side pipes.

We went on a nearly thirty-minute drive down toward the beach, and I was convinced before I turned around and headed back that I was going to purchase the vehicle. It had been years since I'd driven a stick, so it took me a mile or two to get a feel for the clutch, but once I did, it was as easy as spreading butter over bread. She ran wonderfully too. It had the typical rough idle of the C3 Stingray. It wanted to go fast.

Richard Pratt didn't talk much on our drive. He just sat in the passenger's seat, that devilish grin on his face.

By the time I pulled the car into my driveway, I was already trying to figure out which mutual funds I could pull from to make the purchase. For once in my life, I was going to do something without agonizing and calculating about it. I was living for me and me alone.

Finally.

3

"I want it," I said after I stepped out of the car. I left the key in the ignition and left it idling.

Richard nodded but stood there without saying anything. It seemed like he was waiting for something.

"Did you hear me?" I asked. "I said I want it."

"Yes." He closed his eyes, exhaled slowly. "I think this is going to work. I think the car likes you—and I think it likes the place you have here."

"Alright, then. You want seventy-four?"

"That's what I'm asking."

"Consider it done," I said. "Any chance you can meet me tomorrow at Arlo's Car Repair in Downtown Long Beach? I have a friend who works there. I'd like him to do a quick diagnostic, if you don't mind. And I need to transfer some funds. Personal check okay?"

"As long as I can verify the funds are there, perfectly fine. Tomorrow will be great. Call me and let me know the time. I'll meet you at the shop. I'll bring the paperwork."

"Will do."

Richard climbed back into the Corvette and sped down the street.

I couldn't believe that by tomorrow, assuming a clean bill of health, the car would be mine.

4

I was barely in my front door when Tommy, the ten-year-old kid who lived next door, stepped out of his house. He had seen the Corvette outside, watched it speed off, and wanted to see it with his own eyes. He was a gearhead in the making, I was sure of it. We'd talked cars a few times in the past.

"Mr. Phoenix, that was a Stingray!"

"It sure was, Tommy. I'm buying it."

His eyes went wide. He looked just as excited as I was. "Can I come see it sometime?"

"Anytime, Tommy!"

"That's great, because I was hoping—"

He stopped abruptly when the sound of screaming came from his house. I'd heard it before. His dad, Stanley, was yelling at him. Tommy's family had moved from the Midwest less than a year ago, and only months after settling in, Tommy's mom was diagnosed with a brain tumor. Glioblastoma. Not good.

Tommy's mom was at home on hospice, dying, and even though Stanley was on leave to tend to his ailing wife, I think he spent most of his time self-medicating on beer and whiskey.

I grieved deeply for the kid.

Stanley kept yelling for Tommy to get back inside, and he looked at me sheepishly. "Can I come over later, Mr. Phoenix, and talk to you about the car?"

"Anytime, Tommy."

I went back to my house and, sure enough, thirty minutes later, Tommy showed up with a skateboard under his arm.

"Dad wanted me to put away dishes," he explained.

I invited him inside, and we sat at the table and looked up pictures of '69 Corvette Stingrays on my laptop.

But after a while, I knew why Tommy really wanted to come over.

He was hungry. Stanley had been too drunk to get something for dinner.

"Why don't I grill something?" I said and went to the fridge. I felt so bad for the kid that I made him two burgers, and when he didn't finish the second, I told him to take it home.

Who knew when Stanley would be sober enough to make another grocery run?

Chapter Eight

64.89 Liters of Fuel Remaining

1

I went to Arlo's garage the following morning.

It was a little auto shop in Downtown Long Beach and was run by Arlo himself, the sole proprietor. The local joint in my neighborhood, ACS Automotive, was overpriced, and I didn't trust them; years before I had taken my Lexus to have the rotors changed, and they wanted to charge me an arm and a leg. It upset me. When they showed me the quote, I stood in front of the counter and sarcastically asked, "So let me get this straight—I either mortgage my house or drive my car again?"

Ever since then, I went to Arlo.

Even though he worked in a little shop that was virtually hidden in the shadows of the buildings around him, he was impeccably honest. I'd taken my cars there many times over the years, and he always shot straight with me. Sometimes he even told me to keep my money if the car didn't need the work.

When I walked into the shop, Arlo greeted me.

There wasn't a front desk here or anyone working it. Arlo pretty much did everything.

"Charo!" he said, grinning, and approached me. He was a little guy, dark hair, dark skin, wearing his mechanic's jumpsuit, and even though he had a little grease on his hand, I went in for the shake anyway. Why not? He grinned widely. That was the thing about Arlo—he was a hard worker, and he was always smiling about it. "You bring in the 'Ray?"

"Yep, it's right there."

Arlo looked outside just as Richard pulled the Stingray into the parking lot.

"Wow," he said. "Looks beautiful."

"It is."

"Well, give me a little time. I'll take a look. Let you know what I think."

"I trust you," I said as Richard walked into the garage.

2

Arlo's diagnostic check took about two hours.

I found a small coffee shop a block away and invited Richard to join me while we waited, but he had several calls to make. He was outside most of the time on his phone while I went through a couple of coffees and a brownie, skimming through a copy of the *OC Register* I found on one of the tables inside. Right around when it was time to head back, Richard came inside, apologized for being tied up with some work calls, and ordered a coffee himself.

Arlo phoned me. He was done.

Richard and I chatted as we walked back to his shop.

"What do you do for a living?" Richard asked while we waited at a crosswalk.

"Oh, nothing that interesting," I said. "Invested in some commercial real estate when I was younger, and it panned out well. Currently I co-own two storage facilities with a friend of mine. One here in Long Beach and another up in Bellflower."

"Nice. I've heard those can be quite lucrative."

"Yeah, we've done well."

"And kind of low maintenance," he guessed.

I laughed. "Well, you'd be surprised. There's always something. What about you?"

"Just as boring," he explained. "I'm a manager at the Alamitos Energy Center."

I knew where that was. The power station was right along the San Gabriel River Bike Trail, not far from where I lived.

When we got back to the garage, Arlo walked out to meet us, wiping his hands on a rag.

"So how does she look?" I asked.

"I gotta tell you," Arlo said, shaking his head, "it looks like that engine was dropped in yesterday. Perfect condition. Never seen a '69 like this that wasn't a mess and dropping oil on the garage floor. Must have steam-cleaned the engine. Fluids good, tires good, the whole deal. I can't find anything—and trust me, I looked."

"Wow," I said, and turned toward Richard.

I held out my hand, and we shook.

"I think we have a deal," I said. "Mind if we head over to Triple-A? There's an office there. We can complete the transaction and finalize the sale."

3

We discussed the details in the parking lot of AAA.

But I balked at a couple of things.

"Did you bring any of the maintenance records?" I asked. "A vehicle history report?"

He shook his head.

I hesitated.

"Well, I think I'd like to see some of the records and the history report. How do I know this car hasn't been in—"

"Don't have them," he said simply, "and I have another buyer on deck if you're not interested. I'm just not meticulous like that."

I thought about it.

"Your guy just gave it a clean bill of health," Richard said. "Doesn't that mean anything? Look, I'll drop the price to seventy even. I'll cut four grand off the price just to get on with this."

"Okay," I said.

He was right. Arlo had signed off on it, and I wanted it. I was a walking cliché of a man going through a midlife crisis, but I chose to embrace it.

He signed over the title, filled out the bill of sale, and I wrote a personal check for seventy thousand. When he questioned whether I had enough money in my account to cover the charge and asked if he could call the bank just to verify the funds, I gave him my blessing, and when he got off the phone and gave me a thumbs-up, we headed into the building.

It didn't take long, and it was infinitely better than the DMV.

I was worried there would be some kind of snag. What if there was a lien against the Stingray, or something like that, and I couldn't register it? What if it was on some stolen list? But things when smoothly, and when we walked out of the building, I had new plates, new tags, and I was officially the new owner of the Stingray.

"Hey," I said, "why don't I give you a ride home?"

"No, that's fine. I'm going to Uber."

That was when it occurred to me. I had two cars in this parking lot—the Stingray and my Lexus. I guessed I'd drive the Stingray home and then Uber to come back and pick up the other car.

"Are you positive you don't want a ride?" I asked.

"Yes. You're the owner now."

We shook hands again, and I headed toward the Stingray.

Richard waited behind, his phone in his hand, most likely hailing an Uber.

He looked at me as I pulled away, and I saw what I could only describe as utter guilt flash across his face when I pulled out of the parking lot. This wasn't the look of a man who had just dropped seventy grand in his bank account. This was the look of someone who had taken something from another person, perhaps something even more valuable than money.

And it would be a long time before I understood why.

Chapter Nine

63.31 Liters of Fuel Remaining

1

I took Kiki to my favorite breakfast place the following morning. I had decided on a breakfast date as opposed to dinner because it didn't seem as intimidating to me—it had been so long since I'd ventured out on a date. Plus, I knew her café was closed today, and I thought she deserved to be served this morning as opposed to serving others.

Ubuntu is a small outdoor café beside the Long Beach Lagoon. We sat at a small table, sipping mimosas on a beautiful summer day. She, as usual, looked wonderful. She preferred casual. Blue jeans, pink blouse. Her freckled, green-eyed smile was as radiant as usual. I was sporting my usual black slacks, blue button-down shirt, black loafers.

"I love the car," she said. I'd picked her up in the Stingray and driven her here. "How much was it?"

I hesitated to answer. Would it be bragging?

"Seventy thousand," I said.

"Seventy thousand?" Her eyes fluttered a little more. "That must be some payment!"

I took a bite of my eggs but didn't say anything. I wasn't sure whether to tell her that I had just written a check. It occurred to me that Kiki—a bit younger than me—had never been in the situation to purchase something like this for cash.

She read my expression. "You didn't buy it with cash, did you?"

I chewed on my eggs. "Well," I said, straddling the line of being proud but not arrogant, "yeah, I did. But you have to understand, I'm a little older and have been fortunate."

"I should have ordered the lobster, then."

We laughed.

"Seventy thousand," she mused, looking toward the lagoon. "I had to take out a personal loan two months ago just to pay the bills. You know, my apartment is only a block from the beach."

"Location, location, location," I said.

She took a sip of her mimosa. "So, what are we doing after breakfast?" she asked playfully.

Our date plans were simple. A quick bite to eat and then a drive down to Second Street, the main strip. Maybe a walk.

We wrapped up breakfast, and, of course, I paid. I was a little surprised that Kiki didn't offer to chip in—but what did I know? It had been so long since I had been in the dating game that I had absolutely no idea what proper protocol was. I was the one who invited her. Maybe it was stupid for me to assume she would offer.

On our walk back to the car, the hernia pain acted up a little. I coughed once, and it went right to my groin.

"You okay?" Kiki asked.

"Yeah, just a groin injury. Inguinal hernia. Usually it's way, way worse than this. This is a good day."

"Still, not fun."

"Yeah. I have a surgery scheduled, but I should have scheduled it sooner. I just don't like the idea of someone cutting into me. But it's pretty routine. Should be in and out."

We climbed into the Stingray, drove to Second Street, and meandered our way along the small restaurants and shops. We dove into a little ice cream shop. I went for the pistachio, Kiki opted for the black cherry, and we carried our cones down the street while talking idly as we gazed into storefront windows.

Twice, she stopped in front of jewelry stores, pointing out her favorites. In the first store, she was absolutely smitten with a V-shaped graduated diamond necklace—so smitten she went inside, asked to see it, put it on, and modeled it for me. I glanced at the price tag: $6,800.

The second store was different. This time, she spotted diamond stud earrings in 14k white gold glittering in the window display. Like before, we went inside, and she tried them on, gazing into a mirror like Cinderella at the ball. And, I must admit, she did look rather beautiful in them. The price tag was even heftier for these: $8,950.

We purchased nothing, of course, and finished our stroll.

Yet I couldn't help but notice her playful comments: "If someone can afford to buy a classic Corvette in cash, I'm sure a little necklace or earrings won't break the bank."

Her eyes fluttered.

I felt a little unease.

There had been so much talk of money on this first date. Was Kiki into me or into my wallet? I guessed time would tell, and maybe I was being overly sensitive. Yet I'd heard stories about men who do this kind of thing. After leaving a spouse, the sucker went out and found a different version of her.

Was that what was happening? Was my picker broken?

Chapter Ten

61.80 Liters of Fuel Remaining

1

Three months with Kiki passed quickly.

I was smitten with her, and the feeling was mutual.

For the first time in many years, I felt youthful and adventurous, and I fell head over heels for her. Was I in love? I wasn't sure, at first. That was a word that definitely needed to be handled more delicately as one got older, but it was safe to say I was enamored with her playfulness and her youth—and she was equally enamored with me.

We went on fancy dates.

Long walks on the sand along the ocean's edge.

We made love. Lots of love.

Kiki was an amazing cook. When she spent the night—and there were lots of those—she made the most fantastic meals and desserts. Lemon vinaigrette pasta salad. Baked mahi mahi tacos. Chicken fajitas. Sesame tahini noodles. Kiki, I learned, was kind of a health nut, so most of what she made was healthy—but somehow, miraculously, it all tasted good.

The fact that she made most of the meals topless while only wearing panties definitely helped the situation.

Where had this woman been all my life?

Suddenly, I didn't feel old. I didn't feel like my best days were behind me.

I felt young again.

And Kiki was the fire that fueled it.

2

I'd accepted that Kiki wasn't really a gold digger. Her clear love for money, I'd learned, was born out of a complete lack of ever having it. She had never finished college, never found direction, and although waitressing paid the bills, she'd struggled to find a clear sense of direction in her life.

And there was Duncan, of course, her abusive ex.

She didn't like talking about him, and I honored that. But it was pretty bad. I think she was ashamed she had remained in the relationship, and that was why she was so silent about it.

Everything drastically altered course one Saturday when Kiki woke me up at eight o'clock in the morning.

She had stayed the night at my house, which she often did on the weekends.

Without a word, she held up the pregnancy test so I could see the result.

Her eyes welled with tears.

I blinked. This had to be a dream, right? It couldn't be real.

"But we used protection," I said.

She nodded.

I held her close to me, and my hands began to shake. This wasn't two people holding each other out of silent joy that they were bringing another person into the world. It was two people holding each other out of fear of what was going to happen next. At least, that was how I felt.

Could I even a raise a child again? My first attempt had been so disastrous.

But Kiki saw things differently. She had always wanted a child. We could make this work. After all, it had been a good three months—no drama, no arguments, just smooth sailing.

That was because there was no kid involved during these last three months, I thought.

Kids changed everything.

3

Later that morning, more news came.

I was sitting in the living room, having coffee, trying my best to swallow the idea of being a father again, when I heard a knock at the door. I answered, and some young man I didn't recognize was standing outside with a clipboard in one hand and a manila envelope in the other.

He handed me the envelope and asked that I sign his clipboard.

I knew what this was. Mara had filed the divorce paperwork, and I was being served.

All a formality, really.

I signed, took the envelope, thanked the young man, and headed back to my coffee.

I opened the envelope and withdrew the paperwork. As I'd guessed, it was a divorce petition filed with the court. From what I read, Mara and I were to attend a mandatory mediation appointment at the courthouse. All cases involving custody of a minor, the letter explained, must meet for mandatory mediation prior to a court hearing.

"But we're not fighting over anything," I mumbled as I scanned the paperwork.

But I was wrong.

Mara wanted full custody of Adam, child support, and an astronomical amount of spousal support.

I gasped.

I was going to pay spousal support when Mara was living with a guy who made more than me?

I only read one page of the petition, which included a rebuke of my parenting and how I was not fit to raise a sixteen-year-old. I stopped there. I didn't want to read any more. The petition was several pages. That was lots of ink to frame me as the Antichrist.

And it was all so petty. Adam was already living with her and her new boyfriend. Did she really have to pay an attorney to pour on the salt and twist the knife?

"I can't believe this," I mumbled. "Adam's sixteen. She's gonna make a fight out of this?"

I couldn't read any more. Not now.

I slipped the papers back into the manila envelope.

4

On top of that, I received another letter that day from Fergus's quack attorney, Buck Valentine.

More of the same thing. He was unjustly terminated. He deserved to be recompensed.

I imagined a bleak future of driving out to Long Beach Courthouse most mornings only to run back and forth between divorce court and civil court. And then returning home to a baby. What if Kiki became more interested in the baby than me? I'd been down that road, and how shameful it was to think that at my age I had made the mistake of repeating history.

That night, I completely lost it.

I needed to get away.

Kiki was back at her apartment, although that was coming to an end too. We had discussed her moving in, but now—being pregnant—it was imminent.

I opened my garage and stared at the black Stingray. I wanted to drive. I needed to get away.

I slipped into the driver's seat, started her up, and backed into the driveway.

Tommy was out front on his skateboard, and when he saw me pull out of the garage and the headlights rise and flick on, he looked as amazed and dumbstruck as if he were witnessing a flying saucer descending from a cloud.

"Whoa, so cool," he said.

I rolled down my window. "I'll take you for a ride soon, okay?"

He nodded.

I cranked up my window—no refurbished electric ones on this car—and headed out onto the road. To be honest, I had no idea where to go. I just headed to the beach and went south. I must have driven for over an hour, lost in thought, trying to sort out the broken pieces of my life, when—somewhere past Laguna Beach—I checked my gas gauge. The red needle was to the far left, just below E. I cursed myself. I had been so consumed in my thoughts, I hadn't even thought to check the gas.

It had completely slipped my mind.

The engine sputtered. The gauge lights flickered.

I looked for a place to pull over, but when I glanced down at the gauge, I saw what I can only describe as sheer impossibility.

The gas gauge's needle slowly moved from E to F, as if gas were being poured into the tank right then and there as I drove fifty miles an hour down the coast.

Chapter Eleven

60.25 Liters of Fuel Remaining

1

By the time I returned home, I was convinced the tank had never actually been empty. There must have been something wrong with the gauge that caused it to dip below E and then bounce back to F. I let the car sit in the garage for an hour as I took a shower, but it kept bothering me: what exactly had happened?

I went back out to the garage, took off the gas cap, and used a liquid dip stick to determine the gas level. Sure enough, this car was totally full. The gasoline float wasn't lying. It was all the way up, and the sender, a wire-wound rheostat with the resistance reading determined by the float position, was conveying accurately that this tank was brimming with gasoline. I was utterly perplexed. I took a seat in my garage, stared at the black contour of the Stingray, and began to question how this was possible. Had Richard Pratt installed a second tank on this vehicle? That was the only possibility I could imagine. Perhaps the gauge had moved from E to F when it somehow transferred to this backup tank. Like an archeologist, I dug through and inspected everything under the hood and crawled under the vehicle, but there was no backup gas tank. I know I would have found it.

I had filled up the tank several times over the last few months, always before hitting E. Everything seemed normal during those fill-ups.

The original sales brochures for the '69 Corvettes claimed they had a gauge "for everything but your blood pressure." Tachometer, oil pressure, ammeter, sweep second rally clock, the usual mileage and trip odometer, and seat belt light gauges all seemed to be in just as fine a working order as the gas gauge, but I had one last thought. The '69 Vette had storage areas under the carpeting behind the seats to house the battery and store the jack and tools, and there was another spot to house valuables. Maybe another gas tank was somehow built into that space?

I checked, but no such luck. The big block R79W battery with vent caps and hoses looked as vintage as the original battery this car must have used, the car jack was in place, and the storage place was totally empty.

By that time it was nearly two in the morning, and I was convinced I wouldn't sleep that night.

And I didn't. I brewed coffee and sat up all night speculating.

When the sun came up, I decided to put it to the test.

I headed out on the road at first light toward Sedona. If this car was anything close to the original—which everything seemed to be—I expected to get maybe thirteen miles per gallon. With a twenty-gallon tank, I could probably get around two hundred and fifty miles or so, considering stops and some traffic.

By normal calculations, I shouldn't have been able to make it to Sedona on one tank, but I decided that I would drive until the Stingray sputtered out on I-10 or, if it truly was a miracle car, before it replenished itself yet again. And even though I hadn't slept a wink, I thought I would be fine for the drive. In truth, I've never been much of a sleeper. And I was so anxious to discover if I was losing my mind or not.

Fortunately, I left early enough to avoid traffic. I made my way through Riverside, Palm Springs, Indio, and then the long stretch on I-10 through Quartzsite and the earthen vastness of open desert.

2

I kept my eyes on the fuel gauge the whole drive. Predictably, as the hours passed, the red needle slowly dipped toward the E. I was just outside of Quartzsite when the car began to sputter. I looked at the gauge. The needle was flatlined to the E, and the engine began to show signs of fuel starvation. The dash lights flickered, and the engine backfired.

So it wasn't a miracle car. There must have been a backup tank.

I looked for a place along the shoulder of the highway to pull over. I'd call AAA, fuel her up, and head back home.

But just as I spotted a safe place to pull over, the sputtering stopped.

I looked back at the gauge.

The red needle, like Lazarus, rose from the grave of E and made its way back to F.

Chapter Twelve

58.70 Liters of Fuel Remaining

1

Two weeks passed, and I kept my discovery secret. I went on several more drives just to make sure I hadn't completely lost my mind, and sure enough, the Stingray replenished itself every time.

Another funny thing happened too. One afternoon I was sitting at home, eating a peanut butter and jelly sandwich, reading the mail—now complete with more letters from Fergus's attorney, Buck Valentine, and my soon-to-be-ex-wife's attorney, Cynthia Brown, when the phone rang. I picked it up. It was a call from my doctor's office. They were waiting for me to get back to them with some of the paperwork for my inguinal hernia surgery. I apologized and promised I would send in the last of my paperwork. But when I sat down and resumed eating my sandwich, it occurred to me: I hadn't experienced much pain recently.

The hernia pain had simply vanished.

I tried to think back to the last time I had felt any pain, and I couldn't even remember. I thought it was my first date with Kiki at Ubuntu.

Maybe I was wrong to schedule the appointment so hastily. I should have gotten a second opinion.

2

After I put away lunch, I found the paperwork I had failed to complete sitting on the kitchen island and, hesitating for just a moment, threw it in the trash. If the pain came back, I'd start the process all over again.

I was about to run by my Long Beach storage facility and check on things when Kiki walked through the front door. She seemed to float across the room more than walk, all giddy with smiles, and she had a bundle of paint samples in her hand. Before I had a chance to ask her what was going on, she spread them across the dining table like a deck of cards.

"I have some ideas for what color to paint the nursery," she said.

"Ah, I see."

I took a seat and wiped some breadcrumbs from the table. We'd avoided having a serious conversation about this. Truth was, I didn't much like confrontation. Even with business, I was never the guy to confront the difficult things. That was Trey's job.

"Okay, well," I said, trying to formulate the right words, "I think it would be a good idea to sit down and really talk about things. There's a lot to discuss."

"Sure," she said. I think she was totally oblivious to my reservations, and I had done a terrible job of addressing them. "I know it's kind of quick, but we have to figure this out, right? And I assume I'd be moving in here, right? We've talked about it before. You wouldn't want me living in my apartment. That wouldn't make much sense."

"No, it wouldn't." I rubbed my hands down my face. How did I get into this situation?

"You're right," she said, gathering the paint samples and stacking them on the edge of the table. "It's just that I'm a bit excited, and maybe I am going a little too fast. We should probably talk about me moving in first, right? We haven't even figured that out yet. And, of course, there's the issue with us being married or not. We probably need to discuss."

"And there's my ex."

"Okay." She blinked. "What about her? You're not talking about getting back together with her are—"

"Her lawyer," I said, pointing to the letters. "You can read through them yourself. She wants half, and she wants spousal support. This is a lot to deal with all at once."

She nodded. "Are you going to be okay? Are we going to be okay? Can you afford this house?"

"Yes, I'm not worried about that."

"Well, that's good."

I sighed and thought I'd cut right to the chase. "Listen, this is all happening so quickly, and really, we haven't been together for very long. Are you sure this is what you want?"

"Of course this is what I want," she said, with hardly a pause. "I've never lived in a house—let alone a house like this. You know how long I've been scraping away in that apartment? This is—well, I don't know how to say it—this is like a dream come true. And this opens up so many possibilities. I can go back to college, maybe, and get my teaching credential—what a relief that would be—and be a stay-at-home mom and finally savor some of my life instead of having to spend every waking moment clawing and scrambling and struggling to keep afloat."

I listened intently. I couldn't figure out where I fit into this dream of hers, other than being its funder.

"And you want to keep the kid?"

She blinked away her shock, and her hand theatrically went to her chest. "What do you mean, do I want to keep the kid?"

"Well, I'm just asking," I blubbered. "I mean, it's a big deal, right? I've raised one, and let me tell you, it's not without its scars. I just want to make sure that you really—"

"You're not suggesting to—"

"No, no," I said, waving away the comment, "I'm not suggesting anything, really, other than if this isn't a good idea, then maybe there are other options that we can explore, because—"

Now she grinned, and she playfully reached for the collar of my shirt and pulled me toward her.

"You know what your problem is, Mr. Phoenix?"

I recognized the sensual pout, the kelp-colored eyes.

"What's that?" I asked.

"You worry too much."

"I know, I just—"

I'm not sure how it happened, but within moments we were on the couch and our clothes were off.

Chapter Thirteen

57.16 Liters of Fuel Remaining

1

Two hours later, I pulled my Stingray into the parking lot of Long Beach Storage Needs, one of the storage facilities I co-owned with my business partner, Trey.

I was disappointed in my discussion—of lack thereof—with Kiki. I should have been more forthright with her, but I just couldn't. What was I going to say? I needed time to think about things and process things.

When I strolled onto the premises, business appeared as usual. Tina, our day manager, was talking to a middle-aged couple in front of one of the sheds. Giving them the grand tour, I assumed. I gave her a friendly wave and went through the main office and into a small conference room.

Trey was waiting for me. He had picked up two coffees at Starbucks—one for him and one for me—and he was totally absorbed in his phone when I approached.

"About time," he said, without looking up. "I should have stayed at the gym longer."

Trey spent a lot of time at the gym. He was a few years younger than me and made it a point to hit the gym every day. The results showed. He was a strong, lean black man, and his dark, healthy skin looked to be the result of routine moisturizer and personal care.

And it worked with the ladies. I could hardly keep track of the women he dated. Never married, Trey lived with the philosophy that marriage was an institution, and he was far too young to be an institutionalized man. In his own words, he was a "bachelor 'til the rapture."

We sipped our coffees and went over several business matters. New property insurance. Company software. We were also going to replace two faulty video cameras that had gone out on our southern structure. We were big on security. In total, we had eighty cameras monitoring the facility.

"You put in the order to have those cameras fixed?"

"Sure did," Trey said.

"Haven't those cameras gone bad a couple of times in the last year?"

"I think so."

"Sounds like faulty wiring or something. Are we using the same vendor? Sentech?"

"Yep."

That was the problem, I thought. They were too cheap. And their work showed it. Eventually, I was going to press Trey to update the whole system and go with a new vendor. Sentech did shoddy work.

My sister Donna wanted us to get involved in some organization called Charity Storage. Her husband was ridiculously wealthy, and both were serial philanthropists. I called her, put her on speaker, and she told us the concept. It was simple. We could allocate one of our storage units as a collection point for donated goods. Tenants, local residents, and businesses could donate items, receive Charitable Donation Receipts, and eventually the unit would be sold at auction. The revenue would be forwarded to various charities.

Trey and I both told her we'd look into it, though I could tell Trey wasn't very interested. Neither was I.

Donna agreed to send us the information.

Before getting off the phone, she asked me, "How's the new Corvette treating you?"

"Not bad."

"Well, we have a charity event coming up over in Duarte. We have a classic car booth. We could use a car like yours."

"Maybe," I said, not thinking much of it. "I'll give you a call soon."

Donna knew what that meant. I really wasn't interested.

Trey and I kept talking, and eventually Fergus came up.

"You still getting letters from that attorney, Buck whatever?" Trey asked me.

"Yes. Buck Valentine."

"Ridiculous. Lawyers are vampires." Trey took a sudden interest in his phone again.

"I'm going to be spending lots of time with lawyers in the near future, it seems," I told him. "You know, I thought my ex was going to go away quietly. When she left, she said she didn't want much. No spousal support. She just wanted her freedom—and now, lo and behold—she wants to take a bite out of everything. Spousal support. Half the house. Half of everything. It's gonna get ugly."

"Of course it is." Trey sipped his coffee. "That's the nature of divorce, especially if lawyers get involved."

That was Trey. Right to the point, and suave while he was getting there.

"And there's another problem." I hesitated, but Trey had been more than a business partner over the years. He was a friend, and while some friends may have fallen into the fair-weather type, Trey was the opposite—he was the stormy- and gloomy- and inclement-weather kind of friend because I knew, above all things, Trey would tell me like it was. "The girl I've been seeing—Kiki Patterson—she's pregnant. I don't know how I did it, but I think I made the situation worse."

Trey didn't miss a beat.

"Well, I know how you did it," he said, "but I don't think you really need me to explain that to you, do you?"

"No, I don't."

In some ways, he didn't look at all surprised. "You sure she's really pregnant?"

2

I was struck by the question.

"Yeah, I'm pretty sure."

"Did you actually see her take the test?"

"Well, no, I wasn't there when she peed on the stick, but she showed it to me."

"I see," Trey said, grinning. "She told you. And you believed her?"

"Well, why wouldn't I believe her?"

"There might be lots of reasons," he explained. "Let's do the math. Single girl who got out of a bad relationship struggling to make ends meet, and along comes you, a guy who is—how many years older than her are you?—and then, suddenly, she's pregnant and—let me guess—already making plans for the wedding or, at the minimum, planning to move in with you. Am I right?"

I didn't say anything, but I think my expression conveyed it all.

"That stuff can be easily faked," he said. "You can buy a fake false pregnancy test online as a gag. It's not difficult. And there are ways to fake it. I read once that some ingredients used to make sodas mimic pregnancy hormones. You dip the stick in your Coca-Cola and, shazam, you're pregnant."

"What makes you think this?" I asked. "You don't even know her."

"Well, you did tell me about her," he explained, opening one of the manila folders he'd brought with him. "And you mentioned your concerns. It isn't difficult to find public information like this online. Intelius. TruthFinder. Instant Checkmate. The list goes on and on. You want to read through what I found, or should I summarize?"

I motioned for him to proceed. "Why don't you summarize?"

"Your new girlfriend has had some issues when it comes to money. She's been slapped on the wrist for check fraud and has been sued for unpaid rent. This was years ago, but still, I thought you should be aware of it."

"Wow," I said, though I wasn't totally surprised. "So you went out and did this? Did this search? Why?"

"Friends look out for each other," he said.

3

Trey slid the manila envelope to me. "Look, I'm not saying Kiki's a bad person, not at all. But sometimes when people are desperate, they do desperate things, and the more information you have, the better, right?"

"Right."

It did make sense for Trey to do this. He always ran the background checks for our employees, and he was the one who warned me about hiring my nephew.

"Wouldn't hurt to check that pregnancy test, if you ask me."

"Maybe I will."

"Now, then," he said, opening another folder and getting down to business. "Let's focus on what we came here for."

"Sure thing."

He got up to use the restroom, and I noticed how stiff he was. I'd seen this before. He put his hand on his lower back as he slowly rose from his chair.

"Back acting up again?" I asked.

"You know it."

"Sucks getting older, huh?"

"As long as I can perform where it counts—the bedroom—I can deal with a little back pain." He laughed. "Got a date tonight. Might have to stretch it out before then."

It didn't surprise me that Trey had a date.

Trey always had a date.

When he left the room, I considered what he'd told me.

Was Kiki playing me?

Chapter Fourteen

55.61 Liters of Fuel Remaining

1

I had barely driven a mile from my storage facility when I got a notification on my phone. At a red light I checked it. My son's band, Pure Evil, was playing tonight at the Whisky a Go Go. Amateur metal night. Sixteen and older. I knew little about the show and had never visited the Whisky, but he had told me they were the low man on the totem pole and were taking the stage first. Considering it was nearly five and it would take at least an hour to make it to Hollywood—perhaps more, considering rush hour traffic—I decided to head straight there and pulled onto the 405 North.

I had completely forgotten. If I had remembered, I would have given myself time to go home and change into something more fitting for a metal concert in Hollywood, but maybe it didn't matter all that much—I was pretty convinced I didn't own anything that would even relatively camouflage myself in what was most likely going to be a much younger, edgier crowd.

I was greeted by a seemingly endless path of red taillights as I merged into traffic.

Yes, this was going to take a while.

The red fuel gauge indicated that I was just above E. The car would replenish itself right around the halfway point of my trip, by my calculations.

I still had no clue as to how any of this was possible. My only guess was that somehow Richard Pratt had engineered this thing to refuel on its own. I had not the vaguest clue as to how, but there had to be some reasonable and logical explanation, right? Cars didn't just replenish themselves without a means of doing so. If indeed he had discovered some technology to do this, he had installed it in the car incredibly stealthily, and I couldn't even imagine the kind of money he could make on such an invention.

"What did Richard do to you?" I mumbled, looking at the dashboard gauges. "What in the world did—"

I stopped.

Why was I asking the car?

I had a better idea.

Why not call Richard himself?

2

The one thing I didn't like about the '69 Stingray was the lack of modern technology. In my Lexus, I could make a call from a small dashboard screen that was connected to my phone via Bluetooth. I didn't even have to take the phone out of my pocket. That wasn't the case here.

With one hand on the wheel, I pulled my iPhone out of my pocket, scrolled through my contacts, and found the one for Richard Pratt.

I hit the call button and waited.

Why would he sell a car like this to me? And why hadn't he told me about this feature? I had been so consumed in my life and everything in it—a divorce, an unexpected pregnancy, a crazy ex-employee out for money—that I had completely forgotten to consider the most fundamental of things. I should have called him the moment I discovered the car's capabilities.

The phone never rang.

Instead, I heard a message: *The number you dialed has been changed, disconnected, or is no longer in service. If you feel you have reached this recording in error, please check the number and try your call again.*

3

The Whisky was located on the corner of Sunset and North Clark Street and was teeming with a long line of people waiting to enter. The large marquee on the front read METAL NIGHT XTRAVAGANZA, and the outer walls of the nightclub featured large, illuminated murals of bands that, I assumed, were up-and-coming. I didn't recognize any of the names, nor the sullen, hermaphroditic faces of the band members. I couldn't tell if half of them were men or women, and it was safe to say I had never heard any of their songs.

Looking at the murals, I wasn't sure I wanted to.

I found a parking lot a few blocks down, paid an exorbitant amount of money to park the Stingray, and paid an equally exorbitant amount of money to get into the venue. Forty bucks.

When the bouncer—a large, beefy guy with a black ponytail and tree-trunk arms—asked for the forty dollars for admittance, I chuckled. "Forty bucks?"

He nodded.

"For amateur night?"

He nodded again.

"Those must be some amateurs," I said, and handed him two twenties.

Inside, things appeared as I had imagined. I looked nothing like the clientele here. Amongst the metalheads, ripped jeans, leather jackets, and mohawks, a middle-aged man in khakis, a green polo shirt, and loafers stood out like a sore thumb.

I made my way to the bar, ordered a Corona, and found a seat on the top level where I could look down. I knew what a mosh pit was and wasn't sure if that was going to happen this evening, but the last thing I wanted was to get caught up in it.

Immediately I recognized my son plugging in his guitar and adjusting his microphone while his other bandmates did the same. Within minutes, Adam introduced himself and his band, Pure Evil, to the crowd and launched into a song that was so heavy and so angst-filled, I'm not sure I could properly categorize it as music.

4

I watched Pure Evil for the twenty-something-minute duration of their set.

As much as I wanted to say I loved it and was blown away by my son's raw talent, it didn't turn out that way. He had painted his nails black for this performance and applied eyeliner below his eyes. Dressed in black jeans, a black shirt, and a flowing trench coat, he reminded me of some pissed off mortician having a temper tantrum. And really, it just sounded like screaming. Every now and then, I could make out a word—*hate, death, evil*—but he sounded like a rabid wildcat in heat.

But I was there, at least. At this point, I just wanted to be supportive.

When the set ended, there was lukewarm applause from the crowd, and I couldn't tell if it was because they didn't like the band or because it was early in the evening and the better, bigger bands were coming later.

When I saw my son and his band striking their set, I seized the opportunity.

I went downstairs and approached the stage, where my son was rolling up a guitar cord.

"Adam!" I said.

He didn't hear me. Too much noise. The house speakers were blasting a Zeppelin tune.

"Adam!"

This time he looked up. He was completely stone-faced. I was surprised. I had driven all the way out to Hollywood to see him perform. Didn't that at least merit a smile? A friendly wave? His mom wasn't even here.

"You sounded awesome tonight!" I said. "Great job!"

He gave me a thumbs-up, picked up his guitar case, and headed backstage.

And that was that.

5

I had just started my Stingray and was about to head home when I saw someone running toward my car. In the rearview mirror, I could see that it was Adam. He was clutching his guitar case in his left hand.

I climbed out of the car.

"Dad, I'm glad I caught you before you left."

"Yeah, just barely. Hey, again, great job tonight. You guys really put on quite a performance."

"Thanks." He moved his guitar case to his right hand and shifted uncomfortably. "Look, uh, any chance you can give me a ride to Mom's tonight?"

"Sure. Why? What happened?"

"Dan's dad drove us here. He's tired. Wanted us to get our own ride if we could."

"Yeah, well, no prob. I can drop you off."

"I'm half-surprised you even bothered to show up tonight," Adam said and approached the passenger side of the Stingray. He tried to open the door, but it was locked.

I felt the sudden urge to confront this situation head-on. I had done too little of this in my life, and now, standing in a parking lot with my guitar-toting, mascara-wearing, rebellious son, I felt the time was right.

"What's the matter with you?" I asked.

"What do you mean?"

"I mean that I drove all the way out here to watch you perform, and the reaction I get is you basically flicking me off."

I saw his crooked grin. The ocher-colored streetlights surrounding the parking lot gleamed in his dark eyes.

A lover of conflict, my son enjoyed this.

"So what do you want, Dad? A medal for showing up to one of my shows?"

"No, I don't want a medal. But a little appreciation would be nice."

"Here you go," he said, and clapped his hands together. "There's your applause. Now can you let me into the car so I can go back to my mom's? You know, the *real* parent, the one who actually took an interest in me growing up."

"There you go again."

"Go again with what?"

"That victim mentality. The world owes you. That's all it ever is with you."

He squinted. "What are you talking about?"

"I'm talking about you. Nothing's ever good enough for you. All you see is the negative. I was there while you were growing up, Adam, in case you forgot. Maybe that mascara you're wearing has caused some memory lapse."

His eyes went wide, and he kicked the side of the Stingray with his boot. It took everything inside me to resist racing around the car and attacking him with my bare hands. I felt blood rushing to my face. My heart quickened.

"Don't kick my car, son."

He kicked a second time. Hard. Now I was nearly seeing red. I was sure those steel-toed boots he was wearing put a dent in the door.

"You damage this car, you're gonna pay for it. You hear me?"

He laughed. "Sure, Dad, whatever you say. This car means more to you than I ever did. Your stuff has meant more to you than I ever did."

"You wanna hitchhike home?"

"It'd be better than spending the drive with you," he said.

We stared each other down.

As pissed as I was, I wanted to drive him home. And as pissed as he was, I think he wanted the same thing. That's the thing about conflict, I suppose; beneath the surface, at times, what fuels so much of it is an unquenched, unrealized desire for reconciliation.

I opened my car door. "Get in the car. I'll drive you to your mom's."

"You sure? I don't want to interfere with your busy schedule."

I climbed in and reached over to unlock his door. Slowly, he got into the Stingray and placed his guitar between his legs. My son is tall and lanky, and he looked cramped in the passenger seat.

"You can move the seat back a little," I suggested.

"It's fine," he said, looking away. As stubborn as he was, he couldn't help but offer: "I'll give you a few bucks for gas money, okay? I don't want to hurt your bank account."

I turned the key. The V8 roared to life, and while we sat in its rough idle, I turned on the pop-up headlights.

"It's not a problem," I replied. "Gas isn't going to be an issue."

THREE QUARTERS
OF A TANK

Chapter Fifteen

54.07 Liters of Fuel Remaining

1

It was truly a miracle.

The on-ramp to the 405 was closed due to construction, and although I could have found another entrance to the freeway, I decided to take the coastal route instead. I hated the idea of dropping off my son without having some of this—even a tiny fraction of it—resolved before I went to bed that evening. Taking a longer route would give us more time to let the coals of our anger cool.

So I took I-10 toward Santa Monica and drove Highway 1 toward home. We didn't talk much at first, and I turned on the radio, searching for some music to make the drive feel less lonely, and came upon a fitting song: "Cat's in the Cradle," an old folk rock song by Harry Chapin.

It was almost prophetic. A song about a father and a son who missed each other in life. I couldn't have imagined something more timely.

The radio signal was a bit staticky, and somewhere around Redondo Beach I reached to turn the knob, but my son surprisingly said, "No. Keep it on. I like it."

"You do?" I was stunned. I assumed he wouldn't like a song unless someone was screaming inaudibly amongst distorted guitars. "You know what it's about?"

"Yeah, I do," he said.

I wasn't going to get a better opening than this. "Adam, look, I wasn't perfect when you were growing up. I know I was gone working a lot, and when it comes to art and poetry and music, I'm not the most—"

"No, Dad, it's okay."

"It is?"

"Yeah." He looked out the window and toward the swirl of blue and yellow city lights passing like swarms of fireflies in the night. "I was wrong to kick your car. And I was wrong to get so upset tonight. I don't know—it's like something came over me—and, uh, I'm sorry. I shouldn't have done that."

I didn't even know how to respond.

That may have been the first time, to my knowledge, that those two words—*I'm sorry*—escaped my son's lips.

2

I was so in awe that evening, I didn't want to go to bed.

Instead, I went out to the garage and took a seat beside the Stingray, marveling at it. Since his teenage years, my relationship with my son had been anything but good. There were occasional breaks in the storm when the clouds parted, but for the most part, it was a bleak and acrid experience.

That was when I got to thinking: why had everything changed this night? I'd taken my son on thousands of drives over the years, many of them not-so-pleasant. So why had one drive down Highway 1 changed everything? Maybe my son would wake up the following day and return to his crabby, distant self, but there had been a genuine connection during that drive. I'd seen it. I'd felt it.

I heard something enter the open garage, and it was my usual visitor.

Chuck strode slowly toward me, looking as fatigued as ever, and made his way to the bowls of water and food I'd put out for him.

"What's up, Chuck?"

He looked up, meowed once, and went straight for the food bowl.

"Tough night on the home front?" I asked.

He went on eating.

"I know how you feel."

My phone beeped. Incoming message. I took a look, and it was a text from Adam. The message was short and simple: *Thanks for coming tonight. Hopefully we can talk soon.*

I stared at the message for what seemed like minutes, and then I looked at the black Stingray sitting in my garage. What had the car done? I knew that it somehow replenished its own fuel, but what if it replenished more than just gasoline? My relationship with Adam had been at its worst only hours ago, and now, somehow, so much had been rectified. In just one drive.

I got up and walked around the car, touching it. I felt its sleek, smooth surface along my fingers.

"What are you?" I whispered.

Then I remembered. Adam had given the car two swift kicks with his steel-toed boots. I hadn't looked—maybe because I was afraid to—but I needed to assess the damage. I bent down and looked at the passenger side, right around where Adam's boot would have made contact.

There was nothing.

No dent. No scratch.

The paint was as black as a moonless, starless night.

3

Chuck looked up from his bowl of food as headlights pulled into my driveway. It was late in the evening, but perhaps Kiki had decided to come by and finish our discussion about her timeline for moving in, what exactly we were going to do, and how we were going to do it. So much was unresolved. So much needed to be discussed and decided on, and I was dreading it.

I walked out of my garage.

It wasn't Kiki.

I recognized the yellow F-150 immediately. Fergus opened the driver's door of the double-cab truck and got out. He was wearing tight ripped jeans and a yellow tank top almost identical to his vehicle.

"What are you doing here?" I asked. I thought of one thing and one thing only: If this got ugly, was there a weapon nearby? Anything? My mind instantly went to the crowbar on my workbench. If this got bad—and I prayed it didn't—that was what I'd pick up.

Fergus walked toward the front of his truck and stood between the headlights.

"You owe me," he said.

"Fergus, you shouldn't be here. Please get in your truck and leave. Do it now."

He laughed and flicked back his blond mullet. "That's the thing about you." He pointed accusingly. "You've forgotten how hard it is for people to get where they want to be. You never appreciated me, Charlie. You never appreciated everything I did for you, and there's nothing worse than a man who can't keep his promises. Know what I mean?"

"There was no promise, Fergus. You lost your job fair and square."

"It wasn't right, and you know it."

"Get a life, Fergus, and move on. And get off my property."

"Move on, huh?" he said. I could hear the rage in his voice. He crossed his muscular arms. "Easy for you to say. You get to go back to all this." He pointed to my house, and then his gaze landed on the Lexus and Stingray parked in the garage behind me. "And *those*. You forgot where you came from, didn't you?"

"Did you hear what I said? Get off my property."

"I see that new sports car of yours somewhere, and I'm gonna key it. You hear me?"

"Fergus, if you key either of my cars, I'm going to—"

"Think of it as my calling card," he said. "A way to think about me when I'm not here, because you must be getting lonely, right? Or maybe not. I know your wife left you, but at least you got that new chick and that cat to keep you company."

I wasn't sure how Fergus knew these things, but he was right.

Maybe he'd been following me. Watching me.

"I'm going to call the police," I said. I pulled my phone out of my pocket.

"I'll get out of your hair, so don't worry," Fergus said. "I just came by to give you a message. I think in-person messages always pack a little more punch. I want my job back or I want a payout."

"There's not going to be a payout," I said. "Get out."

"I'll be watching you and everything you care about in this world. Until I get what I want, I'm going to make sure you know what it feels like to have something taken from you."

He got in his truck, put it in reverse, backed out of my driveway, and peeled out down the street.

I put the phone back in my pocket, realized that my hands were shaking, and went back to my workbench. I needed to sit down, collect myself.

"You doing alright, Chuck?"

The cat didn't respond. He was back at his bowl, feasting.

I took that as a *yes*.

Chapter Sixteen

52.53 Liters of Fuel Remaining

1

The following morning, I sat and tried to put the pieces of the puzzle together. The car could replenish gasoline, and now it seemed at least possible that it could replenish one other thing: relationships.

But how?

I had tried calling Richard Pratt the night before but, just in case, I tried again. I got the same announcement that the number had been disconnected. I had to get a hold of him and ask him some questions.

I only had two pieces of information: his name and a disconnected number. Not much information to go on, but enough, I hoped, to figure out who this guy was and where he came from. Then I remembered. I raced to my office and pulled out the manila file I'd labeled STINGRAY. Inside was the copy of the Bill of Sale.

Richard had drafted the original document, and the good folks at AAA had made us extra copies for our records.

I cross-referenced the phone number with the one saved in my cell phone and, sure enough, it was identical. I checked the address. I didn't recognize the street name, but it was in Whittier. Not too far from my own city.

I entered the address in my phone. I would drive out there this afternoon, knock on his door, and ask him what in God's name he'd sold me. And why had he done it?

I had just finished entering his address when the front door opened.

"Charlie!" It was Kiki.

I headed downstairs, and this time—especially after everything Trey had told me—I was determined to have a real conversation with Kiki and make sure I wasn't just another middle-aged guy getting suckered out of his money.

2

"I think it's time we really talked about what we're going to do with our—um—situation," I explained after she had come in and taken a seat at the dining room table. I poured myself a glass of wine. God knew I was going to need it.

"We can do something else first," she said, winking.

For a brief moment, I was tempted. But I'd fallen for that trap the last time we had this conversation. I was going to do my best to resist.

"Are you sure you're pregnant?"

Trey's words had gotten to me and pierced both flesh and marrow. As much as I hated to admit it, maybe my old colleague was on to something. When it came to business, Trey was shrewd. Maybe he was seeing something here that I couldn't.

Kiki's eyes fluttered. "What?" she asked, her face a half-grin, half-frown.

"I mean…" I struggled for words. "There are false positives, right? Did you take more than one test? Have you gone to the doctor? It's just that—you know—before we start making all of these plans and getting all of your hopes up, it might be a good idea to just make sure everything is honest."

"Honest?" she repeated.

It was my fault. Chalk it up to a Freudian slip, but the word just popped out of my mouth. I'd meant to say a different word, like *accurate*.

"Do you think I'm lying to you?" she pressed.

Tension filled the air. I considered how I could sidestep this but still have some of my questions answered.

"Look," I said, "I'm not accusing you of lying. I just think we should make sure that you are, in fact, pregnant. Have you been to your OBGYN?"

"No, not yet. I haven't made—"

"Then let's make an appointment. I think they do a blood test, right? And why don't you and I both go together? It'll be good, and it's been a while for me, so I probably need a few reminders. How does that sound?" I pulled my cell out of my pocket. "I'll call right now and make the appointment."

I watched as the fun-loving, giggling, youthful Kiki recoiled ever so slightly in her seat. She was soaking this up, trying to make sense of what I was doing. Instantly, I realized there was another side to her. A shadow seemed to pass over her face, and those eyes, usually mesmerizing, were dark and calculating.

"What's happening right now?" she asked as much to the room as to me.

"I'm just trying to set up an appointment." I pointed to the phone, as if it were an exhibit in a court case.

"You don't believe me," she whispered. "You think I'm lying to you."

"Now, hold on," I pled. I tried to think of exactly what to say, but the truth was clear: she was right. She saw right through me, so I proceeded cautiously. "I'm not saying I don't believe you. It's just—sometimes when people want something really badly, they can kind of blindly believe something they want to believe. Know what I mean?"

"No, I don't know what you mean."

I decided to go full throttle. No holding back now.

"How long have you been having money problems?" I asked.

It looked like a charge of electricity jolted her. Her eyes went wide, and her fingers went to her lips in shock.

"It's just that you've had money problems," I said, conveniently failing to mention whatever check fraud she'd been accused of in the past. "You've talked about that. How hard it is to make ends meet. It's totally understandable how someone in your position could start dating a guy like me and how the temptation to—"

She stood up, aghast.

"Kiki, I'm not saying you're lying. Maybe you did take a pregnancy test, and maybe you did think—"

"'Maybe'?" She pointed an accusing finger at me. I recoiled as if it were the red-hot tip of cattle prod. "What do you mean 'maybe'? You think I'm lying?"

"Let's call the doctor. We can schedule an appointment. That way we—"

She sighed and stomped toward the entry table by the front door, where she'd dropped her purse and car keys on the way in. She opened the front door, was about to leave, but she couldn't resist turning back to me.

"To think—after all these years I found someone who I think has some integrity and wants to start a life together. And you think it's all a ploy to get your money!"

I stood as silent as a statue. It felt like liquid shame was being poured over me.

Had I miscalculated?

"Kiki, listen, I'm sorry. All of this has made me so terribly nervous. Maybe I was wrong, and we should just—"

"I'm going back to my apartment," she said. Before closing the door, she looked back at me. "Or maybe I don't really have an apartment. Maybe that's a lie too!"

She cackled like a witch and slammed the door.

I sat in the silence.

When I finally had the energy to move, I headed straight toward my wet bar.

I needed something stronger than wine. Badly.

3

I knew Kiki to be a fireball, and I hoped she would cool quickly.

I sent several texts imploring forgiveness, pleading my stupidity, chalking it up to typical male naivety. The more I thought about it, the more I realized the error of my ways. Since I had started dating Kiki, she had made me dinners, cleaned my house, helped refurbish my wardrobe. Her love language was clearly acts of service. Sure, she liked the money, and I'm sure she romanticized what it was going to be like to have some at her disposal, but I shouldn't have overlooked some of her best qualities.

Whatever trash Trey had dug up on her on the internet, there was probably a reason for it. We all have seasons in our lives we'd rather keep to ourselves.

It was late afternoon when she texted me, and it was sweet and simple: *I understand. I know you are going through a lot. I will call doctor and make appointment. How bout tomorrow night I make you dinner?*

I read the text several times, impressed. Kiki may have been explosive, but it takes quite a woman to make a home-cooked meal only hours after having been accused of lying about her pregnancy. If that wasn't a gem of a human, I didn't know what was. I wasn't sure I even had the capacity for such forgiveness.

I responded with a *yes* and headed to the door. I wanted to drive to Richard Pratt's house and get some answers about the Stingray.

Before leaving, I received a notification on my phone.

I checked it and was reminded that I had a mandatory court-ordered mediation appointment at Long Beach Courthouse tomorrow morning.

"That ought to be fun," I mumbled, and I headed toward the garage where my Stingray awaited.

Chapter Seventeen

50.98 Liters of Fuel Remaining

1

I pulled up to Richard Pratt's house in Whittier. It didn't look like much. It was an old California bungalow, run-down with a front lawn that was mostly unmanicured and unweeded. It struck me as amusing: the guy who had sold me an impeccable Stingray without a scratch on it lived in a house that was a total eyesore.

I got out of my car and walked up to the front door.

A woman was talking somewhere inside the house.

I knocked on the security screen and waited only a moment before a dapper-looking woman in high heels, a pencil skirt, and a green blouse approached the door. I could smell her lilac perfume before she was in view. She glared at me from the other side of the screen door. She wore heavy makeup. Purple lips. Blushed cheeks. Eyes bordered in shadow.

"Yes?" she asked. I could sense the irritation. Maybe she thought I was a door-to-door salesman or, even worse, a Jehovah's Witness.

"I'm looking for someone."

"Yes?"

"Richard Pratt. Does he live here?"

"Used to live here."

I expected more of a follow-up, but no such luck.

"Did he move? What happened?"

"Who are you?" she asked. "And why do you want to talk to him?"

"I bought a car from him a while ago," I said, pointing to the Stingray in front of the house. "I just had some questions about it. I thought maybe he could, you know, answer them. You know how I can get hold of him?"

The woman unlocked the security screen and invited me inside.

"I'm Zora," she said. She pulled a cigarette out of her purse with nervous fingers. I wondered if that was why she wore so much makeup. She looked to be in her late forties, and I was pretty sure she'd smoked a long time. She lit up and brought the cigarette to her mouth with the dexterity and grace of a seasoned professional.

"So, where's Richard?"

"Dead," she said simply, as tendrils of smoke rose from her cigarette.

2

"I probably can't answer any of your questions about a car, but maybe you can find something here," she said, waving her cigarette about. That was when I noticed the entire house was boxed up. It looked like someone was preparing to move.

"I'm sorry. What exactly happened?"

"My brother died several weeks ago," she explained matter-of-factly. I detected a slight accent in her voice. Definitely East Coast. "And, once again, he leaves it to his little sister to clean up his mess. I've been doing this my whole life. Dick wasn't exactly—not exactly the most responsible of guys."

"Dick?"

She nodded. "That's what family calls him, and let me tell you, it's a bit more fitting. I probably sound like a total bitch, huh? Brother's dead and here I am complaining about him. We barely knew each other—that's the truth of it—and it's very sad what happened to him. But now I gotta figure out what to do with this house, his stuff, everything. Still waiting on the death certificate so I can do more than just box things up. Dick had everything in a trust. And I have my own life to deal with, okay? You know any good realtors out here? Once I get this place cleaned up, I'd like to get this on the market and on with my life. I don't know anything about any car, but you're welcome to look through some of his auto files." She pointed across the room to a lone file cabinet in the corner. "Maybe that'll answer some of your questions."

"Actually, no, I don't think it will. What happened to him?"

"You didn't hear?"

"No, I'm sorry, should I have?"

"Well, it was all over the news. He lost a couple friends recently to suicide, and I guess he wanted to join them. I didn't know he was that depressed." She walked to the kitchen island, where there was a stack of newspapers. She grabbed one, handed it to me. "You can read for yourself. I was going to keep some of these, take them back home to family. I don't know. Maybe it's grotesque—maybe it's odd—but I think some of the fam would want to see these. Touch them. Maybe it'll bring some closure."

3

The headline said it all: MAN BELIEVED DEAD AFTER JUMPING OFF GERALD DESMOND BRIDGE.

I skimmed the brief article, and it made enough sense. Richard Pratt, 58, pulled his Chevy truck to the side of the bridge, climbed up the chain-link fence, and then jumped into the cold waters 185 feet below. At least, that was the theory. Two witnesses—drivers in passing vehicles—claimed to see it take place. Considering the freak summer storm that evening, the lack of an officer present to throw a flare into the water to mark the place of impact, and the lack of an immediate call from such officer to contact the Coast Guard, the body had time to drift in the current.

One of the witnesses was traveling with a dead cell phone. The other, a married man who was not named, was allegedly having an affair and on his way back from a sexual encounter with his mistress. He didn't want to get involved—not until hours later, when his conscience would no longer allow it.

A spokesman claimed that Coast Guard and fire department helicopters, as well as six fire department boats and three boats from the port of Los Angeles, were using sonar in an active search to reclaim the body. Surviving a fall of that height was an impossibility.

The article contained detailed and quite graphic information about a suicide fall like this, and why survival was an impossibility. A body falling from such a height would go from nearly eighty miles an hour to zero in a fraction of a second. The force of such impact would cause a person's internal organs to tear loose. In falls like this, autopsy reports frequently detailed lacerated spleens, hearts, and livers. Ribs were often broken, impaling heart and lungs, and broken sternums, clavicles, necks, and fractures to the skull were quite common.

"Wow," I said, lost for words. I handed her back the paper. I'd seen enough.

4

I didn't stay much longer. I imagined Zora had much to attend to with her newly deceased brother: dealing with this property, telling friends and family, forwarding mail, obtaining that legal pronouncement of death—which, I imagined, might be rough without an actual body.

She did allow me to sift through his files. I improvised a valid excuse to rifle through them. I had purchased the Stingray not long ago, and although the registration was in my name and all the paperwork had been dealt with, I had never received any of the records. Oil changes. Maintenance. That kind of thing.

His files proved what I already knew Richard Pratt to be: a classic car aficionado. There were several other files for cars in here—a 1966 Fiat, a 1966 Ford Mustang, a 1953 Plymouth, a 1974 Pontiac Firebird—and in the back of the traveling file holder, one last file with the label STINGRAY.

I pulled it out and opened it.

No paperwork inside, only two newspaper clippings. Both obituaries. One was a woman, Sheila Thatcher, and the other was a man, Greg Ellis. I skimmed them. Sheila, mother of two, died eight months ago. Greg, a retired pilot, died a year and a half ago. I couldn't determine the cause of death for either.

"Do you know who these people are? Sheila and Greg?" I asked.

"Those were his two friends. From what I remember Dick telling me, the guy hanged himself. Sad thing. The woman drowned herself in her own bathtub. Can you imagine that?"

"Awful. But why would he keep this in the Stingray file?"

Zora laughed. "You don't know Dick well, do you? Let's just say organization wasn't his strong suit. I wouldn't be surprised if you found his high school report cards in there too."

Chapter Eighteen

49.42 Liters of Fuel Remaining

1

The following morning, I was up early.

I poured myself a bowl of cereal and went out to my back patio, where I took a seat.

I hadn't sleep well. The mandatory mediation appointment I needed to attend this morning wasn't going to be fun. I had no idea how Mara and I were going to come to any rational agreement. The amount she wanted for spousal support was absurd, especially considering that she was "shacking up" with the guy she'd been sleeping with for years.

I hadn't yet read through the pages of her accusations against me as a parent.

Not enough time nor enough brandy in my cabinet. It was going to take lots of brandy, I assumed, to get through it.

Chuck joined me. I ate my cereal and pondered.

He, near my feet under the table, sipped milk from a bowl I'd put out.

Just two guys trying to make it in the world.

"Well, Chuck," I said, gathering my things. "It's time I head out. Wish me luck, okay?"

2

It was a bizarre situation. I sat in the small waiting room of Department N of the Long Beach Courthouse, sipping a cup of coffee I'd purchased at the small café downstairs, while my soon-to-be-ex-wife sat several seats away from me, stone-cold-silent while looking down at her phone.

A receptionist had told both of us it would just be a few minutes. The mediator would arrive shortly and take us into the back, but I couldn't wait.

"Mara," I said, moving a seat closer to her. "Why are we doing this?"

She ignored me. Stared down at her phone. I think she was doing some online shopping. From what I understood, her new live-in boyfriend could certainly afford it.

"Mara, we don't have to do this."

She looked up me. "It's over, Charlie. The marriage is over."

"No, I get that. That's not what I mean." I sighed, and pointed to the room we were sitting in. "Why court? Why lawyers? This is where pathetic people go who can't work things out on their own. It's like daycare for petty people. We can figure this out on or own. We're reasonable people, and our son is nearly grown. Do we really need to go through all this nonsense?"

She looked back down at her phone.

There was a hardness to her—an edginess—and I wondered why she had changed so much. When she left to move in with her lover, it was all sunshine and rainbows. She acted more like an excited kid leaving for summer camp than a grown parent participating in a marital exodus. Why the sudden change? I questioned if I had said something or done something to initiate this.

"We can work this out together," I pled.

No response.

Frustrated, I went back to my original seat because I think that was what she wanted. Space.

My phone chimed.

I pulled it out of my pocket and read the message. It was from my son: *Hope it goes well today. Told Mom it's dumb to go to court. Need to talk soon. Not even sure I want to stay living here.*

Slowly, I slipped the phone into my pocket and lifted my gaze toward Mara.

Now I knew why she was so pissed.

My son's loyalties were shifting. Adam had been steady in his preference for his mother for many years, but I'd seen firsthand how glacial shifts in a teenager's psyche can happen overnight and without notice.

For Mara—who had long prided herself of being Adam's favorite—there was probably no greater offense in the world.

But I'm sure behind all of her anger and fury, there was fear.

Hot, smoldering fear.

3

"So, let's just go over this one more time," Justin, our mediator said. We were in a back room at a little table, and my wife had just dished out a laundry list of her wants. Justin was a middle-aged guy with oversized glasses and thinning hair, and although he tried to look like an attentive referee to keep us on track, he seemed fatigued. His eyes were weary, and the wrinkled forehead told the tale of a man who had been doing this a long time.

I couldn't imagine spending my days listening to couples bicker about such petty nonsense.

It sounded more like a death sentence.

"So you"—he pointed to Alice—"want primary custody, visitations to Dad every other weekend, court-ordered child support, and spousal support."

"Ridiculous," I said. I'd kept my lips sealed so far, but now I couldn't handle it. "Child support? The kid's sixteen-and-a-half years old. He's not a little kid."

Justin nodded but corrected me: "Child support can be requested any time before a child is eighteen and graduating high school. Legally, the primary parent has a right to request, and unless there is some extenuating circumstance, the court will look at your incomes, time share, and derive support from that. Do you believe there is an extenuating circumstance here?"

"Of course there is."

"And?" Justin readied his pen above his legal notepad.

"Her new boyfriend is wealthy. She doesn't need money."

That must not have been a good answer, because Justin didn't write anything.

"Child support is derived on a parent's income," he said. "A spouse or significant other isn't considered."

"It's not?"

"Not typically."

"Well," I said, utterly frustrated, "is this place full of idiots? You're telling me she can live with some sugar daddy and still milk me for money each month even though she's doing totally fine."

"In the court's eyes," Justin explained, "child support is your child's money. It's not your wife's."

"Okay, so does my son get to decide how to spend it?"

Justin, who had probably dealt with many an angered parent like me, said calmly, "Because Adam is a minor, child support is given to the parent to attend to the child's needs."

I laughed. "Wow, our legal system. It seems like the most educated people in our country have managed to put together the most ass-backwards system imaginable."

"Yes, well," Justin said, pointing to his notepad, "let's get back on track, shall we? What about spousal support?"

"Oh, I forgot about that," I said. "What else am I to give up? My right testicle and left one too? Would that suffice?"

Justin cleared his throat and took a sip of his water. I could tell this was his tactic. He remained calm, neutral, and talked only facts.

"Why am I being asked to pay spousal support? She didn't want to work. For years she didn't want to work. Now I have to pay for it?"

"Well," Justin said, "the court will certainly look at history, time married, professional capacity, and so forth."

I knew this didn't look good for me. We'd been married a long time. My wife had never worked, had no college degree, and—unless you considered shopping to be an employable skill—had very little going on in that department.

But there was one thing that could work to my advantage here.

"What about her new boyfriend?" I asked. "She's living with him. I don't have to pay spousal support if she's living or married to some rich guy, right? I know that much."

Justin turned toward Mara. "He's right. The court will certainly take this into consideration. Would you consider dropping or reducing your court request for spousal support considering these circumstances? Yes to child support but no or reduced spousal support?"

"But I need it…" she said faintly.

"But you do live with a romantic partner? He's gainfully employed?"

"Not exactly."

I shifted in my seat. I didn't like this.

"I don't actually live with him," she said.

Justin looked at me. "Well, your husband says that you are. If this is true, the court has a right to look at this and decide whether—"

"We're just friends," she explained, "and I'm just renting a room until I get my feet back on the ground. I thought this might come up." She opened the folder she had brought and produced copies of several checks. "These are checks I've paid to Shane Miller for my rent. I can provide the court other documentation too, if they request it. At one time Shane and I had a fling, just a fling, but it's not that way. I'm a renter, and I need some help to support my son and myself. We don't have the money to indulge like he does on classic Corvettes."

I sat back in my seat.

I looked her up and down, realizing what this meant.

Asking for child support was one thing.

Asking for spousal support was another.

But outright lies and manipulation?

This meant war.

4

The conversation took another bizarre turn—and, I confess, this one was my fault.

I pushed it.

"All this talk of child support," I said during a brief pause in our unproductive debate. I leaned back in my seat and took a sip of my coffee, which was now lukewarm. "How do you even know Adam is going to stay living with you? He might change his mind. In fact, I had a talk with him the other day, and I don't know…"

I let my voice trail off, let her connect the dots.

I hit the target. I could see the reaction on her face. She failed to blink, and I saw her grip tighten around the pencil she was holding. If she were stronger, she might have broken it. I think it was safe to say my words penetrated her armor.

"I think he's going to stay with me," she said softly.

"I wouldn't be so sure."

It was utterly sad and pathetic. Two grown adults using children as pawns. Sad, but true—but the system created it. It made me wonder if anybody could get through this without blood on his or her hands.

"It probably wouldn't be good for Adam to stay with his father," she said, looking more to the mediator than me. I didn't like how she used that word—*father*—instead of *dad*. There was distance and coldness to it. Clearly, she was setting up for something else. "There's been a history here—a sad history—but nonetheless a history of abuse."

I wanted to grab her by the neck and shake some sense into her. If she wanted to see abuse, I was about to show her.

"What the hell are you talking about?"

She took two labored breaths, closed her eyes, and asked for a tissue. Justin complied and handed her a box of Kleenex. I saw the first of several tears.

This can't be happening, I thought. Like a true thespian, she had slipped seamlessly into her role as victim.

"It's been terrible, and it's been going on for years," she whimpered.

Justin scribbled something on his paper and asked her, "Is primary custody what you are seeking, then?"

She nodded, too weak to speak.

Justin looked at me. "And how do you feel about this?"

"Me?" Anger, confusion, and disbelief swirled in my soul. "I think this woman's lost her freakin' mind, that's what I think. What abuse are you talking about? You've never said anything about abuse until now."

"Most of it's been verbal and harassing," she said. "He's totally emasculated his son, and Adam needs counseling to repair the wounds. It would be terrible for him to live with his father most of the time—even half of the time would be a tragedy."

Justin nodded and looked at me for a response.

I threw up my hands. "Are you on drugs or something?"

"Okay," Justin said, trying to get the conversation back on track, "why don't we go over what both of you are asking and see if we can—"

"I need the assistance animal," she said, turning toward Justin. "I need five minutes. Can I please have five minutes? I'm not doing very well right now."

I had no idea what she was talking about.

"Yes, as we discussed, we'll take a ten-minute break, and I'll see to it that we have an assistance animal available."

He walked Mara to the door and led her to the front, then returned a moment later to let me know that we would resume the mediation appointment in ten minutes.

"What's going on?" I asked.

"The Petitioner has requested ten minutes with a therapy animal to calm down and collect herself," he said matter-of-factly. "It's a service we provide as a court for alleged victims in family and custody matters. Is there anything I can get you while we pause?"

"You're telling me my tax dollars are going toward providing a puppy for people who cry victim when they don't get what they want?"

He ignored my comments. "You don't need anything?" he pressed.

I waved him away.

The door closed, and I was alone.

Wow, I thought. The moment I stepped into this building, I didn't step into a Court of Law.

I'd stepped into a world of insanity.

5

The meeting ended in a blur. We failed to reach an agreement on anything, and because of it, things would be decided at our future court date. Justin informed me that if I wished, I could hire an attorney, file for a continuance, and write a response to my wife's petition. It was ultimately my decision.

I left as I imagine many other divorcees left that office—more confused than when I first arrived.

I found myself standing in front of an elevator beside Mara, and I opted for the stairs instead. Being in a closed elevator with just us two didn't seem like a good idea. I was sure I'd be accused of something by the time we hit the first floor, and Mara would probably need another round of puppy therapy.

When I got to the parking lot, self-doubt started to cloud my thinking.

Maybe I should have been calmer and more collected during the mediation meeting.

Maybe I should have offered Mara more of an olive branch.

I had reached into my pocket and withdrawn my car keys when I noticed Mara in front of me, maybe only fifteen feet or so. She was headed toward her own car. The Jaguar. The one I bought for her.

Desperate, I raced toward her.

"Mara, listen to me," I said as I approached from behind.

She swiveled around instantly.

She no longer wore the face of a victim. This was the face of a puppeteer. A con artist.

Her grin was subtle, but it was there—a thin, knowing curve of the lips.

"I think we need to talk," I said, "but not with that guy there. Just you and me. Just us."

She said nothing.

"Why go through this court system?" I pled. "It's gonna take a lot of money out of you and a lot out of me. Come on. We're too old for this."

"Charlie, you had your chance to negotiate."

"Let's just talk, okay? You and me. No courts."

She studied me like a specimen, and then, with a sense of finality, said, "We'll see each other in court."

She was about to turn, but I think my gaze seized her.

"Just a little talk," I said and looked toward the Stingray. "I'd like to take you for a ride."

Chapter Nineteen

47.89 Liters of Fuel Remaining

1

She never did get in the car.

I pled a couple more times, but she just wouldn't go for it. I left the courthouse feeling more defeated than when I walked in. When I returned home, I contacted an attorney that Trey had recommended. Gertrude Hammer. She was, in Trey's words, a total "bulldog" and everything I'd want in a lawyer. She agreed to take the case, I agreed to write a check for her retainer fee, and she informed me that her secretary would send out a packet for me to complete. Her plan was to have me draft a response to my wife's petition and, to give me time, she would file for a continuance.

After dealing with that, I walked outside.

Tommy was in front of my house, leaning against the garage and petting Chuck. A basketball lay next to him in the grass.

"You doing alright, bud?" I asked. I picked up the basketball and dribbled it a couple of times.

"Just thinking."

"Well, it's okay to think. What are you thinking about?"

"Heaven."

"Really?"

I didn't have to ask. I knew why. With a mom dying of a brain tumor, I'm sure these moments flared up frequently. He was too young for it, far too young. Death was a constellation too difficult to be looked on or understood by a child of this age.

"You hungry? Want some lunch?"

"Yeah, Dad's been…" His voice trailed off.

"Drinking?" I finished.

Another nod of his shaggy mop of hair.

"Come on in. And bring Chuck too. He's one of the guys."

2

"So, what do you think happens when people die?" Tommy asked me. Such a profound question to escape the lips of someone so young.

I thought carefully. "I don't know." We were sitting on my back patio, eating peanut butter and jelly sandwiches and drinking pink lemonade. "But I think—at least,

I choose to believe—that there's a kind of pattern and organization to everything going on in our lives. I tend to think that whatever happens, it's gotta be a lot better than this place, right?"

"Yeah," he said, biting into his sandwich. He was already halfway done, and I'd only taken a few bites.

"Is this about your mom?"

He nodded, looked down.

"I know how you feel, Tommy. I totally get it."

"You do?"

"Yeah, I do." I took a sip of my lemonade and realized I hadn't talked much about this since I was a young man during a time which, in the grand scheme of things, I wasn't that much older than Tommy. "I lost my mom and my dad. Both to cancer."

"Both?"

"Yep. And I—well, I had a son—only two months old. He passed away too."

"Sucks," he said.

"Yeah, it does." I leaned toward him. "What has your dad told you? Do you know how long until she probably—" I stopped, thought through my words carefully, and proceeded delicately. "How long will she still be with you in your house?"

"I don't know," he explained. "But she's really tired most of the time. Dad used to take her out for walks around the block, but now she just wants to sleep all the time."

"I understand."

"Dad wants her to die in her own home and in her own bed. That's what he says."

"I see," I said. Here I was trying to word things softly, and the kid just came right out and said it. In a strange way, I wondered if kids could deal with death and tragedy in ways that adults couldn't. I'd read that before. Kids had a unique resilience that age and privilege stripped us of.

"Can I play basketball outside and use your hoop?"

"Of course," I said and, gathering my cup of pink lemonade, got up. "Why don't I play with you for a bit, huh? I need a workout. Chuck here can referee. Sound good?"

We headed toward my garage, and I couldn't help but think.

I hadn't talked about Seth's death to anybody in years.

Mara had accused me of being an emotional rock—physically there but not very present—and my son would probably say the same thing.

Maybe age had taught me something.

If I was going to be a father again, I was going to do it better this time. And if Kiki and I were really going to be together, I wouldn't let us grow in two opposite directions like what had happened with Mara and me.

"Let's play Horse," Tommy suggested.

"Horse it is."

We played for hours, and it was a great afternoon.

I didn't know why his mom had to die, and I had no idea what happened to people after they shuffled off their mortal coil. The answers to those questions were way above my pay grade.

But I did know this: If playing ball with a kid going through all that made him feel better—even for a moment—I'd play with him all night if I had to.

Because I'm not a monster.

I'm not what they say I am.

3

Kiki and I were going on a date later that evening.

Miraculously, she'd forgiven my early accusations, and as I readied myself in front of the mirror, I began to contemplate the possibilities before me. I was not going to be able to talk Mara into peacefully negotiating this divorce—that much was obvious—but maybe the outcome wouldn't be so bad. Even if I did have to pay child support, a couple of years would pass quickly. And I was willing to bet her attempts at spousal support would blow up in her face. It was obvious they were cohabiting and had been romantically involved for years. Even a third-rate private investigator would be able to figure that out.

Maybe things would work out.

I looked at myself in the mirror. I was never going to be the lean, six three, middle-aged guy I wanted to be, because I'd never been that way when I was young. Half of the girls I dated before marrying Mara were taller than me, sit-ups and crunches never made a dent on the belly, my hair—although still there—was thinner than even a few years ago, and what had once been dark was now flecked with silver.

I was thankful for that, at least. I had hair.

But who knew: by the time I got through this divorce, maybe there'd be none left.

The doorbell rang, and I checked my watch. 5:03. Kiki was early. She wasn't supposed to show up until six.

I put on some cologne—Versace Eros, which Kiki loved.

I checked myself one last time. Black slacks. White button-down shirt. Hair slicked back.

"Looking good," I mumbled and headed downstairs to the front door.

I was a little upset she was early. I was hoping to buzz to the flower shop across the street and buy her some flowers before she arrived.

When I opened the door, it wasn't Kiki.

It was Stanley, Tommy's dad.

I hadn't seen him in a while, and he looked as I imagined a man in that situation might appear. He was wearing jeans, no shoes, and a wrinkled shirt stained with what appeared to be wine. He was bald, unshaven, unkempt, and he glared at me with moist, bloodshot eyes.

He reeked of sweat and whiskey.

"Stanley?" I said, shocked to see him.

He pointed at me and swallowed. "Stay away from my son."

I nodded, trying to understand what had provoked this. "I'm sorry, is something wrong? Tommy came by earlier—he was just bored—and we played a little basketball. Just trying to cheer the kid up, that's all."

"It ain't your job."

I waited. What else was there to say?

"If my kid needs to eat, I'll feed him. Got it? And if he wants to be entertained, he can talk to me."

"Stanley, I know what's going on with your wife, and I just thought the kid—"

"I don't need your charity," he said, wiping saliva from the corners of his lips. "I don't need nothin' from you or anybody else. We take care of ourselves, okay? Stay away from me, stay away from him, and if we want anything, we'll come and ask. Got it?"

"Yeah," I said, "got it."

He turned and went back to his house.

Chapter Twenty

46.35 Liters of Fuel Remaining

.

1

"Great view, huh?" I asked.

Kiki sat across from me. We were in the Sky Room Restaurant, twenty or so stories up, looking over Downtown Long Beach. My doubts about her were vanishing. I'd started to accept that I was wrong about her. Paranoia, it seemed, had gotten the best of me.

"So how are you feeling about everything?" she asked.

I wondered what *everything* she was referring to. There was just so much.

"Well," I said, "I was hopeful the divorce would go quickly and painlessly, but not so much anymore. She wants spousal support, child support, the whole deal."

"How old's Adam again?"

"Sixteen."

"Well, at least that'll be over soon."

"My thoughts exactly."

She stared out over the jeweled lights of the city. "And how do you feel about *other* things?"

"I don't think I was a very good dad the first time around," I admitted. "Sure, there was food on the table. Yes, he was clothed. But at the end of the day, I was pretty checked out. I'm looking forward to remedying that. Call it age, call it wisdom, but I think I'm going to get it right this time. At least, I'm going to try."

Her cheeks flushed, and the wide smile I'd come to love beamed at me from across the table.

"If I heard you correctly, that implies you might actually be excited about this," she said.

"Yep," I admitted. I raised my glass of wine. "I'm as ready as I'm ever going to be, and I'm sorry that I—"

She shook her finger. "You already said you're sorry. My mom taught me very young to only say sorry once. Otherwise, it becomes a tool to control people. The past is the past."

"Wow," I said. "Your mom taught you well. I guess I had a chance to do some thinking and, well, I'm ready to go all in."

Her phone went off, and when she fetched it out of her purse, I saw the look on her face.

She wasn't happy.

"Give me a few seconds," she said, and excused herself to take the call.

2

"Who was that?" I asked when Kiki returned
"Duncan."

No surprise there. This had happened a few times over the last several months.

"What'd he want now?"

"What else? Just wants to plead his case, say how much he misses me, and what a stupid mistake I'm making. More of the same."

"Ever thought of blocking his number?"

"Maybe I will," she said. "But you're right, I shouldn't have taken the call. That was dumb of me."

"Well, you're forgiven."

She grinned.

"I'm a little worried that before long he's going to bother you," she said. "He's not a good guy. Incredibly possessive. Incredibly angry. He did time too. Got into a barfight when he was in his twenties and put a guy in the hospital for weeks. He has this angry streak in him—really angry—but as long as you don't cross him, you're fine."

"How'd you stay with him so long?" I'd asked her different versions of this question before.

"Let's just put it this way: when you've only been treated one way, that's the only thing you know, and it becomes normalized. You develop a pattern, a comfort with what in your heart of hearts you know to be wrong. And trust me, there's a part of Duncan that is incredibly protective and loyal. If he's getting his way, he can be charming and affable. That's why he's such a good salesman. Builds and sells custom bikes. But there's a side to him that's very dark, particularly if he doesn't get what he wants."

"And he wants you? Doesn't he realize you're with me? And you're pregnant?"

"I don't know if he wants me," she said, "so much as he wants to control me. That's what he really wants. He wants the trophy at his side."

"And he got physical with you in the past?"

Kiki had always dodged this question. Strangely, I think she was ashamed. This time she didn't.

"Of course," she explained. "When he gets angry, he's very volatile. Especially when he's on meth. It's a little hobby of his. He pushed me several times and slapped me across the face on a couple of occasions. One time he gave me a black eye."

"That's terrible."

"Yeah, it is. And I didn't tell anyone. Didn't call the police. Nothing."

"I'm sorry to hear it."

"He'll go away," she said. "He's only called a few times, and I think he's been drinking. I think he's hoping it doesn't work out between us and I'll run back to him."

"Well, then," I said, reaching out and taking her hand. "We'll just have to make sure that never happens."

I leaned over and kissed her.

"I think you have a better chance of getting struck by lightning than him bothering you at this point," she warned me, "but if for some reason he does, stay away from him. He's dangerous."

"You don't think I could take him?"

"Maybe," she said, "but not if he's carrying the bat."

"The bat?"

"Yeah, he's always had a paranoid side to him. Always keeps a bat in his car."

"Noted."

3

After my first glass of wine, we moved on to a cheerier topic.

"So, you looking forward to moving in?" I asked.

"Yes," she said. "I've already given notice to my landlord. As soon as I get back from visiting my sister in Baltimore, we'll get packed and get everything to your place."

"You mean our place."

She rubbed her finger along the rim of her water glass. "Yes. I mean our place."

"How long will you be in Baltimore again?"

"Not sure. A couple of weeks, maybe longer. My sister could use the help. I haven't bought a return ticket yet. I'll figure that out when I'm there."

She'd already told me the story. Her sister was going through a divorce and had to relocate. Kiki had managed to get time off work and was visiting to catch up with her and to help get her life resituated.

Now my phone chimed. It was sitting on the table next to me.

It was Adam.

"It's my son," I said. She could probably hear the enthusiasm in my voice. Getting a text from my teenage son was like witnessing a falling star. Quite rare.

I read his text and smiled.

"What is it?" Kiki asked.

"He wants to do dessert tonight."

"He does? Well, we could meet him. I'd love to meet him."

I thought about it. I guessed this was inevitable.

"Alright," I said. "Let's do it."

4

We agreed not to say anything about the pregnancy. Not yet.

I had no idea how to tell my son, an only child, that a woman he hadn't yet met was about to become mother to his much younger sibling. I needed to read a book or some kind of instruction manual before attempting that one.

We met at the same little ice cream place on Second Street where Kiki and I ventured into on our first date. Shockingly, the introduction went well. Adam didn't seem at all fazed by seeing me with another woman; in fact, I think he liked it. Maybe the tide was turning and my son, ever distant, was coming around at last.

"So, what kind of music do you play?" Kiki asked him.

"I like the heavy stuff," he said.

"Your influences?"

"Well, there's so many…" He paused and swirled his spoon through his cup of chocolate ice cream. "I guess I'm a fan of old school. Like, I would probably say Anthrax,

Megadeth, and Metallica are my biggest influences. Like, huge."

"You like their earlier stuff, like before *The Black Album*?" she asked. "You know, like *Ride the Lightning* or *Master of Puppets*? That's always been my favorite—the earlier stuff. And I kinda feel the same about Anthrax. *Among the Living* is definitely my fave."

My son's eyes widened. "You know the albums?"

"Of course!" She laughed, leaned in for a whisper. "I'm not as old as your dad, okay? And someone around here needs to appreciate good music."

Adam smiled.

I leaned back in awe.

Adam's mom may have been able to spoil him rotten by buying him whatever he wanted, but neither she nor I had the ability to talk shop with him like this. I had no idea Kiki knew this kind of music, which was, sadly, a true testament to how quickly our relationship had unfolded and how perversely little we actually knew about each other.

"Do you know Faith No More? Ever hear of them?" Kiki asked.

"Hell yeah!"

"So, you like them?"

"Of course."

"I have an original vinyl of their album *The Real Thing* stored in my garage. Signed by the band. Pretty awesome."

"Are you serious?"

"One never lies over ice cream," she said, pointing her spoon at him. "It is forbidden."

I listened for what seemed like an hour as they talked about music, bands, guitarists, and vocalists about which I knew nothing.

But I didn't mind. I didn't mind it all.

All things considered, I think the meeting went quite well.

Chapter Twenty-one

44.80 Liters of Fuel Remaining

1

When I arrived home, I noticed Fergus's yellow truck parked a block down.

As I sped past, I saw him sitting in the driver's seat. Engine off. Lights off. Waiting for me, most likely.

"Why did I even try to help him?" I mumbled as I pulled into my driveway.

I guessed what his plan was. His last arrival at my house hadn't quenched his anger, and he had returned for more. This time, I was pretty sure I knew what it was. I remembered his words: *I see that new sports car of yours somewhere, and I'm gonna key it.*

I considered avoiding my house and driving on. Maybe he'd walk down to my house, realize I wasn't home, find no Stingray in the garage, and return back to whatever cave he crawled out of.

But that was when an idea struck me.

And it was a profound one.

Fergus was a volcano. Ever since I'd known him as a young man, he was angry and explosive. Once he'd done whatever damage he felt was necessary and satiated his passions, he usually went away.

Maybe I ought to give him the opportunity.

I remembered how Adam kicked the passenger door of the Stingray with his steel-toed boot and how, when I returned home that evening, there was not even the faintest scratch. As my hands gripped the steering wheel of the car, I thought of the pristine interior of the automobile and the engine beneath the hood that hadn't aged a day since this Vette was driven off the lot.

It would replenish itself. I was convinced.

The same way it did with gasoline. The same way it did with the relationship with my son.

I didn't pull into the detached garage at the end of my driveway like I normally did.

Instead, I parked in front of my house.

I got out of the car and headed inside.

"Come and get some," I mumbled as I closed the door.

Let Fergus walk away feeling like he'd done some real damage, I thought. Maybe then he'd leave me alone for good.

2

Like a moth drawn to flame, Fergus did exactly as I anticipated.

I pulled open a small crack in my bedroom blinds and looked outside as Fergus walked toward my vehicle. He circled the Stingray in what seemed to be a strange, predatory ritual, and then he went to work.

He pulled a key out of his pocket and, as he circled the car, he dragged it along the car's exterior. He must have circled the car five times, leaving a jagged EKG-like line of scratched paint, and I found it so difficult to watch that I had to turn away.

I had full confidence the Stingray would replenish itself, but why watch?

It was too painful.

Instead, I went downstairs and poured myself a glass of brandy.

3

I waited until morning to check the results.

If it was the last thing I saw before I went to bed, I was pretty confident I'd be so upset I wouldn't get a wink of sleep.

But sure enough, when I walked outside in my pajamas with my morning cup of coffee, the Stingray looked as new as ever. Not one scratch along the curvature of its sleek body or anywhere near the side louvers that looked, in many ways, like gills. At certain moments, it did look alive. Some chrome-and-steel creature that had risen from the ocean. I saw the reflection of blue sky, clouds, and treetops in the car's hood, and as I sipped my coffee, I wondered more about the marvel parked in front of my house.

What was this thing?

I was about to run inside, grab my keys, and pull it into the garage when I heard Tommy's voice. He was screaming.

"Mr. Phoenix! Help!"

I turned around.

The kid was running from the direction of my garage.

I wondered what had happened. Maybe Stanley was passed out drunk somewhere in his house, or, worse yet, maybe Stanley had done something rash. I dropped my coffee and raced toward the boy.

"What is it?" I asked. "What's wrong? Is it your dad?"

"No," he said, visibly upset. His face was flushed. Tears streamed down his cheek. He pointed to the garage. "It's Chuck!"

4

I found Chuck lying several feet from his bowl along the garage.

At first, I thought he was injured because it looked like he was lying in a small puddle of blood. But as I drew closer, I could see and smell that it wasn't blood. This was vomit. Poor Chuck convulsed as I drew near, and although he looked near death, he managed the strength to look up at me.

"What the—"

I bent down next to him, wishing I could do something.

I ordered Tommy to back away. He'd dealt with enough death in his life lately. He didn't need more of this.

"Hang in there," I whispered to Chuck.

It's sad to say, but watching Chuck suffer like that brought more tears to my eyes than the dissolution of my own marriage. I suppose that speaks volumes to what a sad state my life had been in. I thought about what to do. How was I supposed to help him? There was a veterinary clinic a few miles away. If I could get him there, maybe they could so something.

Then I noticed the blue bottle that had been tossed alongside the garage.

I went toward it, picked it up, and read the label: PEAK ANTIFREEZE AND COOLANT. 50/50 PREDILUTED.

I screamed and threw the empty container at the wall.

Tommy, scared, retreated several steps.

"What happened?" he cried, terrified. "What is it?"

"Nothing," I lied and tried to gather myself.

But inside I was seething. I should have stayed at the window last night and watched Fergus leave. He'd come to my house to do more than just key my car. If I had been more vigilant and watched, this never would have happened. When I looked toward the bowls again, I noticed the water bowl—which I suspected didn't contain water—was half-full and the food remnants were the remainders of wet cat food.

Fergus must have put it there, most likely drenched in antifreeze, because I always put out dry food.

"Is he gonna be okay?" Tommy asked.

"I don't know," I said, thinking. "I hope so."

Never in my life had I tried to move a dying, poisoned cat, so all I could do was improvise.

I ran into my house, grabbed a couch pillow, and brought it out to Chuck. My plan was simple. I would gently pick up the cat, place him on the pillow, move him to my car, and drive him straight to the vet.

It was the only thing I could think to do.

I didn't like how lifeless Chuck felt when I picked him up. His eyes were closed now, and for all I knew, he was already dead. But I had to try.

"Open the passenger door," I told Tommy and threw him the keys to the Stingray.

I followed the boy, holding the pillow, looking down at the lifeless, vomit-drenched feline. When I got to the car, I gingerly laid the pillow in the passenger seat. I noticed the cat convulse once, and then he went completely limp. The feline's almond-shaped eyes slowly opened, slit-like pupils rolled back in their sockets, and more vomit rolled out of its frothy, fanged mouth.

Still in my pajamas, I ran to the driver's side door.

"I told you to stop spending time with my son!"

I looked up and saw Tommy's father, in pajamas too, standing on the front porch of his house.

"Is he gonna be okay?" Tommy asked again, whimpering.

"I hope so!"

I climbed into the car, started it up, and pulled onto the street.

The vet, if I remembered correctly, was only a few miles away. Maybe they could do something. Maybe it wasn't too late.

"Stay with me, Chuck," I said, and when I got onto the main street, I put the pedal to the metal. "Don't leave me."

5

I drove up Park Avenue and made my way to Spring Street. Once there, I headed West. Sometimes I went to the Ace Hardware on this street, and I always passed a small veterinary clinic on the side of the road. It was a tiny white building and very easy to miss.

To say I pushed it is an understatement.

I blew through one red light and hit nearly ninety miles an hour on my way there.

I looked down at Chuck, who lay lifeless on the grey pillow I'd fetched off the couch.

When I pulled into the small parking lot beside the clinic, there were no other cars, so I parked as close to the entrance as possible, jumped out with my key still in the ignition, and headed to the front door. Maybe they'd want to come out and get Chuck? I didn't know what I should do.

But I had barely taken two steps when I realized my plan had been foiled. The building was closed, abandoned, and the sign on the front door told the tale: CLOSED UNTIL FURTHER NOTICE.

"What?" I complained.

But I should have asked *why*? Why did the one veterinarian's office I drove to have to be the one that was shut down?

I tried to gather my thoughts. There was still time. There had to be another practice not far from here. I reached for the phone in my pocket, and that was when I realized there was no pocket—I was still wearing the flannel pajamas I'd woken up in.

Desperate, I raced back the Stingray and checked my seat, but I already knew the truth.

My phone was at home.

I hadn't walked out with it that morning because my only goal was to check on the Stingray.

I never would have imagined this.

I desperately tried to recall the locations of any other veterinary clinics in the area, but I came up with nothing. Chalk it up to never having owned a pet. If I were to drive home, look one up on my phone, and then drive there, it would be too late. It was totally obvious.

Chuck lay on the pillow, lifeless. He was probably already dead, and if he wasn't, it was clearly imminent.

Rage seized me.

"No!" I cried, and I kicked the side door of the car three times.

If I left a dent, why did it matter?

I was sure the car would be just fine.

6

So I drove.

I couldn't go home and face Tommy and tell him that Chuck had passed. The boy had been through so much, and I couldn't bear to tell him. I was willing to bet that if I drove straight home, Tommy would be sitting in front of my house, waiting expectantly for me in hopes that Chuck was better. I didn't have the heart to disappoint him.

I spent two hours on the freeway. One hour down the 405 South, and the other back up the 405 North.

I didn't cry, but I stared straight out the window and never once looked down at Chuck.

I've never been a crying man.

But as I drove, Chuck's death brought to the surface so much of my angst and so many of my questions. Why did the cat have to die? Perhaps more importantly, why did all things have to die? Why was my marriage dead upon arrival? There had never been life in my marriage with Mara. And why had my relationship with Adam, which had been good when he was a little boy, rot like a corpse over the years?

Did all highways and roads in this life eventually end in loss and grief?

Were there no off-ramps?

Two hours later, I pulled into my garage. Fortunately, Tommy wasn't sitting out front, so I had some time. I could grab my shovel, bury Chuck, and think about how to break the news to the kid.

I needed a stiff drink. It was technically morning, but I didn't care. The situation demanded it.

I had just stepped out of the Stingray when I saw Tommy run up my driveway. I was so stunned and disappointed, I didn't close the door to my car. I wished I'd had time to think. Time to contemplate.

"Mr. Phoenix!" Tommy said, out of breath. He'd only sprinted down the driveway, but he looked like he'd just jogged a marathon.

"Hi, Tommy," I said.

"What happened? Is everything okay?"

"Well…" I struggled to find the right words. There had to be some euphemism I could use, some way to break the news lightly.

"Is he alright?" he asked pointedly.

"I…uh…"

And then it happened.

"Yes! He's okay!" Tommy cried, looking past me.

I spun around.

Chuck leapt out of the driver's seat of the Stingray and pranced through my garage toward the backyard. He moved swiftly and with a youthful dexterity I didn't recall him having before that moment.

Tommy ran after him.

Dumbfounded, I looked once again at the dark, sleek machine Richard Pratt had sold me.

I moved my hand along the smooth, steel surface of the hood and closed the driver's door.

"Impossible," I whispered.

Chapter Twenty-two

43.26 Liters of Fuel Remaining

1

I had to test the theory.

All day, I paced around my house, asking whether I was losing my mind. To believe a car could replenish its own gasoline was one thing. To believe it could replenish relationship was another. But this? To bring something back from death—if only a cat—was something utterly divine. Or maybe the cat hadn't been dead? Maybe Chuck was at the very edge—just above E—when the replenishing took place.

Whatever the case, I had an idea. I had to know.

I picked up my phone and called Trey.

His back pain had been excruciating lately.

It was time to take him for a ride.

2

Trey agreed to meet me for dinner at one of our favorite restaurants on Second Street. Open Sesame was a Lebanese restaurant where Trey and I occasionally met to go over paperwork. He was free for the evening and loved the food, so it didn't take much convincing.

On my way over, Kiki called.

"Hello, sweetie!" Her voice was youthful and warm.

"What's up?" I asked.

"I just wanted to let you know that I called a moving company. Everything is dialed in, so if you can come over and help me box up some things when I get back from my sister's, that would be great. I'll need a ride to the airport too."

"Okay. I will put my amazing physique to work for you."

She giggled. "And I made an appointment with my OBGYN for when I come back. Can you come? They're gonna do an ultrasound. You can hear the heartbeat."

Wow, I thought. This was real.

"Of course I'll be there," I said.

As unexpected as all of this was—as clumsy and maybe foolish—there was life in it. And God knew I needed that lately.

3

"So, you still seeing Kiki?" Trey asked me over his plate of Chicken Tawook. We were sitting outside on the patio of Open Sesame, each with a glass of wine—his white, mine red—enjoying a warm summer sunset.

"That I am."

"And she's still pregnant?"

"Yeah, she is. It's for real, Trey."

He nodded. "You ever look into that stuff I told you? You know, about the financial stuff?"

"I talked to her," I explained. "I think she's had some hard times, that's all. Kiki's a good person, I think. I have a feeling it's gonna work out."

"I hope so," Trey sighed. "There are lots of women out there who are good people who would sure like to get into your wallet or my wallet, if you catch my drift. Just be careful, okay? But I'm glad you're both doing well. You're going to have quite a life adjustment coming up. If you need anything, I'm always here."

"What about you, Mr. Casanova?" The waitress returned and asked if we wanted a second glass. I said yes and turned my attention back to Trey. "How's it going with your most recent girl?"

"Beth?"

I chewed my food and thought about this. "I thought her name was Sarah. No?"

"I'm kinda seeing both," he said coolly.

I laughed. "Ah, I should have known."

"Beth owns a beauty salon in Seal Beach. Beautiful woman. Body to die for. Still manages to spend five days a week in the gym. Sarah is nice too. Economics professor at Cal State. Amazing in bed, let me tell you. The ones who are kinda nerdy, read a lot, and seem reserved are totally wild in bed. It's almost a guarantee."

"I'll have to remember that."

"And both self-sufficient," he said. "That's the best part about them. They don't need me to buy them things all the time and tell them what's what. They have minds of their own." He took a couple more bites of his food and, in a rare moment, looked mildly apologetic. "Sorry, Charlie. I'm not trying to make a point about Kiki."

"I get it." And truthfully, I did. If I had Trey's physique and height—and his perfectly moisturized dark skin—I'd probably have a couple of girls on the side too. But those weren't the cards I was dealt.

"Speaking of which," he said, "if, for some reason Kiki doesn't work out, you ought to consider a little nip and tuck. Might draw a few more hummingbirds toward your nectar."

"Nip and tuck?"

Trey wiped his mouth with his napkin. "A little botox never hurt anyone," he explained. "Takes care of the crow's feet and the forehead creases." He studied my face. "And a little microdermabrasion might be in order. Think of it as a gentle sanding of your skin. Gets rid of some of those fine lines."

"Micro-what?"

"Microdermabrasion. It's what they call it."

"Wow," I said. The waitress set a fresh glass of red wine in front of me. "And how do you know about all this?"

He leaned toward me, pointed toward his own face, and said firmly, "The Taj Mahal wasn't exactly built in a day, nor was this. It takes a bit of time and effort at our age. But if you're willing to put in the work, the benefits are unparalleled."

4

"So, was this just a catch-up dinner?" Trey asked after we were done and sat waiting for the bill. "I thought you had some news for me regarding the facility or maybe the new night manager, Zeb. Everything going okay with Zeb?"

"Yeah, it's not that. He's fine."

"Everything okay with your nephew, Fergus? He still giving you a hard time?"

"He's being the normal prick he is," I explained, "but I have a feeling he's not gonna be bothering me much longer. We had this argument—and in my own way, I kinda let him win—but I think it'll keep him out of my hair."

"Well, that's good." Trey picked up his near-empty wine glass, swiveled it in circle. "Sometimes the better part of valor is discretion."

I assumed that was some literary reference. Whatever it meant, it went over my head.

I adjusted my position in my chair. "Actually, I wanted to talk to you about something not work-related."

"Okay."

"It's my new car."

"The Stingray?"

"Yeah, the Stingray. I…uh…" I had no idea what to say. What was I going to tell him? *My car replenishes its own gasoline. It mends relationships with people. It brings cats back to life.* Trey would think I had totally lost my marbles, and I wouldn't blame him. So I tried a different route. "How's your back doing?"

"Unfortunately, the same." He had brought his lumbar support pillow to dinner with him, so I probably didn't have to ask the question. "Still looking into surgery. But, you know, it comes and goes. So, we'll see."

"I've heard Stingrays do a great job alleviating back pain."

He laughed.

But I pressed. "No, really, why don't you come for a ride with me? Hell, you've never even been in the car. It'll do you some good, and I read this funny article the other day about how the vibrations of some V8s actually have a soothing effect on the body. Why don't we go for a quick cruise down PCH? You'll love the car."

"Yeah, I'm sure I will." He picked up his phone and scrolled through a few messages. "But I've got a late date this evening at nine. I wanna get ready."

"Nine?" I protested. "You still have a couple of hours. Is it Beth or Sarah?"

"Ava."

"Ava? Who?"

Trey grinned. "Rule Number One: If you have two steaks in the fridge, keep one in the freezer. You never know when unexpected circumstances might call for it."

"Wow," I said. This guy was living the dream.

Or maybe it was a nightmare. Juggling three women? One was hard enough.

"Alright, you talked me into it." Trey got up from the table and grabbed his lumbar pillow. "Let's see what this new Corvette of yours is made of."

5

We drove down PCH through Seal and Sunset, then turned around a little after Huntington Beach. It was a beautiful summer evening, and we looked out across the blue waters as the sun dipped below the horizon. The sunset was majestic. A fading blue canvas smeared in splotches of blood red and royal purple.

Trey enjoyed the ride, and although we discussed our business a little during our conversation, I couldn't get my mind off how the drive was affecting him. Was it working? Would the ride be long enough?

I dropped him off at his car on Glendora Avenue, a few blocks down from Open Sesame.

Thanking me for the ride, Trey shook my hand, got out of the car, and grabbed the lumbar pillow he'd used during the drive.

"So, you enjoyed?" I asked.

"Very much," he said, standing outside the car, holding on to the passenger side door. "Nice ride here. We'll have to do it again sometime. I've been thinking of getting a classic sports car myself soon. I have a few ideas. I'll have to hit you up for advice."

"Anytime." I smiled. "How's the back treating you? Did those V8 vibrations do the job?"

Trey moved his hand to his back. I saw the look on his face, the recognition.

"You know," he said, tweaking his body a little to the left and then to the right, "it's feeling pretty good right now. But that's the thing—it comes and goes. I guess right now it's mainly gone."

"Gotta thank the V8, huh? It's a magical healer."

"Well, I don't know about that," he said, laughing. "But I'll tell you what—if I ever get cancer, I'll call you up for a ride, okay?"

"Anytime."

He laughed again, waved goodbye, and headed toward his car. I watched the way he walked with his lumbar pillow in his left hand.

He walked surely, confidently, without the slightest strain. When he climbed into his own car, he threw the lumbar pillow in the passenger seat. It seemed, for now at least, he didn't feel the need to use it.

I pulled onto the street, and when I hit a red light, I thought about what he'd said: *If I ever get cancer, I'll call you up for a ride.*

He'd laughed when he told me that, but I realized, as the light turned green, there was nothing to laugh about.

I thought of Tommy, and I thought of his mom.

And I had an idea.

Chapter Twenty-three

41.71 Liters of Fuel Remaining

1

My plan was fairly simple.

I had no idea if it would work or if it were ethical, but I went forward with the belief that it was for the greater good. So many times, it seemed, life was like that. Sometimes you simply had to venture off the narrow road and make your way through the thorny brambles and vines, and this was one of those times.

The morning after I took Trey for a ride, I walked over to my neighbor's house and knocked on the door.

I waited nearly a minute and almost turned around to head home because I thought Tommy and his dad were still asleep.

The door opened. Tommy stood there, rubbing his eyes, still in pajamas.

"Hey, Mr. Phoenix," he said.

I hadn't considered how early it was. I was so anxious to try this, I hadn't paid much attention. It was only half past seven.

"Hey, Tommy, how you doing?"

"Good. I was just getting up and—"

A shadowy figure emerged from behind Tommy, placed a large hand on the boy's shoulder, and nudged him out of the way. It was Stanley. He wore nothing but boxers and a white T-shirt, and his hair—like his son's—was unkempt and unbrushed. He looked at me with dark, marble-like eyes and scratched the rough bristle on his chin.

"What do you want?" he asked. He squinted at the unwelcome sunlight the open door let in.

"Hey, Stanley. I'm sorry to come by so early. I just wanted to—"

"Didn't I tell you to stay away from my kid? We don't need any of your charity, okay?"

"Yeah, I know, I got that." I tried to compose myself. "I know you guys have been going through a lot, and I know how hard it is being a dad and everything. I'm sorry I made it seem like you couldn't provide for your own kid. I come with a peace offering, okay?"

"A peace offering?"

"Yes, a peace offering." I revealed what I had been holding behind my back. It was a 750ml bottle of Johnny Walker Blue Label. A blend of rare malts from selected casks around Scotland. I was gifted the fine whiskey at a birthday party two years ago and had held on to it for a very special occasion. I never imagined it would be this.

"What is it?" Stanley asked, taking the bottle. I imagined him to be more of a Budweiser and Jack Daniels kind of guy, so he eyed it suspiciously.

"That is a very fine bottle of whiskey," I explained. "What you got there is selected from some of the rarest stocks in the Johnny Walker reserves. Let me tell you, after a bit of that, it'll be hard to go back to anything else. Think of it as an apology."

"I see," he said, reading the label.

For someone who was a self-proclaimed hater of charity, he certainly had no problem with me gifting him a free bottle of rare whiskey.

In a matter like this, he was clearly willing to make an exception.

"And I just wanted to say—you know, it's hard to know what to say—I think about your wife a lot. I wish the best for her. For you. The whole thing."

"Yep," he said, looking down.

Kind words fell on him like acid rain. I don't think he knew what to say or do, but he nodded and said, "I'll see if I like it. In the meantime, if my kid's hungry, just send him back home. I got food in the fridge."

"I'll do that. Let me know if—"

Still admiring the bottle, he mumbled something that sounded like "thanks" and closed the door.

I didn't take offense.

In all honestly, I think that was his way of being courteous.

2

A few hours later, I looked out the window of my home and saw Tommy outside playing with Chuck. The kid was building a fort made of Legos and, from what I could surmise, Chuck was supposed to be the Godzilla-like creature who was threatening it.

But the cat didn't look like much of a threat. Chuck lay in the sun, half-asleep.

I walked outside with a glass of cool lemonade in my hand.

"Hey, Tommy," I said.

"Hey, Mr. Phoenix. Wanna see my city? Chuck the Gigantic is threatening to wipe it out."

"He looks very dangerous."

Tommy didn't get the sarcasm.

"Listen," I said, hunkering down beside the kid. "I wanted to ask you something. You've told me in the past how your dad falls asleep early. Passes out sometimes right there on the couch."

"Yep. He drinks too much."

"I see. Listen, tonight when he passes out, I'd like you to come over. I have a suspicion—and I could be wrong—that he's gonna pass out harder than usual. Don't tell him you're coming to see me. It's our secret, okay?"

"Okay," the boy said. He was still working with his Legos and barely looked at me.

I wasn't sure if he really understood. "Does that make sense, Tommy? Do you know what I'm asking you to do?"

"Yep." He snapped a couple pieces of his city into place and admired his work. "When my dad passes out tonight, I come talk to you. Right?"

"Yes, that's right."

"Why?" Now he looked up at me, his face scrunched with wonder.

"I'd like to take you and your mom for a ride in my new Stingray. I think it might be good for her to get out of the house for a little bit. And my car—I can't explain it, Tommy—it heals people."

"It does?"

I nodded, and Tommy, satisfied with my answer, nodded back.

Oh, to be a child again. How unworn one's capacity for belief is in those days.

"But don't tell your dad, okay? He can't know. This is just between you and me."

"I don't know if it'll work. Mom's really sick."

"I know," I said. "Tonight, we're gonna try to change that."

How terrible it looked.

Yes, I handed a bottle of irresistible liquor to a man drowning in the vice of alcoholism.

Yes, I told a young boy to keep a secret from his father.

But it was the only way—and it was the right thing to do.

3

"Are you sure he's asleep?" I asked Tommy.

As promised, the boy arrived at my house at a little after nine o'clock and told me his father had gone into his room and collapsed on his bed. Out cold, Tommy told me.

Now we were standing just outside his front door, and I wanted to make sure.

"I'm positive," Tommy explained. "I even tried waking him up, but he just rolled over and mumbled something."

"Okay." That sounded pretty legitimate. If Stanley were to wake up and discover me sneaking around his house with his own son, it wouldn't be good. "Listen, we're going to wake up your mom and get her out to the car, okay? But we have to do it quietly."

Tommy nodded. "Okay. But sometimes she doesn't really wake up well, and sometimes she doesn't know who I am."

"That's okay," I said. "Let's just be super, super quiet. Okay?"

"Okay." He was about to open the door, but he peered back at me. "You really think this will work, Mr. Phoenix?"

"I'm counting on it."

He smiled and opened the front door. I followed him inside.

As I suspected, it was a mess. Dishes were piled in the sink and covered in flies, and old pizza boxes, fast food bags, and half-eaten plates of food were strewn about. It was musky and rank. Not so much from the food but the closed windows, the lack of sunlight, and, I imagined, the lack of showering on Stanley's part. This truly did look like a man cave, and quite an unkempt one. It turned out I was right about Stanley being a Budweiser guy. A trash can was overflowing with Budweiser cans.

But I was wrong about his choice of whiskey. No Jack Daniels. Instead, several bottles of Maker's Mark stood on the dining room table, all empty.

Amazingly, I saw the bottle I'd gifted Stanley only hours ago on the same table. Only one third of its contents remained.

The plan worked, I thought. And that much whiskey in that short a time? Quite impressive. I was pretty sure I wasn't going to see Stanley come out of his bedroom anytime soon, but still, I resolved to be very, very quiet and cautious.

"This way," Tommy whispered, and he led me down a hallway.

The house was carpeted, so that helped for quiet movement, and as I walked down the hallway, I noted several pictures of Stanley and his wife, Jaysa. One was of their wedding. Husband and wife stood at the altar, facing each other, exchanging vows, I presumed. My cursory glance suggested that Stanley looked quite younger then. He had hair, more chiseling of the jaw, eyes still electrically alive with youth.

Other pictures I assumed were from vacations. White water rafting. Camping. In one picture, husband and wife stood on the beach of some tropical paradise wearing leis—I assumed Hawaii—while little Tommy, maybe only three then, grinned widely at the camera. I looked at the picture closely. Jaysa was a brunette with large curls, a square jaw, and a strong, athletic build.

Why, I wondered, did this have to happen to her?

Why did she have to be brought down below E?

Tommy, several feet ahead me, quietly opened a door.

I followed him into his mother's room. She resembled nothing of the vivacious woman I had seen in the pictures. Thin and frail, she lay in the bed, her face turned toward me, eyes closed. This room was musky too, but it was a different kind of musk—the smell of encroaching death, of depleting life.

"She's sleeping," Tommy whispered. "She sleeps all the time."

"I understand."

I moved toward her. On the table beside her bed were several plates, some with the remnants of food, others polished clean, along with at least a dozen paper cups. As if reading my thoughts, Tommy said, "Dad brings her food, and sometimes she eats, sometimes she doesn't. She's just so tired."

"Sure." That was what Stanley's life was like these days, I assumed. Take care of the wife all day, feed her when she's able, and then—at night—drink away the memory of it.

I got it. I'd probably do the same if I were him.

I leaned toward the woman and whispered into her ear. "Jaysa, can you hear me? Can you wake up? Jaysa, can you wake up?"

Nothing. She was stone silent.

"It's hard to wake her up sometimes," Tommy explained.

"Okay." I reached for both of her shoulders and gave her a little nudge. "Jaysa, can you wake up? Can you please wake up?"

A slight stir, but hardly anything.

"Mom!" Tommy said, trying to help out. I warned him to keep the volume down, but somehow it worked. Maybe it was because it was his voice, the voice of her son. Slowly, like heavy doors on rusted hinges, her eyelids opened. She looked at me and then Tommy. I saw no recognition in those dark tunnel-like eyes.

"Mom," Tommy said, "this is our neighbor, Mr. Phoenix. We're taking you somewhere tonight."

"Microwave," she said, eyes creaking shut.

I had no idea what she was talking about—and I don't think she did either.

"Tommy's right," I whispered. "I'm your neighbor. We'd like to get you up and out to the car. I can help you."

"Drive-in movie," she said. "Is it new? Can I sit by the microwave?"

"Yes," I said. "You can sit by the microwave. And it's new. Very new. Can I help you to the car?"

More awake, she sat up in bed, and I could tell what great effort it took. She studied us for several moments, eyes blinking. She looked around the room as if she had never been here before.

"We're going to the movie?" she asked.

"Yes," I said. "Let's go. But we go quietly, okay?"

She scratched her head. "Quietly?"

"Yes, very quietly." I hadn't thought this through. Total improvisation. "There's a dog here sleeping, and it's kind of a mean dog, so let's get up and go quietly, okay? Can we do that?"

She swallowed. Her eyes struggled to stay open.

"Are you an angel?" she asked.

I paused. "Tonight, I am kinda that." I took her hand. It looked like she was wearing long pajamas. That was good. There would be no need to change her clothes. She could go in that.

"I'm glad you're an angel," she said, and then, pointing at her son, she leaned toward my ear and whispered, "Who's that one? He kind of scares me."

4

I put my arm around Jaysa, Tommy held her hand, and we walked the frail skeleton of a woman through her house. She staggered forward like a sedated prisoner.

We managed to get Jaysa outside and into the Stingray quietly and unnoticed.

As I helped her into the passenger seat, she yawned, told me she was going to go to sleep, and asked me what movie we were going to see. I told her it was a surprise. As the car had no back seat, Tommy climbed into her lap. He was wedged in tight, but as frail as she was, and Tommy being just a kid, it worked.

I started up the engine.

All three of us, in the glow of the dashboard lights, waited while the engine loped and loudly idled.

I pressed in the clutch, shifted into reverse, and, slowly applying pressure to the gas while easing off the clutch, backed into the street.

I noticed Fergus's yellow truck parked across from my house. I couldn't believe he was there, but apparently he'd come back for more—as if vandalizing my car and killing my cat weren't enough?

I drove past him without any acknowledgement.

Within five minutes, I was on the 405 with open road before me.

"Where are we going?" Tommy asked. "Are you sure this will help Mom?"

I looked at him, looked at her.

He looked wide-eyed at the freeway before him; Jaysa was asleep and snoring.

"I sure hope so."

I accelerated to eighty. I was going to drive as far as I could until it worked.

"Come on, baby," I said, looking across the dashboard at the Stingray's luminescent gauges, "do your thing."

5

When I pulled back into my driveway, the sun was just coming up. I had driven all night, up and down the freeway in hopes that something would happen, but alas, nearing daybreak, I realized it wasn't working. Tommy had slept for hours, pressed into his mother for strength and warmth, and Jaysa remained submerged in deep slumber.

There was no resurrection this time.

And I couldn't understand why.

I got out of the car when I pulled into my driveway. Mom and son were still asleep in the Stingray, and I cursed the vehicle. If it could bring a cat back to life, why couldn't it help her? I knew there were people in the world who loved animals more than people—was my car one of those?

Frustrated, I woke up Tommy and got him out of the car.

"Did it work?" He rubbed the sleep out of his eyes.

"No," I said, "not this time. Next time, we'll drive farther."

I assumed that was the problem. I hadn't driven far enough. Or fast enough. In her condition, she simply needed more.

I helped Jaysa out of the car, and she, disoriented, dazed, and utterly delirious, walked with me to her house. With my arm around her, I was virtually carrying her. I was glad she was still alive. During my drive, I'd imagined how terrible it would be if she passed away on the 405 and the replenishing hadn't worked. Taking my neighbor on a Death Drive along the 405? How would I explain that to the authorities?

"Let's get her back in bed," I told Tommy, "and let's do this quietly, okay?"

Tommy yawned and nodded.

Hopefully, Stanley was still asleep. I don't know what would be worse: dealing with him or the police.

Quietly, we ushered Jaysa back into her bed. Her eyes were barely open, and even though she had been asleep during almost the entire drive, it appeared to have exhausted her.

I left her as I found her—unconscious and near the edge of death.

Tommy walked me to the front door of his house. Before I left, I bent down to look him in the eye. I felt so utterly grieved, and not just because it hadn't worked. I had planted hope in the boy's heart, and now that hope had been extinguished.

"I'm sorry, buddy," I said. "We'll keep trying, okay?"

"Okay." He nodded.

"You get some rest. And remember, if you need anything—"

"Tommy!"

I heard the voice from the other room.

It was loud, clear, and utterly cognizant.

I flinched, because my first thought was that it was Stanley. We'd woken him up.

But this wasn't a man's voice.

It was Jaysa's.

6

Hunkered down in the side yard, I listened outside the open window of Stanley and Jaysa's home.

"Mom," Tommy said.

"Tommy, what happened? I had a dream—an amazing dream last night. You and I were driving the street somehow, and these lights were passing by, and every time a light passed by, I felt myself getting—"

"Mom, you're not supposed to be out of bed. Aren't you supposed to—"

"I know," she said, "but I woke up and—well, I don't really understand—but I feel okay." A pause. "My God, look at me. I'm so skinny. Are you hungry? I'm hungry. Can we eat? And look at this place. I know I've needed some rest, but really, this place is a pigpen. Can't your dad at least take all these beer cans out to the recycling?"

"Mom?"

"Yes?"

"Is it really you?"

"Yes, hon, it's really me. Don't be silly. Who else would I be?"

"I've just never seen you so—"

"I know. Maybe this is a good day, huh? The doctor said there might be some of those. Let's make the best of it, huh? Where's your dad?"

I didn't hear Tommy say anything, but I imagined he pointed to the other bedroom.

"Why don't I wake him up today? Give him a surprise, huh? I think he'd like that."

"I love you, Mom. I really missed you."

"Me too, Boogers."

Boogers? A nickname, I guessed.

I'd heard enough. I walked back to my garage, placed both my hands on my hips, and admired the Stingray.

"Well done," I said.

I had driven all night and should have been exhausted. If I were driving my Lexus, I'm confident I would have wanted to crawl into bed and sleep away the day.

But I didn't feel the slightest bit of fatigue.

The Stingray must have recharged me.

Chapter Twenty-four

40.17 Liters of Fuel Remaining

1

After I'd showered and had a light breakfast, Kiki called.

"Hey there," I answered the phone.

"Hey, sexy," she said. "I wanted to call you before going into work. I just finished doing some packing for my Baltimore trip. I'm really looking forward to seeing my sister. Just wanted to see how your night was last night and what your thoughts were for today."

"Interesting night," I said.

It was a cold truth: I hadn't told Kiki about the Stingray and what it could do. There were several reasons, of course. I was worried she wouldn't take me seriously, and how could I blame her? She would think I'd lost my mind, until, of course, I was able to prove it to her. I could probably find some injured animal along the highway to pick up and take for a spin, but it just seemed like such a hurdle to get over. I wasn't ready. Not yet.

The other reason was more troubling, and although I had tried to stave it off, the thought was there: What if the only reason Kiki was into me was because of the car? We'd gone on several drives together. Had the car intoxicated and—in some ways—falsified my relationship with her?

I just didn't know.

"What'd you do last night?" she asked.

"Just went on a long drive."

"In the Stingray?"

"Yep."

"Wow, you sure are loving that car, aren't you?"

"You bet I am."

"Well, I sure wish I could have been there when you got back last night."

"Yeah, and why is that?"

"I think your performance is a little better after you've gone for a drive," she said, giggling.

"Ah."

I hadn't thought about it until that moment, but I think she was right. I would love to say that middle age hadn't ebbed some of my desires and my "performance," as Kiki had put it, but in truth it had. As I thought back to our last couple of encounters, they had been directly after a quick drive to or from somewhere.

And the performance had been good. Very good. A V8, four-hundred-something-horsepower kind of good.

"Well, I'm not going to be able to come over tonight, unfortunately," she said, a tinge of theatrical mourning in her voice.

"Oh yeah, why?"

"I have a date with a young man."

"A date? You do? Are you talking about—"

"Yes, Adam. I'm gonna take him to Amoeba Music in LA. It's epic. Every young connoisseur of music like him should go. Then we'll grab a bite after. You know, I don't want to be a stranger to him. I want him to know me."

"Wow." I was shocked. Pleased but shocked. It wasn't every woman who would take an interest in another person's teenage kid. "I got a feeling Mara's not gonna like this all that much."

"Well, Mara doesn't need to know the whole truth just yet. She thinks he's going with some friends."

I liked her theory about one's needing to know the whole truth. It made me feel better about not dishing out all the dirt on the Stingray.

"Well," I said, "I think that's good—"

Incoming call. Speak of the devil. It was Adam.

"Hey, I'll call you later. It's Adam."

"Sounds good. And don't forget, I need a ride to the airport." She giggled. "Maybe we can make out in the car while I wait for my flight."

"Tempting. Talk to you soon."

I clicked over to the other line to talk to Adam.

2

"So, I hear you have a hot date this afternoon," I jested.

"Yeah," Adam said sluggishly. I wasn't sure if he smoked pot, but half the time he sounded like it. Maybe it was just a teenage thing. "Kiki's pretty cool, Dad. I gotta admit. We're going to Amoeba Music."

"I heard."

"Cool place. And listen, I don't have long but…" He adjusted his phone, maybe to the other ear. "Is there any chance I could come over or maybe we can go out to dinner or something like that? I'd like to talk. I've been thinking about some things and…"

"Sure," I said.

I took a seat on the couch because, truthfully, my son's words knocked the wind out of me. Even though he hadn't said anything, I knew what he was talking about. He wanted to move in.

Perhaps the Ice Age was coming to an end.

And I had to tell him too. I needed to tell him about the pregnancy.

"Let's find a time when we can do dinner."

"That sounds good, Dad. I'll call you—"

Another incoming call. This time Mara. When it rains, it pours.

"Hey, it's your mom calling," I told him. "We'll talk soon."

3

"What is this record store business all about?" Mara asked.

I could tell from the tone of her voice that this wasn't going to go over well. I took a seat on my couch and braced myself.

"What are you talking about?" I asked.

"The fact that *your* girlfriend is taking *my* son to some record store in Los Angeles. I overheard the whole thing. I'm his mom, Charlie, in case you forgot. He's *my* son."

"Yeah, I get that Mara. It's just a record store. It's not a big deal."

"It's a big deal to me."

"Listen," I said, "Adam's sixteen now. The umbilical cord was cut a long time ago. I was there, remember?"

I shouldn't have gone there, but I did.

And it didn't help.

"You know, Charlie, I've tried to be really nice and understanding. I wanted this divorce to go smoothly, and you're the one making it difficult."

"Me?"

"Yes. Who else would I be talking to?"

"I don't know. I'm not the one making outrageous claims and ordering therapy animals. Listen, if you don't want Adam to go to the record store, then tell him no. Forbid it."

She paused, and I knew why.

She would never tell Adam no. She had always cared too much about his approval, and now, with the divorce and being the flighty teenager that he was, she'd give the kid anything if it elevated her standing with him. If the kid asked for drugs, I'm sure she'd struggle to say no so long as it kept them enmeshed.

"Look," I said, trying to shift the conversation, "I'm actually glad you called. I still think we need to talk. We don't need to do this through the courts. Lawyers are bloodsuckers. They'll suck the money out of you and me and whatever soul we have left. We can do this on our own. Why don't we go for a drive and talk? I think we can—"

"You could have settled right there. We were in the room with a mediator."

"Yes, but what you're asking for is ridiculous."

"It's ridiculous to help provide for your son?"

"No, of course not," I said, "but come on. The circumstances are a bit ridiculous, right?"

"This is why we need lawyers," she said matter-of-factly. "You don't know how to have a productive conversation."

And then the line went dead.

4

"So how's she doing?" I asked Tommy later that afternoon. I was on my back patio, drinking lemonade.

Tommy had come over with a drink of his own. A can of Cherry Coke.

"Good." He had a gleam in his eye. One I hadn't seen in a while. "Can I ask you something, Mr. Phoenix?"

"Sure thing. Why don't you grab a seat here at the table?"

Tommy climbed into the seat, took a chug of his cola.

"Mom's doing well today. Dad is excited, but he told me the doctors said she might have good days. This might be one, but Dad's not sure, because she hasn't had a day this good in a long time. I think Dad is going to take her to the doctor—just in case, you know, the sickness is gone."

"Maybe."

"That's what I wanted to ask you."

"Okay. About the sickness?"

"Yeah." Tommy set his can on the table. "How does the car do it? You know, like, how does it heal people?"

"That is a good question." I looked toward the Stingray. It was in the driveway today. I had pulled it out of the garage earlier to make a grocery run. "To be honest, Tommy, I don't know. There are some things in this world there are no answers for. But I think God—if there is one—creates things that are, I don't know, special. I guess that's what I think. I think it's a gift from beyond, I guess."

"Like an angel?"

"Maybe. That's a good way to think of it."

"If I ever get sick, will you let me ride in the car?"

"Of course." I laughed. "Hey, if that Stingray has the power to bring back Chuck and your mom, I'm pretty sure it can handle a little troublemaker like yourself, huh?"

He chuckled, grabbed his can of Cherry Coke, and got up. "Thanks, Mr. Phoenix. I should go. Dad still doesn't like me spending time here."

"That's okay," I said.

Tommy headed back toward his house, and as he did so, I noticed a figure standing just beyond the gate. It was Fergus. He had been standing there the whole time, watching, listening, and as he walked forward, he grinned slyly.

5

"So," Fergus said, strolling into my yard, his hands buried in the pockets of his jeans. "I thought I'd stop by."

This time, he didn't seem upset. Not at all. Just curious.

I didn't think this would get violent.

His posture suggested he wasn't here to fight. I guessed he wanted to talk.

"Nice paint job on that Stingray," he said, motioning to the Corvette which sat, like a shiny drop of black ink, on the white driveway. "What, you got two of them or something?"

"Two Stingrays?" I laughed. "Not likely. Fergus, haven't you had enough? Just get outta here, okay? Do you really think harassing me is going to entice me to give you your job back? You need to get it together, okay? I'm done."

"I get that." He took his left hand out of his pocket and pointed toward the Vette. "But what I don't get is what happened with that car. I saw it with my own eyes. There's no way you could have found someone to fix it—to make it look like that—so quickly. What'd you do? Some kind of spray-over or something?"

I grinned, because it occurred to me that I had the upper hand here.

He really was confused.

"I dunno, Fergus," I said. "Maybe you didn't scratch it up as much as you thought you did."

He nodded. "I'd believe that before those crazy stories you're telling that kid. You ought to know better than to spread lies like that to the kids in the neighborhood. Especially about a kid's mom who's dying. Charlie, I don't even go that low. But really"—he looked at the car, then back to me—"how'd you do it?"

I got up from the table and headed toward my back gate. He stepped back into my driveway.

"Get out of here before I call the police," I said.

Just then, Chuck strolled into the backyard. He was chipper that day, and he bolted across the grass and toward a hole in the wooden fence, which he quickly disappeared through. There one moment, gone the next.

Before I shut the gate, I noted the expression on Fergus's face.

It was the look of a man who'd seen a ghost.

Chapter Twenty-five

38.62 Liters of Fuel Remaining

1

As I went to bed that night, I kept thinking about that look on Fergus's face.

It was priceless.

After I got out of the shower, I threw on a pair of pajamas and headed to bed. I was pretty beat, and although I planned to put on a Netflix show or something to lull me to sleep, I doubted I would make it through much before totally conking out.

I received a text. It was from Kiki. A selfie of her and Adam standing in front of Amoeba Music, holding on to two records: *Appetite for Destruction* by Guns N' Roses and *Rocks* by Aerosmith.

She also sent a message: *Had a great time with Adam. Don't forget. Ride to airport tomorrow morning. Make-out session planned for parking lot. Be ready.* ☺

I shook my head in disbelief. I didn't know how she'd managed to connect with Adam so well and in so short a time, but she had. I was impressed, to say the least.

I was half-tempted to forward the picture to Mara with the message, *UMBILICAL CORD HAS POSITIVELY BEEN CUT*, but I thought better of it.

It might feel good for a second, but it wouldn't help the situation.

My phone rang. I didn't recognize the incoming number. It was a 518.

I let it go to voicemail, but a moment later, just after I crawled into bed, another text came through. This one from the same 518. It was short and to the point: *Charlie, this is Zora. Please call me.*

2

"Hello," I said.

I assumed Richard's sister was calling because she'd found some files related to the Stingray. I'd asked her to contact me if that were the case.

"Sorry if this is late," Zora said in greeting.

"No, it's fine."

If Zora was home on the East Coast, it would be much later there, for sure.

"This question might strike you as strange," Zora said. She sounded just a tad bit tipsy. A slight slur of the words. "Have you by any chance seen or heard from Richard?"

"What?"

"I told you, it's a strange question. Even in supposed death, my brother pisses me off."

"I'm sorry, Zora, I'm confused as to why you're calling me. Richard died. Right? Am I missing something?"

"Perhaps," she said. Now I heard the tinkling of ice in a glass and the sharp flicker of a cigarette lighter. Smoking and drinking. I imagined her sitting in a kitchen or some dark living room in Upstate New York, drink in one hand, cigarette in the other, phone tucked between chin and shoulder. "A declaration of presumed death was about to be issued, but that changed yesterday. A private boat's security camera caught someone, a mile or so from where he jumped, climbing onto the docks. It raises suspicion."

I sat up in bed. "Was it him on camera?"

"They don't know. They haven't shown me, of course, but they say it's pretty grainy and it's being looked at. They're also going to contact other boat owners in the marina to see if they can come up with some footage from, I don't know, other boats."

"I see."

"Yeah, well, I hate to be so blunt about it, but it's hard to move things further along—like life insurance policies and his trust—without some kind of death certificate."

"I get it."

And I did. I assumed Zora was the beneficiary of the life insurance policy. Made sense. Richard had no wife. No kids.

"So why are you calling me again?"

"I'm just trying to find out if Rich—Dick, that is—faked his death because he wants to get out of Dodge. Have you heard from him? Seen him? You have any reason to believe he might be alive? You bought a car from him, right? Didn't you have some connection with him?"

"No, I just bought a car from him. That's all."

"Well," she said as I heard the tinkling of ice draw near the phone, "call me if you hear anything. I have bills to pay, okay?"

"Sure, I will."

I hung up, and as I lay my head on the pillow, I couldn't help but wonder: Was it even remotely possible for someone to jump off that bridge, at that height, and live?

3

The following morning, I noticed something when I got into my Stingray. The odometer read 111,268. Strange. That was thirty miles less than the car had on it when I purchased it, yet I knew that the odometer packed on miles like it should have while I was driving.

I had a simple theory. Every evening, the car "replenished" its mileage and landed here at 111,268. Richard's advertisement had stated this number as the mileage. I don't know why the Stingray liked to "reset" at that mileage, but it did.

Whittier, where Richard had lived, was about thirty miles away.

That explained those additional miles on the day I purchased it. I was sure it also would have explained the additional thirty miles on the day Richard drove the car to my house and I first saw it, but I had been too unobservant and hadn't noted the mileage that day.

After thinking about this, I drove Kiki to the airport.

We were running late, so there was no quick make-out session in the parking lot. I pulled into Long Beach Airport, she kissed me goodbye, gave me her keys for safekeeping, and told me she'd give me a call when she got there.

And she was off.

I went back to my quiet house and did some yardwork. By that evening, after two glasses of wine, I was beat. I crawled into bed early and was nearly asleep when I heard my bedroom door slowly open.

I sat up instantly. It was Fergus. He strolled into my bedroom, holding a gun at his side.

Shocked beyond words, I recoiled.

"Get out of the bed," he ordered.

"Fergus, what are you—"

"I said get out of the bed."

This was beyond comprehension. Fergus may have been the stereotype of an angry ex-employee, but as appalling as killing cats and keying cars was, this was an entirely different level. A gun? In my house?

Out of choices, I followed his request and got out of bed.

"I want the car."

"What?"

"You heard me. I want the car. Where are the keys?"

My throat was dry and coppery, and my heart pulsed in my chest. I swallowed and tried to think of a way out of this. There was a gun in my closet, locked in a gun box, but there was no chance I could get to that now.

"The keys are downstairs by the—"

"Get out of the bed and show me where they are, and don't try anything. Got it?"

"Yeah, I got it," I said, standing up.

With my hands in the air and Fergus directly behind me, I walked slowly down the stairs and to the kitchen drawer where I kept the keys. I reached to open it, and Fergus reminded me, "Don't try anything."

"I'm not." I opened the drawer and reached for the leather key ring with the silver handcrafted Corvette symbol embedded in it. One lone key dangled from it. I had another key to the Vette on my own keyring. This was the spare.

I began to hand it to Fergus, but he greedily snatched it from me. His two beady eyes gaped at the key like a vulture's, and an enormous smile spread over his flushed face. He took a deep breath, and a couple of beads of sweat trickled down his face and along the curvature of one lone, pulsing vein in his forehead.

I noticed one of the windows in the living room was open. It must not have been locked. My mistake. I assumed that was how he'd crawled in.

He still had the gun pointed at me, but he backed a couple of steps toward the front door.

"What'd you do to it?" he asked, sniffing.

"What do you mean? Do to what?"

"To the Stingray."

"I didn't do anything to it."

"Well, someone did." He looked down at the key in his right hand, then stuffed it in his pocket. "Nobody can do a paint job that quick. And that cat shouldn't be alive.

Then I saw that neighbor of yours walking with his wife. She didn't look good, no, but she was walking."

"You don't really believe all that, do you?" I asked, half-laughing. I've never been a great liar, and I was pretty convinced he could see right through me. "That stuff I was telling Tommy—it's not real, Fergus. You have to realize that. You're acting crazy right now."

"Then give me another explanation for it."

I paused, but it was enough for Fergus to pick up on. That was all he needed.

"You call the police, and I'm gonna go after more than your cat next time I come over here," he said, and, opening the door, he was gone.

4

I called 911.

Just as I heard the Stingray peel out of my driveway, someone answered the phone. It was a woman. In her telephonic world that must have been ripe with violence and brutality, she sounded remarkably calm.

"911, what's your emergency?"

"A theft," I said. "Someone stole my car."

Chapter Twenty-six

37.08 Liters of Fuel Remaining

1

A police officer arrived at my house not long after my call. The short, balding Hispanic man flashed his badge and wrote down a detailed description of the incident as well as a description of the Stingray, which included the license plate and VIN. It was nearing midnight by then, and even though I'd downed a couple of glasses of brandy to calm my nerves, I felt shaky.

"Any distinguishing marks on the vehicle?" he asked. "Dents? Headlight or taillight out? Anything like that?"

"Definitely a negative. It looks as good as new."

"Wow, sounds like a nice car. We'll get right on the search. This address you gave me for Fergus Hart—you believe it's current?"

"Yeah, should be."

"Great. Did he say anything as to where he might be going?"

"I have no idea. He didn't say."

"Got it." The officer closed the notepad he'd been writing on. "Get some rest. We'll begin an immediate search for the vehicle, and we'll be in touch. We're also going to have a unit in front of your house for the next several hours, if that helps you feel at ease."

I closed the door behind the officer, went into my living room, took a seat on my couch, and called Kiki. She was as shaken as I was, maybe more so, and I had to remind her that I was fine and there was nothing to worry about. It was a good thing, as it took my eyes off myself.

Sleep didn't come easy.

I remained on the couch. I watched news on my phone's CBS Los Angeles app, surfed Netflix, and although I might have fallen into a sort of twilight sleep, I never really went under.

All I could see was Fergus. Standing there. Sweat dripping down his face. The barrel of the gun swallowing me whole.

The birds were just beginning to tweet outside and the first shafts of purpled, morning sunlight were beaming through the windows when my phone rang.

I didn't recognize the incoming number, but it was a 562. Maybe it was the police.

"Hello," I answered.

"Is this Charles Phoenix?" It was a woman's voice. Severe and cold.

"Yes." I sat up.

"I'm Detective Serena Grimm with the Long Beach Police Department."

"Great. Did you find the car?"

"I'd like to talk to you about Fergus Hart."

"My nephew, yes. What is it?"

"I think it would be better to talk in person," she said. "Can you meet me this morning at the station? Nine o'clock?"

2

I found myself sitting in a small interrogation room with a Styrofoam cup of coffee. It tasted terrible and, for a moment, I understood the stereotypes I'd seen on movies and television shows of cops frequenting local donut shops. Maybe it wasn't for the donuts. Perhaps it was to escape terrible, burnt coffee like this.

The whole situation seemed odd.

I wasn't sure why I was sitting in an interrogation room. Fergus had stolen the car from me at gunpoint. He was the one who deserved questioning.

Detective Serena Grimm entered the room. She wore a black double-breasted blazer, a black pencil skirt, and high heels that clicked on the tile floors. Her hair was equally dark, straight, and just below shoulder length, and her eyes—the color of coffee with cream—looked at me severely as she took a seat across from me in the only other folding chair in this room. She placed a folder of papers on the table. If she hadn't decided to go into law enforcement, she probably would have made a good Armani Beauty model. Her smooth, olive skin appeared as impervious to the elements as my Stingray.

"Thank you for coming," she said without looking up.

"Yeah, whatever I can do to help. Were you able to locate the car?"

"We'll get to that." She picked up a pen, wrote something on a yellow notepad. "I'd first like to hear about your relationship with Fergus."

"Oh yes, Fergus."

"He's your nephew?"

"Last I checked." I chuckled, but Detective Grimm looked up at me and didn't crack the slightest bit of a smile. This woman was all business, that I could tell.

"I read the report about the robbery," she said, looking over several stapled papers. "He woke you up while in bed, walked you down the stairs, got the keys from you, and then headed out to the car. Is that accurate?"

"Yeah." I nodded. "That about sums it up."

"Was there a physical altercation of any kind between the two of you in the home?"

My eyes went to the corner of the room as I thought, but I didn't know why I was thinking so hard about it. There was no mystery here.

"No, none at all," I explained. "He had a gun pointed at me. I wasn't going to start a fight."

"And you're absolutely positive, Mr. Phoenix?" she asked, her eyes narrowing into slits. She seemed to be implying something, but I wasn't sure what.

I felt like a butterfly on display; her eyes were two needles pinning me down by the wings.

"Look, I'm one hundred percent positive. There was no altercation whatsoever, at least not physical. He got what he wanted, and then he left. What's this all about?"

"Just dotting our I's and crossing our T's, Mr. Phoenix."

"Did he tell you that happened or something? I don't know why he would, but if he did, he's lying. Is that what he told you?"

"That would be impossible," Detective Grimm said. "Fergus is dead."

3

"Dead?" I gasped.

Grimm's curveball had disoriented me, and I sat at that table with the coffee cup in my hand, utterly perplexed.

"Yes, as I said, he's dead."

"How?"

"Well, it's really no secret anymore," she explained matter-of-factly. "The neighbor heard a gunshot, broke into your nephew's rented house, and found Fergus dead in his garage. By all measures, it appears at this point to be a self-inflicted wound to the head from his firearm."

"Suicide?"

"At this point, it appears that way."

"Wow." I sat back in my chair and crossed by arms over my chest. "I'm sorry, I'm just—I'm just—I don't even know what to say."

"Why don't I ask you a few more questions, then, okay?"

"Sure."

"After Fergus left, did you follow him to his house? Did you have an altercation with him there? Perhaps in that very same garage?"

"No, of course not. I was home."

"What did you do?"

"Well, I made a call to my girlfriend, Kiki, and then I fell in and out of sleep for most of the night, watching Netflix. I barely slept last night. I was pretty shaken."

"Okay." She scribbled something on her notepad. "Can anyone else corroborate that you were home alone last night? Did you make any phone calls later, did anyone come over, anything like that?"

"No, of course not. It was the middle of the night."

"I see."

4

"So you were the last person who saw him?" Detective Grimm asked after peppering me with more questions.

"I suppose. I don't know where he went after leaving my house."

"I have one more possibility," Grimm asked. "Could you have driven to his home in a second vehicle, had an altercation there, and then gone back home?"

"Of course not," I protested. "What sense would that make? I would have taken my Stingray home. Not called the police."

"Possibly," she said, "but people who come through that door say lots of things, don't they?"

I was stunned. I felt my heart fall into my lap.

"I'm utterly confused," I said, my hands on the table. Episodes of *Dateline* flashed through my head. Was this when someone should ask for a lawyer? Even someone as innocent as me? Or would that just make me look guilty? "I didn't have any idea all of this had happened until you told me, and I can assure you that I had nothing to do with it, as you seem to be implying."

"Implying?" Detective Grimm looked at me quizzically. "Are you suggesting that I'm implying you were involved?"

"No, I just—" I caught myself and stopped. I had a feeling Detective Grimm would twist whatever I said in another direction. "I really don't know what happened. I just want to pick up my car."

"Yes." She looked down at her papers. "If you don't mind, we'd like to keep your Corvette and look through it. Would you mind if we held on to it for a day, maybe two?"

"Um, yeah, I guess that's fine."

"And you're sure there was no altercation inside the vehicle between you two?"

"I couldn't be more positive."

"One last thing," she said, gathering her papers. "Do you know of any other person who would want Fergus dead? Any enemies out there?"

I thought about it. "I think Fergus has probably made lots of enemies over the years," I explained, "but nobody that I know of who would want him dead. I'm confused, though. Why are you asking this? You told me it was suicide."

"Dotting those I's and crossing those T's, Mr. Phoenix."

She gathered her papers and led me to the door.

Chapter Twenty-seven

35.53 Liters of Fuel Remaining

1

I was shaken up with everything that had happened, but I decided to keep my dinner appointment with Adam.

I drove my Lexus, and on the way to pick him up from his mom's new house, I couldn't help but wonder: What led Fergus to do it? Assuming it was really a suicide as Grimm originally claimed, why, after stealing the Stingray, had he decided to take his own life? It didn't make sense—but then again, so many things in this world made no sense. I saw it on the news all the time. John Doe, millionaire who has it all, takes his own life. It was as predictable as the changing of the seasons.

But why Fergus?

And if it wasn't a suicide but a murder, then who?

As I pulled up in front of my soon-to-be ex-wife's new house, I caught a glimpse of Mara and Shane, her long-time lover. He was getting into a taxi, luggage in tow, but before he got into the car, he and Mara exchanged a long, passionate kiss that must have put at least another buck on his taxi fare. Shane was a tall guy, athletic, broad-shouldered—in so many ways my antithesis—and I didn't want to get close. I pulled my car to the curb a block away and let them engage in their PDA. I didn't need a front seat to that show.

When they were done, Shane got into the taxi, Mara went back inside, and I pulled my car in front of the well-manicured lawn of her new estate.

I texted Adam to let him know I had arrived.

As I waited, I thought about that long, drawn-out kiss in front of the taxi.

"Just a renter, huh?" I mumbled. "Yeah, right."

2

We headed to Simmzy's, a local restaurant in Belmont Shore that was on Second Street. Adam loved the burgers there, and I was pretty hungry myself.

There was a Simmzy's in Huntington Beach too, and if I'd had the Stingray, I would have opted for the longer drive along PCH. I could have used those miles with Adam sitting beside me in that car; without it, I felt like I was going into battle without armor or weapons. I hoped the conversation wouldn't veer into the wrong lane and descend into bitterness and argumentation like it so frequently did.

Only a couple of minutes into the drive, my phone went off twice in my pocket. Someone was calling. I fished it out and checked the missed calls. Both were from Mara.

What now?

I couldn't even take my son to dinner without being harassed.

I decided to return the calls after dinner.

3

As I stuffed my phone back into my pocket, Adam said, "I'm kind of glad you picked me up in this car and not that new one you bought."

"You mean the Stingray?"

"Yeah, that one."

"Why?" I was utterly shocked. "A young guy like yourself cruising down the street in a '69 Stingray. Are you kidding me? You know how many young guys your age wish they had that option?"

"It's just not that comfortable to drive in," he explained, looking out the window.

His words did have some merit. The Stingray wasn't a luxury car with extra legroom and plush seats. Adam was tall, having inherited his height from his mother's side, and probably missed that extra space.

"And the radio," he said, "no Bluetooth connection. Not like this one. Just kinda limits things, you know?"

"Hmm." We drove a minute or two in silence. "You know, Adam, life is interesting. You may find one day that just because something is new or novel, it doesn't mean that it's better or more valuable. You may find it's often the other way around. Things become more valuable—more beautiful, even—with a little age and rust."

"Really?" He must have thought I was speaking a foreign language.

"Yeah, it's like that vinyl you bought with Kiki," I explained. "You could have bought those songs online, right? But you didn't. You wanted something authentic, something classic—and it takes time for something to become that."

"I guess," he said, but I could tell that had struck a chord with him. "I do agree that when you listen to something on vinyl it has, well, more of a warm sound to it. I guess that's how I would explain it. Kinda warmer."

"There you have it," I said, smiling. "The '69 doesn't ride as well as this, the seats aren't as comfortable, and it's a louder, bumpier ride, but to me it's warmer. Think of the Stingray as my vinyl record, okay?"

"Gotcha, Dad." He snickered. "I actually thought you were gonna turn this whole talk into a metaphor for yourself. You know, the whole I-get-better-with-age kind of thing."

"Well, that goes without saying," I said, and as I turned left onto PCH, I reached out and playfully slapped him on the shoulder. "I am as vintage as they come. A full V8 of masculinity and performance that cannot be outmatched."

"Oh geez," Adam said, rolling his eyes.

I drove a block down PCH. From here, I could turn right onto Second Street, or I could keep going down PCH toward Huntington Beach.

"It's a nice afternoon," I said at a stoplight. "I was going to go local, but why don't we head to Huntington? A nice drive down PCH sounds good."

"Yep, it does."

When the light turned green, I accelerated without making the turn, and for the first time a thought occurred to me.

What if I never needed the Stingray?

4

"So, Fergus is dead?" Adam asked.

We were sitting in the patio area of Simmzy's in Huntington Beach, looking out at herds of scantily clad bikini- and trunks-wearing pedestrians, many oiled up and carrying surfboards, who were crossing PCH en route to and from the beach. The sun was about to set.

"You heard?"

"Yeah, Mom told me. Uncle Ben called her."

As I sipped my glass of red wine, I could almost smell the salt from the ocean mixed with the sweet fragrance of cocoa butter sunblock. The scents of summer.

"Pretty crazy." I browsed the menu and decided, like my son, to go for a burger. "Shot himself in his own garage. But there must have been something shady about it. This detective questioned me, and it was a little intense. I'm not sure why, but I guess they suspect there might have been foul play involved."

"Do you think there was?"

"Who knows?" I said. "But I doubt it. I mean, he had just stolen the Stingray, so I have a hard time believing that someone just happened to be waiting there to kill him. But maybe I'm wrong. People like Fergus have messy lives—and when you live a messy life, you often have messy consequences." I waited a moment, then decided to go a little deeper with Adam. "So, how's it going living with Shane? He's okay?"

"Yeah, he's alright, I guess." Adam swirled his straw through his cup of soda. "He's out of town right now. Some business trip."

"Ah, that explains the taxi."

"Yeah. When is Kiki moving in?"

Just then, my phone went off.

It was on the table, facedown, and when I turned it over, I saw a text message from Mara. It was blunt and all in caps: *YOU NEED TO CALL ME RIGHT NOW.*

I turned it facedown again.

"Pretty soon," I said. "She's out of town this next week or so, but we're gonna start getting things ready for the move. Speaking of which, look, I know this is a lot of change for you—a lot of change in a small amount of time—and I just want to know how you're doing with everything. It's okay. You can be honest with me."

Adam hesitated. He looked down at his soda, strangely subdued.

This didn't seem at all like the kid who gave my Stingray a quick kick with his boots. Two of them, in fact.

"You know, I've been wanting to ask you something," he said.

"Yeah, well, this is as good a time—"

My phone rang.

I didn't have to turn it over to know who it was, but I did anyway. Sure enough, it was Mara. Two calls on the way here, a text at the restaurant, and now a third call. I didn't know what was going on, but I hoped it was actually something important and not just an attempt to thwart the little one-on-one time I had with my son.

"Hang on one second, okay?" I told him. "I need to take this call. Order me the same thing you're getting. A burger sounds good."

I walked out of the patio area and to a side street where I had some privacy.

This call could go in any number of directions, and I wanted to be away from people and earshot of my son.

5

"What's going on?" I asked.

"It's *your* son. That's what's going on."

My son?

I'd learned a few things during my years of parenting with Mara.

If she referred to Adam as *her* son, he had done something exemplary.

If referred to as *my* son, he'd gone off the rails.

Referring to him as *our* son, which was infrequent, indicated she wanted money.

"Well, what happened? What did he do?"

"You want to know what I found in his backpack today?"

I nodded, as if she could see.

"I was going to do some of his laundry, so I moved his backpack out of the way, and when it hit the floor, I heard the sound of glass. I opened it to see if something broke, and guess what I found? An empty bottle of rum, a pipe, and a plastic baggie. There's even a little bottle of Visine. He's been smoking pot, Charlie, and drinking. Your son!"

"Okay, calm down," I said.

Mara and Adam had always been close—utter enmeshment—but that didn't mean they were without conflict. Adam had become her surrogate companion growing up, and I blame myself for being distant and aloof and creating that void. They bonded over her issues, whatever they might be at the time, and I knew she confided in Adam about her long-term affair for years. The secrecy created an electric bond between the two, but with it came surges of total dysfunction.

No wonder my kid played in a band called Pure Evil. He needed some outlet.

"What are you going to do?" she asked.

"What do you mean?"

"I mean you need to do something. You're his dad. He's your kid. And Shane is getting tired of having to be the bad guy and provide on every level for Adam. It's time to step up to the plate, Charlie."

"Step up to the plate?" I asked. "Are you kidding me? I'm still standing at the plate. You took the ball and went off to another field."

"Oh, that's very clever of you, Charlie."

"It's true. It's not my fault that Adam—"

"You know," she resumed, "I'm going to get off the phone now because it is exactly this type of emotional abuse that has gotten things the way they are."

"Emotional abuse? Are you kidding me? A baseball metaphor is emotional abuse?"

"You expect me to resolve this divorce with you instead of using the courts?" She sighed. "Get it together, Charlie. And discipline your son, okay? He needs it. Step up and be a man."

She hung up.

I wanted to walk straight back to my table and reengage with my son, but I couldn't just yet.

I needed ten minutes to walk it off.

6

When I returned to our table, I realized how long I must have been gone. The burgers had been served, and Adam had already made a dent in his.

When I slid back into my chair, Adam barely looked up at me. He looked pretty sullen and morose, and I suspected he knew both who I was on the phone with and the purpose of the call.

"Burger any good?" I asked.

"It's okay," he said without looking up. He chewed quietly, his eyes glued to the table.

A toddler was having a temper tantrum at the table adjacent to ours, and both parents were trying unsuccessfully to quiet him and spare those in the vicinity from his wrath.

I heard them dish out threat after threat to no avail. The little boy wailed on, and his parents looked like POWs, wearied and beaten.

I grinned. Been there, done that.

"So that was Mom, huh?" Adam said, breaking the ice.

Swallowing a mouthful of burger, I wiped my chin with a napkin. "Yes, it was."

"And she told you?"

"Yep, she did."

This was normally when I would lay into Adam. I would start with school, his grades, and why he never took any of it seriously, and from there I'd move on to his hobbies—things like playing in his band—which would, of course, ultimately lead to his sour choice of friends. I would talk about his not-so-good trajectory—a word I'm not even sure fully he understood—and, if history proved correct, it would go nowhere.

I took a long sip of my wine and looked out at the Pacific Ocean.

This time, I decided to switch lanes and go another way entirely.

"Rum, huh?" I asked.

He nodded, hardly looking up.

"What kind?"

"What?"

"What kind of rum did you get? I'd like to know that my son at least has decent taste in rum."

Now he looked up. He held his burger in both hands and stared at me in bewilderment. A couple slices of pickle and a splash of sauce fell from the burger onto his plate.

"Um," he said, "I don't know. I think it was that Malibu coconut stuff."

"Ah, okay. Technically, from what I've read, it's not really a rum—more of a flavored liqueur. Personally, I would opt for Bacardi or Coconut Cartel. The proceeds go to a good cause too. Coconut Cartel comes out of Guatemala, and producing it has opened thousands of acres of coconut farmland. Your Aunt Donna told me about it."

Adam hadn't taken another bite. His eyes said it all: *Who is this man sitting before me?*

"Are you mad?" he eventually asked.

"Not mad." I leaned over the table and whispered, "You think you're the first kid to be caught with a bottle of rum and some pot in his backpack? I think not. And do you know all the crazy, stupid stuff I did as a kid? It's a miracle I'm here."

"You? Doing stupid stuff? You always talk about how a responsible person is—"

He stopped talking when I broke into laughter.

It was clear that, even at age sixteen, Adam had about as much insight into human nature as the toddler at the table next to us.

"I've made a lot of dumb decisions in my life," I said. "Particularly when I was around your age. And considering your parents are about to go through a divorce, your mom is shacking up with a guy, and I'm about to—well, how could anyone blame you? This reminds me of my friend Doug too. We were good buddies as teenagers. His parents went through a divorce when he was about your age. The same thing happened. His dad found some stuff in his room. Pot and some drinks."

"So I'm not getting in trouble? Mom said she was going to tell you, and you were going to lay into me."

"Maybe," I said. "But sometimes punishment doesn't drive people into complying. You know what I mean?"

"Yeah, I think so."

"So I'm going to think about it. We'll circle back, okay? You're not off the hook—don't get me wrong—but for now, I just want to know how you're doing. What's going on inside you? How are you taking all this?"

Adam nodded.

He'd evaded the executioner's axe, and I saw the victory on his face.

When the waitress returned to ask if he wanted a refill of his Coca-Cola, I jested to her, "Just cola, okay? No rum."

She nodded and looked at me quizzically while Adam, embarrassed, covered his blushing face with his hand.

7

I dropped Adam off at his mom's after dinner.

He opened the passenger door, but he hesitated before he got out. He hadn't asked me the question all night, and now I could almost feel it seething inside him.

"Dad," he said, "I never had a chance to ask you. I've been thinking about…"

He faltered. I wasn't sure why it was so difficult for him just to come out and ask. Maybe it was the result of being caught between two parental tides of loyalty. No matter what he chose, someone got hurt.

"You're thinking about moving in with me?"

"Yeah," he said, nodding.

"Have you talked to your mom about it?"

"No, not yet."

"I see." I wanted to tell him right then that the answer was a clear *yes*, but I still needed to tell Adam some things. Particularly about the pregnancy. It could alter his decision. "I'll tell you what. Let's set up another night to sit down and talk. I have some things I'd like to talk about, and if you feel the same way after that, we can find a way forward. Sound good?"

"Yeah," he said, getting out of the car. "Sounds good. Oh hey, you never told me what happened with your friend, Doug. Did he get busted for what he did?"

I was glad Adam had asked.

"He died," I said.

"What?"

"A few years after college. He developed a habit, and it got the best of him."

"Oh."

"Yeah. Our decisions have consequences, Adam. All of them. Never forget that. I'll give you a call. We'll talk soon."

I pulled onto the street, and I was only a few blocks away when two thoughts, like rapiers, clashed together in my mind.

The first: Somehow, I had managed to connect with my son.

The second: I had done it without the Stingray.

Chapter Twenty-eight

33.99 Liters of Fuel Remaining

1

The Long Beach Police Department called me the following morning to inform me that the Stingray was cleared to be picked up. I decided to Uber there, and when I walked in, a young brunette at the front desk took my name and information. I waited for several minutes until Detective Grimm emerged from a back room.

She had that same severe expression on her face. The look of a predator closing in on its prey.

"Thank you for coming, Mr. Phoenix," she said.

"Of course." I tried a little humor on her. "Been roughing it in the Lexus."

It didn't work. Not even a thin grin on her lips.

"So," I said after an awkward silence, "any chance I can get those keys?"

"Yes. But first I'd like you to come into the back room for a couple of questions."

2

I found myself in the same interrogation room, sitting in the same chair.

"I wanted to give you one more chance," Detective Grimm asked me. Today she was wearing a business suit, her jet-black hair in a ponytail. "Was there any altercation whatsoever in Fergus's house before his death? I'd like you to think very carefully."

I couldn't believe I was back here.

"I've already told you this. No, I wasn't there. I was at my house. He stole my Corvette, and that's why I called you. I don't know how much simpler to make this."

"It appears," she said like a straight-faced poker player adept at not showing all her cards, "that there was some kind of struggle in the garage before the gunshot."

"There was?"

I was sincerely shocked.

"Yes," she continued, "and I would like to be absolutely certain that you don't happen to recall something different than what you told me the last time we spoke."

"I have no idea. What kind of struggle?"

"I'll tell you what you need to know, okay? I find it very strange that the same man who is threatening to sue you ends up dead and you're the last person he saw."

"Well, whatever happened, I had nothing to do with it. Don't you have a forensics team? Go ahead and search for my DNA and my fingerprints—whatever it is you guys do—but I assure you, I've never even stepped foot in his garage."

"Working on it," she said. "This isn't a television show. Forensics takes time."

I took a deep breath and tried to take this in. "Are you saying this is a murder now? Is that what you're telling me?"

"No. I said there appears to have been some altercation in the garage—at least at this point—and we are doing our due diligence to determine what really happened. Just following the breadcrumbs, Mr. Phoenix."

"Yeah, dotting those I's and T's, right?"

"Right."

She reached into the pocket of her suit and withdrew the key to my Stingray.

"I think that'll be all for today," she said, "but we'll be in touch."

3

After I returned home, I was so disturbed that I decided to go for a walk.

I was sure Detective Grimm was just doing her job. I'd seen enough episodes of *Dateline* to know that when detectives were investigating a murder—or, in this case, a suspicious suicide—they had to take off the gloves. Still, it unnerved me, and I felt restless. A couple of miles of brisk walking might help me think and get my mind off things.

A block or two into my walk, I turned the corner, and there were Stanley and Jaysa, out on a walk of their own.

Jaysa was still frail and worn, but she was, at least, outside.

Stanley had his arm around her for support, and I think it was the first time I'd seen him look bright-eyed and sober in a long while. It even looked like he'd shaved.

"Nice day out," I said casually as I prepared to pass.

"Yes, very nice," Stanley agreed. His former angst seemed to be gone—at least for the moment. "I never did get a chance to thank you the other day. That bottle of whiskey. I appreciate that."

"My pleasure," I said. Yet I felt like I had to say something more. I looked squarely at Jaysa and acknowledged her. "So good to see you out. You look great today."

"And I feel okay too," she said, although her voice sounded weak, like a snapped guitar string.

"Yeah." Stanley clutched his wife tighter. "We're making the most of it. Doctor said the steroid injections sometimes improve things, but this has been better than we imagined. Trying to enjoy the day, you know?"

"I totally understand."

I noticed Jaysa studying me. Her already weathered forehead crinkled into an atlas of lines, and she squinted in deep suspicion.

"I remember now," she said, looking me up and down.

Oh no, I thought.

"What is it?" Stanley asked. "What do you remember?"

"You drove me in some car. A black car. All night long with Tommy." She pointed a thin, skeletal finger at me.

I tried to decide what to do and how to respond but came up with nothing. I stood there with my hands in my pockets, most likely a dumb open-mouthed grin on my face, but fortunately—before I said something that incriminated me even more—Jaysa kept talking.

"A dream," she said. "A real strange one."

"Dreams can be that way," I agreed, and silently thanked the stars that I'd dodged that bullet.

HALF A TANK

Chapter Twenty-nine

33.01 Liters of Fuel Remaining

1

After bumping into Stanley and Jaysa, I began to seriously consider the ramifications of everything. The Stingray had the ability to replenish anything inside of it, and, for whatever reason, this gift had been entrusted to me. I had to do something good with it. Something responsible. Something that would help other people.

If it could recharge Chuck, Trey, and Jaysa, then why not others?

I called my sister, Donna, that evening. We chatted briefly, and then I got right down to brass tacks.

"Are you and Caleb doing that car stuff for charity any time soon?" I asked.

"Of course," she said. "Doing one this weekend, as a matter of fact, at the City of Hope."

"What kind of cars are you bringing in?"

"A '67 Maserati, a '71 Ford Thunderbird, and a '70 Chevrolet El Camino. I also have some engineer bringing in a DeLorean, but it's a *Back to the Future* lookalike. Has the flux capacitor and everything. The kids will love that one, for sure."

"Got it." I walked with my phone out to the back patio and took a seat. Chuck was there, soaking up some rays. "And what do you do at the event again?"

"Well, it's really a chance to get the patients—at least, the ones who are well enough—out of the hospital so they can enjoy the day. It's Patient Appreciation Day. There are booths, food, games, stuff like that. I run the classic car tour. The patients get to see the cars, look through them, and we take them on rides—just ten or fifteen minutes each—and let me tell you, they love it. Especially the gearheads. When you've been sitting for days on end in a hospital room, it means the world to them."

"Perfect."

"What? What sounds perfect?"

"It just sounds like a really good event to put on."

"Charlie, are you okay?" my sister asked. Having grown up with her, I immediately detected the sarcasm. "I've been trying to rope you into more charity events for a long time. Did it finally occur to you that it might be worth a little of your time?"

"Yeah, I guess it did."

"Is this Kiki's effect on you?" she asked. "If so, now I'm even more excited to meet her."

"You will soon. She's out of town."

"So would you like to come help out?"

"I think I would," I explained. "I think some of the patients might enjoy a ride in a '69 Stingray. I'd love to help out. Sign me up."

"Great."

"I just have one question for you."

"Sure. Shoot."

"Ten minutes or so seems an awfully short time to spend in such a nice classic," I said. "Can we increase that time limit a little? Why cut short such a great experience?"

2

A couple of days later, I was en route to City of Hope when my phone went off. It was Kiki. We'd talked a couple of times over the last several days, but she had been quite overwhelmed with helping her sister move. I took the call only a mile or two away from the hospital.

The chat was brief and pleasant, although she was still stunned and troubled by the news of Fergus. The fact that I'd been questioned so forcefully also didn't sit well with her.

I missed her. The house seemed empty and colder without her in it. Her moving in would be a good thing. Life and light would return to the mausoleum my home had become over the years.

"So, where you heading?" she asked as I was about to end the call.

"City of Hope," I answered honestly, but at the same time I acknowledged to myself the depths of my own deception. I hadn't told Kiki about the car. Tommy was the only one who knew. I considered telling her right then, but I had the suspicion that telling her wouldn't pan out very well. How would she respond to that news? How would anyone respond to such news? I thought it best to explain by actually showing her.

Without seeing it, I was worried she'd chalk me up as a nutcase.

"I think that's a great charity to be involved with," she explained. "Just don't turn reckless when you take the patients on joyrides, okay? Why the sudden change? You've told me about your sister and her charitable causes. Why now?"

"Well, I…" My voice faltered.

I pulled onto the off-ramp of the 605 and found myself at a complete loss. I didn't want to lie, but I couldn't tell her the truth.

"Charlie, are you okay?"

"Yeah, I'm fine," I said. "I think when you're back, we need to talk. There's something…well…just something I need to tell you."

"O-kay." She said the word slowly, stressing both syllables. I was sure it sounded cryptic to her, but it was the best I could do.

That was when she caught me unaware.

"Me too," she said softly.

"What?"

I heard her sigh and breathe into the phone, and I knew this sound. The foreshock before the quake. The unsheathing of the sword before the attack.

I pulled to the side of the road, right in front of a fire hydrant. "What is it? What's wrong?"

Another breath into the phone. "There's something I need to talk to you about too," she said. "I don't think I've been completely honest. Uh, it's hard to—listen, when I get back, maybe we just need to sit down and talk. That kind of thing."

"Um, sure, yeah."

"I should go," she said.

"Yeah, me too. I'll call you later, okay?"

The call ended.

I sat in the red in front of that fire hydrant for I don't know how long. I knew I'd been hiding the truth of the Stingray from Kiki, but what had she been hiding from me?

And then, all at once, a terrible thought occurred to me.

What if Trey had been right? Was she just a gold digger and I her latest catch?

I tried to wash the thoughts—the doubt—out of my mind, but I couldn't completely. They festered there like mold, and as I pulled back onto the street, a previous suspicion struck me: Kiki and I had done quite a bit of driving in my car. Maybe she had never loved me. Maybe the car had done it to her.

Even worse, what about me?

Had the Vette done this to both of us?

Chapter Thirty

32.44 Liters of Fuel Remaining

1

It really was a city, and it was my plan to bring it a little more hope than usual.

When I pulled into Lot G on the northern end of campus, I was struck by how large the facility was. It wasn't just one or two buildings, as I had imagined; it was several buildings, both for research and for patients, with gardens and parking lots and various facilities in between.

When I found a parking spot and killed the ignition, I could see the festivities in the distance. It looked like a small fair was taking place. People gathered near Platt Conference Center, and in the distance, I could see all the balloons, the banners, the booths, and along with the sounds of music—I guessed it was The Beach Boys—I could smell the summer scent of barbecue: grilled burgers, hot dogs, and kielbasa. I had only had a piece of toast for breakfast, and picking up a plate of food and maybe an ice-cold lemonade seemed in order.

I had just begun walking toward the commotion when Donna came toward me. She'd told me to park here and had been watching for me. She was her usual self: short skirt, high heels, bouncy hair that defied the laws of gravity, and she gave me a warm hug and kissed me once on each cheek with her freshly botoxed lips.

"Can't believe you made it," she said. Her eyelashes were long and flamboyant, her eyeliner equally dramatic. "I never thought I'd see my little brother at a charity event."

"Yeah, well, there's a first time for everything."

"So that's it, huh?" She turned her attention to the Stingray. "Really nice. You're definitely gonna have some people sign up for this today. It looks beautiful. Not a scratch or defect on it."

"Yeah, it's about as authentic as they come."

"Great. Well, why don't you move your car over to our area, okay?" She had a clipboard in her hand with a map of the campus. She pointed a long purple fingernail toward an area on the map where the words CAR EXHIBIT had been written and circled with a black Sharpie. "Pull around this corner, and you'll see the other cars there. Just park alongside them. We'll start doing our tours in about"—she checked her Rolex—"fifteen minutes or so. Sound good?"

"Yeah. Is Caleb here?"

"No," she said disappointedly, "he had a previous engagement this weekend."

I could only imagine what the previous engagement was.

It was no real secret that Donna and Caleb had an open marriage. It'd been that way for years, and they'd become even less quiet about it since Caleb's tech company joined the big leagues. There'd been a few dinners and happy hours and glasses of wine over the years when some of the details slipped out about vacations in Italy and jaunts over to Whistler with certain "friends," and I did my best to reserve judgment. They were grown adults, and they could do what they wanted, but sometimes it struck me as strange. I guess that was what a certain degree of wealth could do to some people: turn them into devoted philanthropists while simultaneously eroding the marital monogamy that once was.

They didn't have kids, and they didn't seem to fight about it, and that was good.

There was some wisdom in that, perhaps.

"Okay," I said. "I'll pull the Vette over to the area. First, mind if I grab a burger? I'm starving."

2

After devouring a burger, I went back to the Stingray, pulled into the side parking lot, and parked it next to the Maserati, the Thunderbird, the El Camino, and the *Back to the Future* DeLorean. It didn't take me long to figure out how this worked. Former patients, current patients, and the families of both strolled around the fair, and when they came to our little neck of the woods, they walked around the cars and admired them.

Donna stood at a table and signed up those who wanted to be taken on a quick drive in the vehicles. She had several sheets and clipboards, and patients could sign up for whichever car they preferred.

I talked shop with the other car owners, who were middle-aged guys like me. The owner of the DeLorean was an engineer at Northrop who, in his free time, had designed the car himself to look exactly like the one in the movies. He was here because his sister had recovered from breast cancer several years back, and this was his way of paying it back. I was no expert at cinema, but the car looked spot-on to me, and it didn't surprise me at all that the slots for his car were filling up fast.

It wasn't long before Donna told us the rides were about to begin.

I had three sign-ups.

The first guy introduced himself as Armann. He was a tall man who, he told me, was born in India and came to the United States as a teenager to work for a family member's print shop in Carson. Like many of the other patients here, he was skinny and frail, with no hair on his dome, and he looked longingly at the Stingray before he climbed inside it.

I drove.

We pulled out of the parking lot. It was only midday. The 605 South was known for terrible traffic, so I headed to the 210. At this time of day, I thought I still might have some open road and the chance to pick up some speed. I might have been wrong, of course, but for whatever reason,

I associated the car's healing abilities with speed. It just made sense to me.

Armann didn't say much. I think he was tired. He just looked out the window like a kid on his first ride at Disneyland.

"So why this car?" I asked. "Not a *Back to the Future* fan, I take it."

"I've always loved Corvettes," he said. "I grew up in Mumbai, and I told myself—before I ever moved to the States—that I would buy myself a Corvette one day."

"That's a good goal. Did you?"

"Yes. Two. An '87 Corvette, which I traded later for an '89. I made a mistake on the color. Red. Got speeding tickets in both of them."

I laughed. "Well, I've been known to push the limit myself. What do you say? Should we push it a little?"

His eyes went wide, but his smile was infectious. I could tell he loved it. Being outside of the hospital, away from what I imagined were nothing more than white, sterile rooms, machines, and hospital gowns, invigorated him. I could see and feel it in him.

His formerly sleepy eyes now looked alive.

"Yes," he said, looking at the open freeway ahead. "I think a little speed would be nice."

"Okay." I cranked the gear into fourth. "If I get a ticket, you're paying, okay?"

He chuckled, and I floored it.

2

My second passenger was Burt.

Armann walked away after thanking me profusely for the ride, and I hoped the drive did something to him. Please, I thought, let the replenishing take place.

I just didn't know if we had enough time and miles together.

Burt was bald too, although I had the impression Burt had always been this way. With or without chemo. He was chatty too. Much chattier than Armann.

"Last two weeks here," he said proudly as I pulled out of the parking lot. "Doc says things are looking good and I can go back home. I tell you, you look a bit younger than me, but if you ever feel something strange going on down south in your undercarriage, don't be an idiot and wait too long like my sorry ass. Doc says I probably could have saved a lot of time and heartache."

"I see," I said. Testicular cancer, I assumed, or something like that. "So why choose the Vette?"

"How could I not?" he said. "I had myself a Stingray once when I was a kid. Second car I bought. Always loved 'em."

"Really? You had one of these?"

"Oh yeah, only mine was a '68. I liked the '69 too, trust me, but never got one. Don't get me wrong, I'm definitely a '69 man—I just keep that for the bedroom, if you know what I mean."

I wasn't sure how to respond to this.

"I actually lost my virginity in that same '68," he said with the pride of a man who had climbed Everest. "Yes, sir. She was good too, let me tell you. Name was Candice. A friend at school told me all I needed to do was get her inside that car for a drive, and those clothes would fall off just like leaves in the autumn." He laughed, looked out the window. "Oh yes, good memories."

"I can tell."

I tried to figure out how one could lose his or her virginity in a cramped '68 Corvette without a backseat. Not exactly the most spacious, comfortable of places, but I guessed with a little youthful imagination—and the youthful flexibility that accompanied it—anything was possible.

"So where we headed?" he asked.

"Let's do a little drive down the 210. Sound good?"

"Sounds great."

He was more awake, more alert than Armann had been.

Maybe that was because he was further along and near heading home. I wasn't sure if Burt needed the drive in the Stingray the way that Armann did, but I knew enough about cancer to know that it could come back. Maybe this drive would eliminate that possibility.

I pulled onto the 210, and on the more open road, I decided to push the speed.

"Beautiful day out," Burt said. He nudged me with his elbow and jested: "Let's slow down if we pass any good-looking women, huh? It's not every day I get to ride in one of these."

"I'll try," I said, "but this thing has a mind of its own. It loves speed."

3

I wasn't ready for my third and final passenger.

At least, not emotionally.

After I dropped off Burt, I saw Billy—a gangly twenty-year-old wearing jeans, a white T-shirt, and a beanie—standing in front of his parents. The kid was so skinny, so frail-looking, a gust of wind might blow him over. His parents stood behind him, and it was the inversion of everything life was supposed to be. The parents, probably my age, seemed alive and vibrant. Mom, with tanned skin and blonde curls, wearing a bright blue dress, stood behind her son with her hand on his shoulder. Dad was next to her. Tall, strong, wearing white pants and a blue polo shirt, he had a full head of hair, a chiseled jaw, and his hand was on his son's other shoulder.

I thought it fitting that both parents had their hands on their son. I assumed they spent every possible minute holding on to what the world was cruelly trying to steal from them.

"Ready for a ride in the Stingray?" I asked.

He was shy, but Billy nodded.

His parents nodded too, both beaming with joy that their son had a chance to do something other than what I imagined his life normally entailed. Both of their eyes struck me. They were moist, glistening in the sunlight, but as I walked toward the Stingray with their son and looked back at them, I realized there was sadness too. Their eyes were deep wells of insurmountable grief.

As a parent, I could only imagine.

"I'll have him back in no time," I said and waved to the parents, but as I got into the car, I knew I wasn't going to keep that promise.

Not at all.

4

Like Armann, Billy was a little quiet. I had the feeling the kid wouldn't say anything unless I started a conversation, so as I pulled out of the parking lot and onto the main street, I tried to get him to open up.

"So," I said, "how old are you? Mind me asking?"

"I'm twenty."

"One year from buying your own beer, huh? Legally, that is."

That earned me a wide grin.

I looked over at him. If his face hadn't been so emaciated, his body so skinny, he might have looked like some cool punk kid rolling down the street in my Stingray. He looked tired too. His eyes were at half-mast, his cheeks sunken. Still, there was a gleam of youth in his eyes. A pearl in deep waters, fighting to glimmer.

"You ever ridden in one of these before?"

"No," he said plainly.

"Okay," I said, "so what have you driven?"

"Nothing, really."

"Nothing?"

"No, I've been here a long time."

I thought about this. The kid was twenty. If he'd been dealing with this for years and spending most of his time fighting here, clinging to hope, then things like getting a driver's license fell to the wayside.

It felt so wrong. So absolutely wrong.

"So, what are you into? Any hobbies?"

"Not really." He looked at the dashboard of the Stingray, surveyed the gauges.

"Come on, there's got to be something. Something you're into."

"Well, I like writing."

"Okay, nice. What kind of writing? Action-adventure? Science fiction? Romance? If you're into romance novels, I'll need to get some tips from you, because that hasn't always been my strongest department."

"I'm definitely not into romance," he said. "I don't know anything about that."

I knew what that meant. The kid who'd been so busy fighting this battle that he didn't have time to learn to drive certainly didn't have the opportunity to find a pretty young lady.

It angered me. I gripped the steering wheel tighter.

Why did Burt get to lose his virginity in a '68 Stingray and Billy didn't even get a fighting chance?

"So, what kind of things do you write?" I asked again.

"Comedy."

"Comedy?" I was stunned. It wasn't what I would expect from a kid who'd spent most of his adolescence in cancer wards. "Wow, that's great. That's absolutely terrific."

"Yeah, I even like comic strips a bit." Billy opened like a sunflower. "I dabble here and there in short stories. But I like comic strips the most. You know, capturing the little slices of life that are funny."

I was on the 210 now and pushing ninety. Billy didn't seem to notice.

"So why comedy? What led you to do that?"

"Leukemia."

I was silent.

"You have to find the humor in things," he said simply, looking out the window at the blue skies above. "Leukemia is no fun—that's for sure—but if you only focus on the bad stuff, it makes it worse. It's like being dead before you're dead. That's what my mom tells me, and I think she's right. Know what I mean?"

I wasn't sure if Billy noticed, but I wiped a tear from my left eye. And I'm not a crying man.

"I actually have an idea for a comic strip," he said. "I want it to take place in a cancer ward. Everyone thinks cancer wards are dark and depressing places—and there is a lot of that—but there's a lot of humanity too. Lots of funny things that go on. There's another kid, David, who's in my condition, and his parents came to decorate his room the other day with balloons as a birthday surprise, but I guess there was some mix-up with the balloons they bought. When David walked into his room, there were a bunch of balloons hanging from his bed that said CONGRATS, IT'S A GIRL!"

Billy laughed.

I loved the sound of it, and I promised myself that I would remember it.

Still, I had to look out the window, because if I looked at him, I might lose it altogether. My eyes were twin dams, holding back torrential waters.

"I think that'll be the concept of the comic," he explained. "The thing I want to get across to the reader is that we're all in a cancer ward, some of us just realize it more than others."

"Wow," I said. "That sounds so creative. My son's creative too. I'd love to see your work sometime."

"Okay." Finally, he noticed the speedometer. He looked at me quizzically, then at the gauge. "How fast are we going?"

"Oh," I said, looking down at the dash, "just a little under a hundred."

"Wow, uh, you think we'll get a ticket?"

"I'll cover if we do, okay?"

I'd actually lied. We were doing over a hundred. Amazingly, the road was pretty clear, and I wasn't going to miss the opportunity.

"You have any important reason to be back quickly?"

"Uh, no, I don't think so."

"Let's push it a little then, huh? It's not every day you get to ride in a Stingray. Speaking of which, why this car? Why didn't you pick one of the others?"

I saw the little boy in him when he answered: "It looked fast."

"Oh, it is." I raised an eyebrow. "Why don't we take the long way back and see exactly how fast it goes?"

5

Billy's parents were a bit worried when I pulled back into the parking lot nearly forty-five minutes after I left, and Donna was outright pissed. She'd tried calling me twice on the drive and I hadn't answered. When I got out of the car, I explained that Billy had really enjoyed the ride and I just wanted him to get as much out of it as possible.

I think Donna wanted a better excuse—flat tire or overheated engine—but that was my story, and I stuck with it.

I just hoped it was enough to make a difference.

Before I left, I shook hands with both of his parents and told them what a great son they had, and I asked for their number. Billy, I explained, enjoyed the drive, and I would love to take him out for another spin if there was another day and time that worked for them. They were profusely thankful, we exchanged numbers, and when I left The City of Hope, I desperately wished that those drives had done something for Armann, Burt, and Billy.

Not far from home, I pulled to the curb on some random street and put the car in neutral.

All of the emotion I held back on those drives—particularly the one with Billy—seethed within me.

"Why?" I mumbled.

The kid hadn't looked much better when I pulled away from the parking lot. I was convinced I didn't have enough time with him, not enough miles.

Why did Armann get the chance to move to America to live out his dream, when most likely Billy's would be snuffed out before it even began? And why did Burt get a youth that he could look back on with fondness?

Why?

And why didn't my son Seth get a fighting chance?

A flash of anger arose in me, and I hit the steering wheel with my fist several times.

Then I sat in silence as the V8 rumbled beneath the sleek black hood of the Stingray.

My vision went blurry, and everything—the dashboard gauges, the windshield, and the wide world beyond it—became wet, smeared paint on a canvas, and I wept hysterically in a way that I never had before.

If only Mara could have seen me.

For years, I'd been accurately accused of being emotionally distant. A closed box with an iron lock. But here I was, a grown man, broken down in tears, weeping for a kid I barely knew.

But I was weeping for more than just Billy.

I remember leaning over the steering wheel, crying, and when I opened my eyes, I saw the Corvette logo in the center of the steering wheel was wet with my tears.

That was when I realized, for the first time, that there was one thing the Stingray couldn't remedy: grief.

Chapter Thirty-one

30.90 Liters of Fuel Remaining

1

I am at Long Beach Municipal Cemetery, standing in front of Seth's gravesite marked by an infant headstone. It is a cold, gloomy day, and a drizzle of rain falls on me, falls on the grass, falls on the granite plaque with the white imprint of two baby's feet and the words ON ANGEL'S WINGS YOU WERE TAKEN AWAY, BUT IN MY HEART YOU WILL ALWAYS STAY.

The year he died is on the plaque too. The same year he was born.

I kneel down and touch it.

It is cold and wet with rainwater. White roses, alstroemeria, larkspur, and pink spray roses overflow from the small basket I place beside the grave.

For an eternity I kneel on the grass, dirtying the knees of my slacks, and I contemplate how to grieve for memories that never happened and for laughter that was never given the chance to be heard. It is a different kind of grief, a darker corner of that chamber, often neglected and overlooked. But I do my best, and I kneel, and I reflect, and I wonder what could have been. Mara is behind me, clothed in the black garments of mourning, but I think she's judging me because her grief is loud and messy and flamboyant, and mine is quiet and subdued and, in her words, not real grief.

Eventually, I get up and walk back toward where she is waiting for me, but I hear a sound.

It sounds like someone knocking impatiently on a door, and it's muffled.

Where is it coming from?

I walk back toward the headstone and listen.

Silence. Just the drizzle of rain, the whistling of wind through tree limbs.

And then I hear it again. Yes, it sounds like someone knocking feverishly on a door, but there is no door here, and it sounds muffled, like it's underwater.

I look down.

It can't be, but it is.

It is coming from beneath the soil, beneath the grass, and now I hear words. A little child's voice.

"I want a ride!" the voice cries. "Take me for a ride! I don't need flowers! Daddy, please take me for a ride!"

I take two steps back, terrified.

Replenished: A Novel

I turn around, and Mara is standing there, a grim smile on her face, holding out the keys.

"Take him for a ride, Charlie!" she says.

The Stingray is there too in its parking place, both doors open, headlights on, beams like silver shafts cutting through fog and drizzle.

I step away from her.

I step away from the grave.

Both scare me.

But I still hear the rabid knocking from the tomb and the voice that I never heard enough to recognize as my son implores me: "Take me for a ride, Daddy. I'll be good, I promise. Please take me for a——"

2

I sat up in bed, dripping in sweat.

For a moment, I felt disoriented and confused about where I was and what was happening. The dream had been so real, so vivid. I lay back down, closed my eyes, and hoped sleep would quickly envelop me and pull me into a much different dream, but I found, after lying there, that I couldn't sleep.

Dawn slowly spilled in through the windows. I heard the sounds of birds and life outside in the trees.

I knew why I couldn't sleep.

The dream, as awful as it had been, had given me an idea.

And it was a most terrible, grotesque one.

3

I spent the entire day thinking about it.

Kiki called me twice, and I didn't answer either call. Maybe I was wrong, maybe whatever secret she wanted to tell me was something minor and along the lines of normal. Maybe she had some credit card debt she hadn't told me about or a DUI on her record, something I could deal with. But there was something in her voice—I distinctly sensed it—that convinced me her dishonesty went deeper than that. Had Trey been correct? Was the whole pregnancy a ruse to secure her place in my home? We hadn't been to our appointment with the OBGYN yet, and I wondered if she would come up with some reason why the appointment had to be delayed or pushed back.

I tried to beat away the doubt and the suspicion, but I just couldn't.

Adam texted me a few times that day.

Two of the texts were to complain about his mom being, in his capitalized words, THE WICKED WITCH OF THE WEST, and I sent back a couple of texts to tell him to hang in there, she was his mom, and she loved him. I knew all too well how quickly everything could change.

All Mara had to do was take him down to Guitar Center, buy him a new guitar or something, lay off on the punishment for the booze and pot she'd found in his backpack, and once again they'd be thick as thieves.

Then he'd be sending her texts about me in capital letters, calling me things like SATAN or LUCIFER.

I did make one call. Billy's parents. I wanted to stay in contact with them, let them know I really cared, and, most importantly, let them know that I was serious about taking him out for another ride in the Stingray. So much depended on it.

The conversation was brief, pleasant, and they loved the idea of another ride.

"All he did was talk about what a good time he had," his mom told me. Her voice, like sunshine, nearly beamed through the phone. "He doesn't talk about it to a lot of people, but he really does love cars. Especially Corvettes."

"Well, it was my pleasure to host him."

"In fact, he had one of his best days yesterday afternoon. Even this morning. I haven't seen him with this much energy in— It's like, wow, I can't even remember when."

I sat down on my couch, closed my eyes, and breathed in the sound of those words. "That is so wonderful."

"I'll talk to him, call you back, and we'll put something on the calendar," she said. "He would love a quick ride, and we're very thankful for the offer."

"Quick?" I said. "It doesn't have to be quick."

When I got off the phone with Billy's mom, the world felt more balanced on its axis.

4

When it was dusk, I went out to the garage. I grabbed my shovel and a pair of gardening gloves and threw both in the passenger seat of the Stingray. At that point, I'm not convinced I was thinking. I was an animal, nothing more, and working on raw instinct.

Chuck strolled into the garage, looked at what I was doing and, seeing nothing of interest, headed toward the backyard.

As I watched him walk away, I just couldn't help but wonder.

I pictured my deceased son's headstone: *ON ANGEL'S WINGS YOU WERE TAKEN AWAY, BUT IN MY HEART YOU WILL ALWAYS STAY.*

Was it possible?

5

I pulled my Stingray into the parking lot of Willow Springs Park, a wetlands restoration project complete with a walking loop and acres of habitat with native plants and trees. It was just north of the Long Beach Municipal Cemetery and, being near the end of the day, I was sure that if I wandered off the walking loop and headed south for just a few minutes, I would come to the cemetery.

Sure, there'd be a fence of some kind, but maybe I could find a way over it.

Did cemeteries have electric fences? Barbed wire? Security cameras? I had no idea, but I assumed they had something.

I didn't know how common grave robbers were or weird gothic people who for their own macabre reasons wanted to wander around graveyards, but it was a wild world out there, filled with bizarre people, and I anticipated some kind of problem.

Perhaps, I thought, it would be better to stroll the perimeter first. Scope it out, so to speak.

My son's grave was on the northwest end, away from most things. If I could get to it, if I had enough time…

I got out of the car and paced.

Some obvious problems confronted me.

Six feet down? How long would it take me to dig it up? I wasn't even sure if I worked all night long, without breaks, it was possible. And would I have the strength? My arms felt sore sometimes while weeding the backyard, and this—well, this was much more than that.

And what would I find if I did?

Could I even dig around the small coffin and lift it up?

Or would I have to pry it open, and if so, what would remain inside? It had been fourteen years.

Could I really come back to the Stingray with nothing but dust and bones and a fragment of hope and pull this off?

6

The sun went down as I stood there, leaning against the driver's door of my Stingray.

And as the sunlight fled, some of my sanity returned. I had been foolish and hasty to come here, and as I remembered myself gathering the shovel and gloves and putting them in the car, it was like I was watching another person, some intoxicated madman on a fool's quest.

I placed both hands over my face and slowly rubbed my forehead, my eyes, my jaw.

"Idiot," I mumbled.

I got into the car and drove out of the parking lot, but I found myself, almost unwillingly, pulling back to the curb.

Putting the car in neutral, I looked back at the graveyard one last time.

Was it possible? Could I—

"No," I said with finality. I shifted into first and pulled onto the street.

Some things, I resolved, are better left dead.

Chapter Thirty-two

29.35 Liters of Fuel Remaining

1

My impulsive drive to Long Beach Municipal Cemetery convinced me of one thing: The Stingray had a hold on me, and I needed to find out more about it. Who made it? Where did it come from? A thousand and one questions raced through my head.

I went through my files and took out the little paperwork I had on the vehicle.

I had the VIN number, and now that Richard Pratt was dead—unless they found more video footage that determined he had, somehow, miraculously survived that jump—that VIN was about the only thing I had to work with. I went to my laptop, logged in to Carfax, and generated a vehicle history report on the Stingray. Unfortunately, the information wasn't very helpful, at least in regard to finding the identity of the previous owners, but I did learn a few interesting things.

The report indicated that the car had three owners. That made me the third, Richard the second, and whoever he bought the car from must have been the first. Under the column for OWNER THREE, I saw the comment TITLE ISSUED OR UPDATED along with the date that I walked into AAA with Richard. Under the column for OWNER TWO, I saw the date that Richard must have bought it five years ago along with the same comment: TITLE ISSUED OR UPDATED. Above this, alongside OWNER ONE, I saw the date 12/23/1968 and the comment TITLE ISSUED OR UPDATED/FIRST OWNER REPORTED. The report detailed no accidents, no service information, and no mileage samples. It was quite thin.

"Wow," I said. "I'm only the third person to own the car."

But how, I wondered, could I find out who the first owner was? There had to be a way.

2

I tried a few other car websites. Autocheck.com. Its-a-lemon.com. Same thing. I found very little information and, most importantly, no name of the first owner.

After searching for an hour more on Google, I kept running into dead ends.

Most of the searches advised me to do the same thing I had been doing—try websites like Carfax.com—but the people posting such advice clearly hadn't tried it themselves.

I even gave Trey a quick call. Since he was the self-proclaimed research junkie who had done a background check of his own on Kiki, I thought he might be able to shed some light on the situation. But it was another dead end.

"No idea," he said after I explained the details.

"Bummer. Okay. By the way, how's the back pain?"

"Doing okay. A little better."

"That's good. Everything else okay?"

"Yes, sir. Scored a date with Belinda tonight. Been eyeing her for a while, so gotta get moving."

"You're a busy man, Trey."

And he was. Belinda? Apparently, if I recalled Trey's metaphor correctly, he liked to keep more than just one steak in the freezer.

Out of luck, I sat back in my chair and stared at the computer screen.

Then, out of nowhere, I had an idea.

3

I found Arlo at his garage.

When I walked in, Arlo was hunkered down in front of a Solara, giving me and the rest of the world a bright glimpse of his rear end. His ass might as well have been hanging right out of his pants. He had just finished replacing the front rotors of the car, and he was getting ready to replace the pads when he heard me walk in. He got to his feet, pulled up his jeans, and with his big, close-eyed grin and white teeth, he greeted me in his usual, cheery way.

"Charo!" he said.

If I hadn't caught him in the middle of things, he probably would have given me a warm handshake, but he was too busy wiping his dirty hands with a shop rag.

"Hey, Arlo."

"What brings you here? Another 'Ray?"

"No, not another Stingray. One is plenty for me." And was the truth of it. I barely knew what to do with the one I had. "I thought you were the person to ask, and since you're always too busy to answer the phone, I thought I'd swing by. I'm looking to find the original owner of the Stingray. I know who the former owner is, but I'd like to find the first one. You know how to figure out something like that?"

"Hmm." He looked like a man who had been asked a very difficult calculus question.

"Yeah," I said, "it's a tough one."

"You could probably try Carfax or something like that."

Apparently Arlo had been taking advice from the same websites I'd searched.

"Yeah, I already tried that. I could figure out how many owners it's had—there's been two of them before me—but I'd like to find out the first one's name and contact information."

"Oh, I see." Now he looked like he'd been handed an even more difficult calculus problem. "Privacy issues," he mumbled. "I see."

He continued to wipe his hands on his shop towel, mumbled to himself for a few seconds, looked down at his shoes, and appeared to be thinking so hard that I could almost hear the wheels and gears turning and grinding in his head.

"Anything in the car?" he asked. "You know, receipts or something like that? It's amazing what you can find in a car under the seat or stuffed back in the glovebox. Something like that might give you a clue."

"It's been pretty cleaned out." I'd been all through that car, and there was nothing. I was sure of it.

"I dunno then," he said, shrugging. "Now that I think about it, I guess there is that law. What's it called? Oh yeah, the Driver's Privacy Protection Act. I think that's what it's called. It makes it illegal to attach personal information to a driver's vehicle. I think there's exceptions, like if there is a court case or something. So yeah, the online search stuff probably won't work. I don't know what to tell you."

"Okay, I appreciate the help."

He looked past me and saw the Stingray in the parking lot. "Well, since you got her here, you want an oil change or something like that? I got some time in between this here Solara and my next job."

"No, I'm good," I told him and headed out.

I sat in the driver's seat for a long time, holding the steering wheel, thinking how simple a thing this was. I simply wanted to know who had owned the car before Richard Pratt. In a world where so much was public— too public, in my opinion—I couldn't figure out why this information was so private.

Ridiculous.

The online car reports had been pretty cheap. I'd pay big money to figure out this one simple piece of information.

I pulled onto the street, and when I was about halfway home, I thought of something.

"Money," I said. The idea came to me all at once, and it was worth a shot.

4

I called Zora, Richard's sister, on my way home. We chatted briefly, and I learned the authorities were still holding back on any kind of death certificate because of the ongoing investigation into her brother's death. As far as she knew, they could call her anytime with an update. She had no clue what direction it would go from there.

When she asked why I'd called, I spun some serious yarn.

"I've been really enjoying driving the Stingray I bought from your brother," I said, "but a crazy thing happened the other day. I was going through some of the inside compartments under the seats, and I found something. It's a woman's wedding ring. Beautiful ring, actually, and has an inscription and date on it and everything. It says, *For Dora 11/19/72.*"

"Oh wow," she said.

"Yeah, it looks like it's worth something too. Big rock on it and everything."

"And it was just there in the car?" she asked incredulously.

"Well, it was in one of the storage compartments under the seat, wedged in a gap. I was taking it apart. It's the only reason I found it. I don't know, maybe the husband was taking his wife's ring to be resized and it got wedged in there. Maybe she was driving the car and took her ring off for some reason. Who knows? But I think whoever it was and however it happened, I really need to get hold of the previous owners. Or if they're deceased, maybe their kids. It could mean a lot to them."

"Gotcha, but why are you telling me about this? What can I do?"

"Well, that's where I was hoping you could help me out." I tried to lay the pathos on heavy. "I just can't imagine how much this could mean to someone who thought they lost their wedding ring years ago. I'd like to give the previous owner a call and see if I can get it in the right hands."

"That's very kind of you," she said, "but I don't know who he bought that car from. You might as well have called up a stranger. I don't know any more than you do."

"Yes, that's true," I said, "but you have access to his bank accounts."

"His credit union?"

"Yes, his credit union. You mentioned a Living Trust when I met you at the house, and you're the trustee, right? If he bought the car five years ago, you could go back and look for an expense out of his checking account. I assume it would have been a very large one. It's worth a shot, at least. Many banks keep digital files of cleared checks for seven years after they've been cashed. Could you do a quick check and, if you find the check, give me the name of who it was made out to?"

There was, of course, the possibility that Richard didn't pay with a check, but I decided to cross that bridge when I came to it.

Zora sighed. "I'd love to help you out, but don't you realize I'm still in the same bind?"

"What do you mean?"

"No death certificate. No presumption of death. Until that happens, my hands are tied. I don't have access."

I slapped my forehead in defeat as I made a left onto PCH. How stupid of me. I should have known better. No credit union or bank was going to give her access without that document.

"I see," I said, feeling like a complete idiot for not realizing this plan wasn't going to work. "Okay, well, if something happens and you gain access, if you'd let me know, I would appreciate it."

"I'll do that," she told me. "I missed a call earlier from the Vital Records Office. They're going to send the certificate digitally if this ever happens, and the credit union is just waiting for that one document, so maybe something will happen quickly. Or maybe they just called to give me more bad news. Either way, I lost a wedding ring once, so I know how that feels."

I ended the call and desperately tried to think of another way.

5

I stopped at a red light, rolled down the window to let in some air, and tried to think of some other route to take. Who knew when the investigation would end and they'd issue a death certificate, and who knew how long it would take for Zora to get access to his accounts. And then, of course, I had to consider when and if Zora would ever follow through. I didn't think a wedding ring in an old car her brother once owned was going to be very high on her list of priorities.

As I waited for a red light, a little silver car pulled up beside me. I glanced over. It was a Toyota two-seater electric vehicle, but it looked more like an oversized kid's toy than anything else. I remembered passing it earlier, and the back of the little vehicle was a shrine of progressive bumper stickers. SAVE THE FORESTS. PROUD LIBERAL. SAVE THE EARTH: THERE'S NO PLANET B. VEGETARIAN ON BOARD. The list went on.

The driver was a tall, skinny guy with shaggy hair who barely fit into his seat. He wore a tie-dye shirt and a pair of round-rimmed John-Lennon-like sunglasses. As he brought his car to a stop, I noticed the air freshener dangling from the rearview mirror was shaped like a cannabis leaf. The woman sitting in the passenger seat was skinny too, with long, straight blonde hair parted right in the middle, and she had on a green headband.

The window was down, and I heard music. "In-a-Gadda-Da-Vida" by Iron Butterly.

I snickered. They looked young, probably in their twenties, and if they planned to have kids anytime soon, this car without a backseat was going to have to be seriously rethought. But then again, maybe they weren't planning to have kids. Based on their bumper stickers and the thousand causes they seemed to be into, maybe they'd decided to forgo having children in hopes of lessening their carbon footprint or something. Who knew?

The driver looked over at me and frowned. Not very hippie-like.

Since my plan to hunt down the original owner of the Stingray had been thwarted, I was quite grumpy. I looked back at the driver of the electric car, shifted into first, and with the clutch down, I pressed down on the gas. The V8 revved. Vibrations emanated from the motor, through the steering wheel, and into my hands.

The female passenger looked over.

I revved the engine again. Louder. Longer.

"You know," the driver of the electric vehicle said, nearly poking his head out of the toy-sized window of his car, "you ought to take a look at what your car's doing to the environment, pal!"

I just smiled. Pressed down on the gas pedal again.

"Gaz guzzler!" he cried as the light turned green.

"Oh, you have no idea," I said.

I released the clutch, peeled out, and left the electric car in my wake.

No way was I going to be bested by a two-seater electric car. Despite my recent problems, at the end of the day, things could have been worse: I could be driving *their* car.

Chapter Thirty-three

27.81 Liters of Fuel Remaining

1

When it rains, it pours.

I had spent so much time engaging in bizarre, obsessive behavior lately—things like heading to my son's gravesite with a shovel and my desperate attempts to hunt down the original owner of the Stingray—that I thought it very fitting to continue. When you're on a borderline psychotic roll, why stop?

Three days passed, and I didn't do much more than sit around my house. Kiki was coming back soon, and although we'd exchanged a couple of meaningless texts, it was clear there was something wrong. Her keys hung from a hook in the kitchen along with my other keys. She'd left them with me for safekeeping. Why take them with her to Baltimore and risk losing them?

Although our plan was to wait until she returned to begin her packing, the keys pulled at my soul with a near-gravitational force.

If I could get inside her apartment, it might help me determine whether this whole thing had been a charade. Maybe secrets could be found there. The more I thought about it, the more I realized we spent almost all our time at my house. Very little at hers. That left a wide gap. There was so much to learn about people by seeing inside their home, their medicine cabinets, their desk drawers. I had done little of that with Kiki. It was a phase we had skipped over, a chapter we had flipped past.

And to think: I was going to have a child with this person!

Or was I?

The evening the thought came to me, I was sitting at my dining room table, sipping a glass of red wine, and staring at her keys.

"No," I said to myself, "you're not going to go snooping on Kiki. It's not right."

I resolved to resist the temptation.

But by the time I finished my glass of wine, I'd changed my mind.

I fetched the keys and headed out to my garage.

I moved quickly, before I had a change of heart.

2

The apartment was just as I remembered it. Small. Only one bedroom. Decorated in what she referred to as "beachy" style, which was quite fitting since the little apartment was nestled on the Peninsula and only a stone's throw from the Pacific Ocean to the south or the bay to the north. It was a shoebox of an apartment, and had it not been in such a desirable area, I doubt she would have chosen it.

I walked into the living room. The white couch was covered with copies of *Eating Well* and ocean-themed images—seahorses, seashells, mermaids—were embroidered on the large throw pillows. A giant painting depicted the Huntington Beach pier at sunset. The pier stretched out over the water, and the pylons looked like the long feet of a wooden caterpillar. The sky, teeming with silvery fish-scale clouds, was saturated in the color of rust, while frothy white waves crashed like foam onto the shore. It struck me as funny that she had a painting like this. Perhaps it wasn't as dramatic, but if I looked out the window of this second-story apartment, I could see the ocean myself. On a beautiful evening, you didn't really need the painting.

I stood in her living room and wondered where to look. I didn't have much experience at snooping.

I went into the bathroom. I had a feeling the medicine cabinet was a decent place to look.

I rifled through the contents and found the usual things one might expect. Toothpaste. Listerine. Floss. Deodorant. Tweezers. Nothing of any real significance. If

I had found medication for something like schizophrenia, that would have been concerning.

Leaving the bathroom, I went into the bedroom. It was small, like the rest of the apartment, and Kiki had neatly made the queen-size bed. The blue-and-yellow blankets were without wrinkle or obstruction except for a lone pair of socks that I assumed Kiki had forgotten while packing. There must have been at least ten pillows on the bed, which corroborated what I knew of sleeping with her. The woman liked her pillows. There were four on my bed, and according to her, that was not enough.

The wall décor was similar in here to the living room. Starfish hung from the wall behind the bed, and there were small paintings of the ocean, ships, and sailors.

I looked at the nightstand beside her bed. It was barren. Usually, I knew, she kept her iPad there. She brought it over to my place on most occasions because she had a hard time falling asleep without putting on some show or podcast.

"Bummer," I mumbled.

If I could access the iPad, it might slake my curiosity.

I was about to turn around and chastise myself for being stupid enough to come here when I noticed something sitting beside the desk in the corner. It looked like a black messenger bag. I picked it up, took a seat on the edge of the bed, and opened it.

It was her MacBook.

3

I fired it up.

This was quite fortunate. I assumed she'd taken the iPad on her trip, and in doing so, decided not to bring this. She prided herself on being a light traveler—just one carry-on, thank you very much—and now that I thought about it, I remembered that when she kissed me goodbye at the airport and scurried off toward her departure gate, I had seen the iPad in her voluminous white purse.

I cracked my knuckles as the log-in screen materialized.

"Password," I mumbled.

I had one shot here. I knew the password for the iPad. Many a night, while she brushed her teeth and flossed, she'd reminded me of it so I could set up one of her shows or podcasts. It was simple: 6820. She'd chosen it because that was the temperature the Pacific reached along the Southern Coast during the summer months—68 degrees Fahrenheit, 20 degrees Celsius.

If the devices had matching passwords, I'd be in luck. It was possible. Maybe even likely. I duplicated passwords all the time to make things simple.

I typed in the password and hit enter.

It worked. I was in.

4

I investigated her calendars first.

She was utterly meticulous in scheduling things, going so far as to color coordinate events that fell under the categories of work, play, and miscellaneus. Her work schedule was here, along with meetings and appointments. I saw her trip to Baltimore with flight details, a dentist appointment, a hair appointment, a meeting with some friend named Betty, and on and on.

My first concern came as I realized what *wasn't* here.

There was no appointment with an OBGYN.

How was that possible?

Kiki had the time and energy to add appointments for her hairdresser and dentist, but not her first appointment with the OBGYN to address her pregnancy?

"You've been duped," I could hear Trey tell me. I was sure if he were there, that was exactly what he would have said. *"She's not pregnant, Charlie. Never has been."*

5

Okay, I thought. Stay calm. Just because she didn't put her OBGYN appointment on the calendar didn't mean anything. A lot had been going on in her life recently, and this trip to see her sister only made her busier. She probably just hadn't put it on this calendar.

It was entirely possible.

I opened her Gmail and scrolled through several messages. Most were totally uninteresting. A notification from Chase Bank. Calendar reminder notifications. An ad to save 15.5% on her Dropbox subscription. That same friend, Betty, had sent her a link to some article called "Bio-Hunters Capture Picture of Rare Bioluminescence Phenomenon in New Zealand." It actually looked interesting, and the pictures were phenomenal.

There was one email that I did find troubling.

The subject was in bold letters: DEBT COLLECTION.

I skimmed through it. It was from a collection agency called United Collection Bureau writing on behalf of Capital One. It was a letter in PDF format, and after skimming through it, I surmised that this was the last of several attempts to reach Kiki, that she was failing to contact the collection agency, and the ultimatum was right there in black and white: "If you want to resolve this matter without a lawsuit and further damaging your credit rating, you must, within five working days of receipt of this, either pay the outstanding balance of $18,772.32 or contact Capital One Credit Card Services and work out arrangements for payment."

I was stunned.

I scrolled through several more emails and found a nearly identical message. This time it was from a collection agency called ASA Debt Recovery. And this time it was a Mastercard, and the total debt was $9,540.52.

"Thirty thousand dollars in the hole," I said, sighing, "and you never thought to tell me."

"Because she's lying," I imagined Trey's response. *"The whole thing is a sham, Charlie."*

6

I tried, once again, to gather myself.

Things didn't look good. The count was 0 and 2, for sure, but there might still be some explanation for this. It was hard for people to talk about money, even people who had been married for years, and maybe she just hadn't gotten around to telling me yet. Maybe she even had some means to pay it off and was going to take care of it discreetly and never tell me.

It made some sense, I thought.

I opened her Safari browser and went into her search history. I highly doubted I would find something scandalous here—like weird porn sites for bizarre fetishes—but I was intrigued, again, with what I didn't find. There were no searches about having a baby, about finding an OBGYN, or anything that I would have expected.

"Calm down," I told myself. Again, there was an explanation. She might have done searches like that on her phone or tablet. It was possible!

I decided to search for the word "pregnancy" in her search history. Maybe I'd missed something.

When I did, there was one match.

A Google search: *How to fake a pregnancy.*

7

Now I was angry. Completely outraged.

How had I not seen this earlier? How had I been so blind? I was the stereotypical middle-aged male who had gotten caught up with a younger woman, a gold digger who pulled my strings and manipulated me like the pathetic marionette I had allowed myself to become.

There was one last thing I wanted to see.

I clicked into her Messages app. There were all of her iMessages, synced to the computer. I scrolled through the most recent ones, and there were several between her and Mandy, her sister. They were what I would expect to find. *Can you pick up salsa at the store? OMW. Are you awake yet?* That kind of stuff.

But I saw something else that deeply troubled me, as if this whole situation wasn't already troubling enough.

There were several messages between her and some contact named Xavier.

I thought about this. I had never heard Kiki mention anyone by that name.

I read through the last several.

> *Kiki: What time do you want to meet tonight?*
>
> *Xavier: Hey sweetie! Let's shoot for six. Restaurant gets busy then. Really looking forward to seeing you.*
>
> *Kiki: Me too.*
>
> *Xavier: Wear that sexy dress, will ya?*
>
> *Kiki. The red one?*

Xavier: Yep!

Kiki: Will do.

Xavier: Can't wait to touch you and hold you again!

Kiki: xoxo

I'd seen enough. I didn't doubt Kiki was visiting her sister in Baltimore, but apparently she was visiting this Xavier too.

I didn't even bother to put the MacBook back where I found it. I tossed it on the bed and headed for the front door.

This relationship was over.

8

Even though it had been a terrible day, there was one consolation prize.

Just as I pulled into my garage, I received a text. When I heard the single chime, I picked up the phone and saw that it was from Zora. It was simple and to the point:

Hours after you called, State issued a declaration of presumed death. Investigation over. Looked into that transaction. $67,000 check made out to Owen Menken. Went through same time Richard bought the car. Good luck.

She had also sent a screenshot of the cashed check for good measure.

"Bingo," I said and headed inside.

Chapter Thirty-four

26.12 Liters of Fuel Remaining

1

The name of the original owner of the Stingray was fortuitous. Owen Menken? That seemed like an uncommon name. If the name were Joe Smith or James Williams, I would most certainly be up a creek and without a paddle.

After pouring myself a glass of brandy, I decided to get to work. I was deeply troubled, of course, with what I had discovered in Kiki's apartment, but at least this kept my mind off that. Distraction was good.

I hunkered down at my laptop and ran a basic name search through the white pages. Owen Menken really was an uncommon name because there were only two matches. One lived in Florida, and the other lived in Newport

Beach, California, which was only about a forty-five-minute drive from Long Beach. The information about the Florida Menken seemed all wrong. *Age: 20s. Other Locations: Maine.* I suspected Richard hadn't crossed the country to buy the Stingray from a guy who could have been a teenager five years ago. The other Menken from Newport Beach matched a little better. *Age: 40s. Other Locations: Portland.*

There was, of course, one problem. If Owen was only in his 40s, then he couldn't have been the original owner of the '69 Stingray.

I thought of what this might mean. Was the Carfax report wrong? I doubted it. Or maybe the car had been stolen or something, and Owen Menken was some kind of middleman.

I scrolled down. There was no address listed, but there was, at least, a phone number.

I tried calling it to see if it was an active number, and it wasn't.

A message greeted me: *We're sorry, the number you have called has been disconnected. Please hang up and try your call again.*

I hung up and thought about it.

It could be an old landline or cell phone. Who knew?

I wished Trey were with me and thought about calling him. He knew all the ins and outs of doing these background checks and the best, most reliable sites to visit. I felt like a totally inept Keystone Cop trying to hunt down a suspect. I didn't know where to begin.

I ran Owen Menken through a simple Google search.

Some images appeared at the top of the search results, mainly what appeared to be family photos of some kind, and when I scrolled through several of them, I couldn't understand their relevance to Menken or which one he was—if he even was one of the people in the photographs. But one of the results caught my immediate attention. It was a brief news article from the *Orange County Register*: "Popular Coffee Makes Waves in Newport Beach."

Okay, now we were getting somewhere.

I scrolled through the article, and alas, no photos of Owen Menken, but there were photos of the coffee shop. It was appropriately called Waves and looked pretty trendy from my assessment of things. The walls of the establishment were covered in surfboards, boogie boards, and all things tropical, and it was adjacent to the beach.

The article was a couple of years old and spoke of the coffee shop's success and most notably its philanthropic mission: thanks to its wealthy, esteemed owner, Owen Menken, every dollar the coffee shop made was put back into the community.

Owen, who the reporter described as quiet and humble, declined an interview and photo-op for the article.

It struck me as interesting. Newport Beach was pretty wealthy. What charitable organizations was he giving to? Boob implants for the needy trophy wives of those wealthy enough to live there?

But I supposed even in Newport Beach there were ample opportunities for charitable causes. The article listed several organizations that Menken and the coffee shop gave to: Balboa Bay Club Scholarship Fund, Newport Beach Arts Foundation, and the CDM Foundation, just to name a few.

Yet what most interested me was how the article ended. I read the lines aloud.

"Menken can be found in the coffee shop most days, helping out staff and talking to his customers."

I closed the laptop.

"Bingo," I said, and headed out to the back patio with my glass of brandy.

Maybe Chuck would be there. We could do a little catching up.

I decided to eat light for dinner and save my appetite.

In the morning there was a certain coffee shop I was going to visit for breakfast.

Chapter Thirty-five

25.89 Liters of Fuel Remaining

1

Waves was exactly as I imagined it would be. I walked into the small, trendy coffee shop on West Oceanfront and was met by a large crowd waiting for their coffees, lattes, and muffins. Lots of young people. Just like in the pictures I'd seen online, surfboards covered the walls, and there was an outdoor seating area where could I hear reggae playing from the speakers. I was pretty sure it was Bob Marley. "Buffalo Soldier."

Avoiding the line, I got the attention of a young girl behind the counter who was restocking the muffins.

"Excuse me," I said. "I'm trying to find Owen."

"Menken?" she asked.

"Yep, that's the one."

She looked at the staff behind the counter. Several workers were hustling to and from cappuccino makers and microwaves. She looked back at me and, shrugging, said, "I don't see him."

Bummer, I thought. Maybe he hadn't come in today.

"He was here just a second ago," she said. "I'm pretty sure he's out back."

"Great, thanks."

She smiled and, done replenishing the muffin display, disappeared into a back room.

2

There were several people sitting out back, enjoying their coffee, nibbling on their muffins.

The only worker was standing by one of the tables, asking a table of twenty-somethings if they were enjoying their food and if there was anything they needed. A reheat of coffee? Another vanilla scone?

He must have been in his early thirties, had shoulder-length, curly blonde hair reminiscent of Sammy Hagar in his prime, and it appeared that his official work uniform consisted of red board shorts, a retro T&C surf shirt, and a pair of flip flops. Clearly, working at a place like this had its benefits.

When he was done chatting with the customers, I got his attention.

"What can I help you with?" he asked cheerily.

"I'm looking for Owen Menken. You know where I can find him?"

"You sure you wanna find him?" He folded his tanned, toned arms across his stomach. "He's a real prick, and don't say I didn't warn you."

"What?" I asked.

He noted my confusion, and, unable to keep a straight face, broke into laughter.

"Just kidding, buddy," he said, slapping me on the shoulder. "I'm Owen!"

3

"So, what did you want to talk to me about?" he asked. He had invited me to a table in the far corner and now sat across from me. The sun was in his face, so he put on his shades.

"Wait a minute," I said. "I'm confused. "You're Owen Menken?"

He wasn't what I'd imagined. He didn't look like he was in his forties—I would have said thirty-five tops—but maybe the bleached curls, the cool shades, and the deep tan kept him youthful.

"Well, I don't know what to tell you, but ever since Mom and Dad brought me home from the hospital, that's what I've been known as."

"Wow, okay. You've got a nice place here."

"Yeah, I like to think so. We've done alright. But really, why are you here? Looking for work?"

"No, not work. Actually…" I leaned toward him as if I were about to whisper a secret. "I came by to talk about a car."

"A car?"

"Yeah, a car." He lifted his sunglasses and perched them on top of his curls. His blue eyes squinted. "I don't get it, dude. Are you here because you want to sell me a car?"

"No, it's a car you sold to someone. Richard Pratt. A '69 Stingray. It would have been about five years ago."

I had difficulty reading him. He just looked at me, expressionless, and I had the feeling he was pondering something. His eyes, for the briefest of moments, looked me up and down analytically. I saw his bronzed forehead slightly crinkle in thought as he studied me.

"I want to ask you about the Stingray. If this is a bad time, maybe we can set something—"

"Who are you?"

"Charlie Phoenix. Sorry, I should have properly introduced myself."

"So you have this Stingray now?" he asked.

"Yes. You see, I bought it from Richard recently and, well, it's an unusual Stingray," I explained. I didn't really want to go into everything yet, because what if Owen didn't know what the car could do? "I thought maybe you knew its history. Maybe you can help me answer some questions."

"I don't know anything about this car you're talking about," Owen said, suddenly curt. "I've never owned a Stingray. Can't help you."

"But it has to be you," I insisted, knowing there was something he was holding back. "I've seen a copy of the check made out to you."

He was silent.

I pulled out my phone and opened Zora's text with the image of the check. I zoomed in on the name the cashier's check was made out to. "There it is," I explained, pointing. "The check was made out to you—Owen Menken."

"I don't know who you are, what you are doing here, or what you want, but as the owner of this establishment, I'm going to have to ask you to leave."

He stood up. Cool Surfer Dude had suddenly become Irritated Business Owner.

"Look," I said, getting up, "I'm not trying to harass you. There's nothing wrong here. I just want to ask you some questions."

"I don't know anything about a Stingray," he said. "And I'm probably not the only Owen Menken."

True, I thought, there was another who lived in Florida, but he fit the puzzle.

"My father," he said. "It probably was my father."

"What?"

"I'm a junior, and he was into cars—not me. And I don't want to be involved with anyone who was involved with him."

"Your dad?"

"Yes, my dad, and I've already asked you to leave. Unless you plan to order something, please leave."

"Can you at least tell me how to contact him? I've never met him. I just have some questions."

He pulled his shades back down. "He's been dead for two years—colon cancer—and after all the nasty things he did and the things he got caught up in, the world's a better place because of it. Do I need to show you to the exit?"

"No, I'll find it."

I left, but as I walked outside, I looked back and saw Owen standing there, staring at me.

I couldn't put my finger on it, but I was convinced, beyond a shadow of a doubt, that Surfer Dude was lying about something.

4

As I walked back to my car, my phone went off.

Speaking of liars, it was Kiki. I didn't answer but instead let the phone go to voicemail. I didn't want to talk to her, but she called several more times, and each time I let the call go to voicemail. The unanswered calls culminated with an urgent text: *CALL ME 911.*

I thought of calling her but decided not to.

I just wasn't ready to talk to her yet.

5

When I returned home, I did make a call to Trey. I tried to keep it brief, but I told him I was trying to hunt down the original owner of the Stingray.

"This guy I met today," I explained, "is named Owen Menken, and supposedly his father is the original owner of the car. I didn't see someone who would match his dad's description when I searched the online white pages, but I don't really know how all this works. There's another Owen Menken too, but he's supposedly in his twenties and lives in Florida."

"Okay, yeah, I can run a background check. Shoot me a text with the name, spelled right, and any other information you have. Let me see what I can do."

"Great."

"Just curious, why are you looking to find the original owner? Problems with the car?"

"Kinda. It's complicated. And technical."

"Gotcha. While we're talking, how are things going with your girl?"

"Kiki? Well, I—"

The phone beeped. Incoming call. Speak of the She-Devil. It was her.

"Actually, she's calling right now. Let me take this. I'll catch up with you soon."

6

I wasn't sure what I was going to say. So much was unresolved. We still hadn't really talked since my drive to City of Hope and my discoveries on her laptop, and I wondered if I was going to be able to hold all of it in. I had hoped to talk to her in person, when I could look her firmly in the eye.

But as I brought the phone to my ear, I could hear Kiki wailing hysterically. She was in the midst of some kind of emotional breakdown.

"What?" I asked. "What is it? What's wrong?"

Whatever she was trying to tell me, she was completely incoherent.

I thought of investigative reports I'd seen on television. This sounded a lot like one of the 911 recordings they sometimes played of someone who'd stumbled upon the body of a loved one.

"Why," she said, nearly panting, "why, why, why?"

"Why what?" I took a seat on my couch. Now I was worried. I was still pissed at her for all the lying—but this had me worried.

She sniffled, and I heard her trying to suck in tears and sobs. "Why didn't you call? I tried—" She paused. I heard her swallow. "I tried to call you."

"I'm sorry, I've been very busy. What's wrong?"

"I've lost it."

"Lost what?"

"The baby," she said, and after a momentary wail, she was back to mild coherence. "I was bleeding this morning. It was heavy—really heavy—and the cramping was really bad. My sister took me to the ER at about eleven, and they did this early pregnancy test, Charlie, and it's gone. It's gone. I should have…"

She mumbled more incoherencies, and I just listened, understanding little of it.

I wanted to join her in her grief, and I almost did. But I couldn't help thinking this was all just part of her show. I was convinced that Kiki had never really been pregnant, and that this had conveniently taken place while she was out of town and I had no way of attending the appointment and corroborating that this had actually happened. I thought of those emails and the statements from collection agencies and, of course, the detailed calendar that included every minute appointment of hers except the one that should have mattered most.

And the web search, of course. *How to fake a pregnancy.*

"Why didn't you call me earlier?" I asked.

"I did," she said, sniffling. "I just told you that. I called you several times, but you never answered."

"No, I mean early this morning. You said it happened at eleven. That would have been eight o'clock my time. You didn't call until after that."

"I—" She paused, and I noted her brief moment of hesitation. The sniffles briefly subsided, maybe because she wasn't a good multitasker when it came to lying—she couldn't feign grief and conjure up an excuse simultaneously. "I, uh, was just scared, Charlie. And I didn't want to upset you. I thought it'd be fine and I was so scared and I didn't know what to do and why are you asking me this? What's wrong?"

You're what's wrong, I thought.

"We'll talk when you get back," I said. "When are you coming back?"

Silence.

"I'm coming back early," she said. "I'll send you the info."

"Yes, of course, just text me the flight info."

"Okay," she said, "but Charlie, what's wrong, why are you acting like this? You sound so—so—emotionally distant."

Emotionally distant? Wow, I thought. She was clearly dipping into my soon-to-be-ex-wife's bag of vocabulary.

"I just need time to think," I said. "I need to go. Just text me the info."

"Charlie," she said, "did something ha—"
I didn't hear the rest of the sentence.
I hung up.

Chapter Thirty-six

25.02 Liters of Fuel Remaining

1

I had a couple of days to consider what I should do with Kiki, but in the meantime, I had another fish to fry. My lawyer, Gertrude Hammer, had emailed me that morning and reminded me that I needed to write a response to Mara's bizarre divorce petition. She needed to get that filed with the court, and we needed to discuss what direction to go in.

From here, she explained, there were a couple options—agreeing to the 780 evaluation or compromising on getting minor's counsel, but she would call me soon and get to that. For now, she informed me, we were running behind, and I needed to get the response to her as soon as possible.

I think that was the only time in my life I poured myself a glass of brandy while eating a bowl of Cheerios in the morning. Truth be told, it didn't taste half bad together, and I knew that I was going to need something to get me through. When I first read Mara's litany of accusations, I'd only read a couple of pages—I just couldn't read the rest because it was so bizarre and from outer space. Or at least from a different dimension.

But this time, with a spoonful of Cheerios in one hand and my Glencairn whiskey glass in the other, I read through its entirety.

2

It was an utter work of fiction.

I struggled, at many points, to find even grains of truth in what was being conveyed.

Accusation: When Adam was a young boy, I didn't give him enough attention and often forgot to put him in a car seat. This was, according to her, indicative of my failure to show love and concern for my son.

What this had to do with parenting him now as a sixteen-year-old, I could only imagine.

Accusation: I was also belligerently angry all the time and stormed around the house with an iron fist. On one occasion, not long ago, I took Adam's earbuds in a burst of wild anger and threw them at him while driving down the 405.

Of course, the account was all wrong. I do remember driving with Mara and Adam down the 405, and Adam was having a serious attitude problem. So yes, I threw the earbuds, but not at him. I threw them past him. I rolled down the passenger window and chucked them outside.

My crime, in that scenario, was more of a littering offense than anything else.

Accusation: I didn't support my son with his studies, and because of that, he struggled academically and needed to be in a home that suited his needs.

Really? I supposed telling Adam not to cheat and look up the answers on SparkNotes but to sit down and do the heavy lifting was analogous to child abuse. In all those occasions, Mara just pointed Adam to online summaries and more than once said, "Nobody actually reads the book, Adam. Not even the teachers."

Accusation: I was a total pervert and frequently viewed explicit material on the large-screen television in the living room in full view of everyone.

I just scratched my head. I had been anal about having adult programs locked down on the television since Adam went through puberty, so while I couldn't hold back the floodgates of filth and pornography from him entirely, I had certainly tried. And me, a pervert? Okay, sure, only a few weeks before I was home alone and flipping through channels when I came across a bikini contest.

I admit, I watched. Guilty as charged.

What a terrible father.

There were other accusations that were so totally irrelevant or strange that I didn't know what to do or how to categorize them.

Accusation: I once visited a hotel with a prostitute.

I did? Really? Good to know.

Accusation: A friend once called my wife with a concern that I might be bipolar.

Huh. What friend? Was this like a therapist friend? And why didn't anyone tell me this until now?

Accusation: The electrical in my house wasn't to code.

Really? Okay, and what did this have to do with anything?

It was safe to say that this nonsensical paperwork was the equivalent to someone picking up a handful of darts and throwing them at the board in hope that one of them might stick.

3

My first obstacle was figuring out how to defend myself from things that weren't remotely true. How did one do that? For example, there weren't purple elves dancing throughout my house, but if I had to write an argument proving there weren't purple elves, where would I even begin? It seemed absurd to engage in it.

So I opened a Word document and started with some of the easier ones, like this car seat business. I acknowledged that I cared about my son, dating all the way back to the car seat days, and he was now here, alive and healthy, so obviously it hadn't been a problem.

I defended myself, stating I was a caring dad, not an angry monster that stormed around the house, destroying things. Sure, I raised my voice at times, and like any dad, I'd lost my cool on more than one occasion, but Adam was here, alive and well.

I wrote a detailed paragraph about what a good dad I was and how I helped my kid with his schoolwork. Sure, he wasn't a good student and had squeaked by with a handful of C's and D's, but it wasn't because I didn't try. I painted a rosy picture of Adam and I sitting in his room, books open before us, while I sagely offered him advice and insight into *Hamlet*, while my attentive son sat pensively in the seat beside me, diligently taking notes. Had it ever happened like that? Of course not. But what was I supposed to do?

And then I grew tired of it and irritable. Writing had always been difficult for me. The words never come easily.

An hour or so into my drafting, I decided to deal with the asinine prostitute accusation.

I have never in my life visited a prostitute, I typed. I took a sip of my brandy, thought, and then in a mad rush of anger wrote, *But maybe I should have. Because having sex with my wife has been a mis—*

No, I thought. That wouldn't help me.

I deleted the line.

All of this made me feel like I had reverted to middle school. Even though this was supposedly going to be a legal response to a custody battle in our esteemed court system, it seemed utterly petty to engage in such mudslinging.

I thought of all the wild directions this could go in. Adam wanted to talk to me about moving in, but his opinion could change. What if he were assigned minor's counsel? The idea of my sixteen-year-old kid being assigned an attorney seemed ridiculous. He couldn't even afford to buy his own pair of shoelaces.

And a 780 evaluation? I'd heard of those. The idea of social workers and psychologists all up in my business didn't sound very good either, and I was convinced that any person, if looked at close enough, could be deemed unfit. Nothing looked good under a microscope.

And to think Adam was sixteen. This was all so petty.

I closed the laptop and grabbed my phone. If Mara and I could reach some agreement, this could all be avoided.

I had one idea. One last hope.

4

"You'd like to take me where?" Mara asked.

"Just a drive," I said. "I'd like to pick you up, take you to a coffee shop or something, and resolve this." I cleared my throat. "You're right, Mara. Totally right. I've totally blown it as a father—I've been totally off my game—and Adam needs and deserves much, much better. You want more child support? I get it. You want spousal support? I get that too. Let's not fight. We can sit down together and work out some of the minor details and disagreements and keep this out of the court."

She was silent, and I knew why.

I'd never spoken this way to her before.

"What are you trying to do?" she asked.

"What I should have done all along. What do you think? This afternoon? I think this won't take long."

Another pause. I wondered if she was contemplating whether I had been drinking.

"I'm free. Pick me up at noon," she said.

"I'll be there."

Chapter Thirty-seven

23.17 Liters of Fuel Remaining

1

The first time I noticed something wrong, I was on my way to the Stingray. I was running late to pick up Mara, and I glanced over and saw Chuck walking across the driveway and toward my backyard.

He looked older, frailer.

I took note, and if I hadn't been in such a hurry, I would have investigated then.

I promised myself I would check on him when I returned.

2

The ride was a little awkward, but not terribly so.

I told Mara that I wanted to take her to a small café in Dana Point called Coffee Importers. They had my favorite bagels, great coffee, a view of the harbor, and a peaceful place where we could work out what I hoped would be an amicable solution. Really, of course, I was hoping the drive there would help. Hopefully, it would patch the relationship enough for her to relent on some of her ridiculous wants.

She was quiet during the first fifteen minutes of the drive. But I noticed, right as we drove through Bolsa Chica, that she started to lighten up.

"Nice car you got here," she said.

"Yeah, she's a gem. Got her for a good deal too."

"I always wanted a Stingray."

"Well, good thing you're still young. Lots of time. Do you have to be back at a certain time?

"No. Adam's staying at a friend's for a couple of nights, and Shane's out of town."

"Still on a business trip?"

"Yes. Work demands a lot of him."

By the time I pulled into the parking lot at Dana Point Harbor nearly an hour later, I was convinced the Stingray was doing its thing. We talked lightly about Adam, about his school, about his music, and I was convinced any outsider who was listening never would have imagined we were two divorcees in the midst of a contentious custody battle.

Just as I pulled into a parking spot close to Coffee Importers, Mara put her hand on my arm. I looked over.

"I'm glad you decided to do this," she said, sighing. "Truthfully, I've been a total bitch. And a liar. Let's make this right for Adam's sake."

"Sounds good," I said. "And hey, nobody's perfect, right? We all have our moments, good and bad."

"That we do," she said.

I killed the ignition, and before climbing out of the car, I leaned forward and kissed the steering wheel.

"Thank you," I whispered.

3

Our meeting was brief and surprisingly smooth.

We sat at a small table overlooking the boats of Dana Point Harbor, ate our bagels, sipped our coffee, and sketched out some of the details on a legal notepad that Mara had brought with her. I was utterly amazed that it went so smoothly and chalked it up to Mara's fortuitous acceptance of going for a ride in my Corvette.

She agreed to fifty-fifty custody. I was, after all, Adam's father, and she agreed that it seemed petty to engage in war.

We made a column on the paper, labeled one Charlie, one Mara, and wrote down everything we could think of that was important for us to keep in our respective columns.

Nearly everything fell my way.

I was going to keep the house, the cars, several of our investments. She wanted a couple of plentiful mutual fund accounts well into the six figures, and although she waived spousal support, she still clung to some form of moderate child support. We agreed on a number, and though it disgruntled me a little, it reminded me that just because a relationship is good—or replenished—didn't mean it was perfect.

There were thorns in every rose garden.

We knew it would take more time, more phone calls, but within a couple of hours, we had sketched out a rough foundation for a peaceful transition into a new phase of our lives.

When done, we both sighed in relief and raised our mugs.

"A toast," Mara said, "to better days ahead. I'll call my lawyer and have this written up so we can move on."

"I'll drink to that."

Our mugs clinked, and it occurred to me that this was the first time I had ever toasted with a coffee mug.

4

The ride back was pleasant enough, and I was truly amazed at how easy it had been.

When I pulled in front of Mara's house, she got out of the car, clutching her legal notepad to her chest. But before she walked away, she leaned down and spoke to me through the open window of the passenger side door.

"There's one more thing I want," she said.

"Okay, what's that?"

"I want the Stingray. This car."

"What? I, uh—"

"I think it's only fair."

"But, Mara, I bought it after the date of our technical separation. This really shouldn't be included in our discussion. I'll tell you what—why don't I pull some money from a fund so you have plenty of money to buy one? Hell, I'll even get it for you."

She pursed her lips, thinking.

"No," she finally said. "I want this one. There's something—I don't know—something special about this one."

"Mara, I don't think that's very—"

"I'd hate to throw away the deal we have," she said, winked, and headed toward her new house.

I couldn't believe it. Why? Out of all the things she could have asked for, she wanted the Stingray!

So typical. Maybe the Stingray could replenish relationship, but it couldn't change who a person was. Mara simply had to have the upper hand.

I waited and watched as she went through the front door of her house.

I pounded the steering wheel several times in anger.

It was the last time I saw her alive.

Chapter Thirty-eight

22.05 Liters of Fuel Remaining

1

When I got home, I remembered to follow-up on Chuck. He hadn't looked good when I saw him before leaving the house, and I wanted to make sure everything was okay. I pulled the Stingray into the garage, got out, and saw Tommy sitting in the grass with Chuck.

I raced over. "What's wrong?"

"I think he's sick again, Mr. Phoenix."

Chuck lay in the grass, looking weak. He looked up at me, his pupils fully black, and his body convulsed as if someone were pumping some serious voltage into his small body. Even his tail went rigid. It must have been a seizure.

After a few seconds of spasming, his body slackened, and he looked up at me again.

"Let me get him in the car," I said.

I picked up Chuck and walked him to the passenger seat of the Stingray. I told Tommy that I'd be back, assured him that Chuck would be fine, and pulled onto the street.

Chuck and I went for a long, long drive.

2

A few hours later, Chuck was back to his chipper self and looking out the window as I sped down the 405. The drivers of a few passing cars looked over in amusement at seeing a cat looking back at them. It happened all the time with dogs, but cats, not so much.

On my way home, when I thought Chuck was adequately recharged, a terrible realization occurred to me. I was pretty sure I knew what had happened to Chuck, and I felt foolish that I hadn't thought of it earlier. The car's abilities had "jump-started" him after being poisoned and brought him back, but as time passed, he was returning to the same state he had been in before the healing. It was an unfortunate truth about life. All things began at F. All things crept toward E. To think that I could change and tinker with that unpleasant reality was utter hubris.

So what could I do?

It was simple, really. I would take Chuck for a drive every week or two and keep him charged, because if I didn't, I was pretty sure he'd return to the same condition I'd found him in when Fergus poisoned him.

That was what I would do. And that would—

A better idea hit me.

I pulled off the 405 and made a stop at Petco.

3

When I got home, I placed the litterbox in the passenger seat of the car and several bowls of food and water in the driver's seat. I'd leave the Stingray in the garage, engine on, and keep Chuck inside it all night every night that I could. I'd keep the garage door open, of course. I knew the car replenished, but I didn't want to complicate things by giving poor Chuck carbon monoxide poisoning in the process. It was a detached garage behind the house, and so long as I closed the driveway gate, nobody would notice. Maybe I could charge Chuck to way above F, and after a few days or weeks of this, he'd be supercharged.

I had always assumed the car had to be driving for it to work, but I wasn't altogether positive. I was sure, even idling, it could do something. Maybe the hours spent in Chuck's Health Chamber would be just as good as a couple of hours hauling ass down the freeway.

He wasn't happy that evening when I put him in the car. He looked grumpy, with his paws and whiskers up against the glass of the driver's seat window.

"I'm sorry, buddy," I told him. "I know it's gonna be a little boring in there, but it's for your own good. I really mean it."

Chuck wasn't impressed. He meowed loudly in complaint.

"See you in the morning, Chuck," I told him. "We'll get through this together."

I left the garage and headed back to my house. Tommy had come in through the back gate and was waiting for me.

"Hey, Tommy," I said.

"Is he okay, Mr. Phoenix?"

"He's as good as new. I'm gonna have him sleep in the Stingray for a few nights. Hopefully that'll fill up his tank. Everything okay?"

Something seemed wrong. I could see it in the kid's eyes, his quiet nature, and the way he fidgeted with both of his hands in front of him.

"What is it?" I asked when he didn't answer. I knelt down to look him in the eye.

"I think my mom needs to go for another ride in the car," he told me. "She's not doing well again."

4

It grieved me to learn that my suspicions were right. The car would replenish, yes, but a full tank was consumed over time. Tommy told me the doctors thought his mom's sudden burst of life was the result of recent steroid injections. That and the fact that the human body simply wanted to live, and the human spirit put up its best fight near the end.

Tommy told me his dad had also regressed into despair. No surprise there. As the kid went back to his house and I returned to mine, I felt terrible. Was it possible to do the same thing once more? Maybe I could bring over another bottle of whiskey, get Stanley drunk, and once again take his wife on an all-night ride up the coast. No, I concluded, I couldn't risk doing that a second time. It was amazing we were able to pull it off once.

Of course, I could try doing the same thing I was doing with Chuck. But how would that work, exactly? I had a feeling if I walked over to Stanley's house and asked for permission to have his wife sleep in my car every night, that would set off a few alarms.

And maybe, in the end, none of it would be worth it.

I could "recharge" her, yes, but if this happened again, I would be doubling or tripling their grief.

I didn't know what to do, but as I paced around my apartment, another thought occurred to me.

If Chuck had dipped and Stanley's wife had dipped, then what about—

"Billy."

I found my phone and dialed his mom.

5

Billy was still young. Too young. I'd take the risk with him. I could take him for a ride once a week, twice a week, whatever it took.

I wasn't going to let him go down without a fight.

The phone rang several times. I was preparing to leave a message and was thinking about what to say when a woman's voice answered. Billy's mom.

"Hello," she said.

"Hey there, I hope you remember me. I'm Charlie. I took your son for a ride in my Corvette at the City of Hope."

"Oh yes," she said, and I should have recognized how frail and distant her voice was.

"Yeah, well, I have this whole week open, and I'd love to get Billy out there on the road again. If you can give me a time that works, I'd be more than happy to oblige."

There was no response.

And that was when I knew.

Slowly, my legs gave out, and I slipped down to the floor.

"I'm sorry," she said, and in weak voice that was not yet accustomed to the words or the reality behind them, she added, "Billy passed away yesterday."

The world went black.

"No," I said, "I'm the one who's sorry. I'm so, so sorry. If there's anything I can do, anything at all—please don't hesitate…"

"Thank you."

I got off the phone and got to my feet.

Mara's accusations weren't true. I was never a violent, angry man, but I was that night. I picked up the glass vase in the center of the dining room table, and in a burst of red-hot rage, I hurled it across the room. It shattered into a million pieces.

That wasn't enough. I took the painting of the seaside village off my wall and hurled it across the room. The frame broke.

In normal situations, I didn't think death provoked anger in most people.

But when you were the one who could have stopped it—and you didn't—there was little left but rage.

Chapter Thirty-nine

21.63 Liters of Fuel Remaining

1

My phone woke me up early the next morning. I had fallen asleep on the couch.

I reached for the coffee table, grabbed my phone, checked the incoming number, and saw that it was Trey.

"Hey," I said groggily.

"You still sleeping?"

"Yep, I am."

"Wow, it's 8:30. Must have been a late night."

"It kinda was," I said.

After my temper tantrum, I'd poured myself a large glass of brandy, sat outside, and just thought about things.

It was well after midnight when I went back inside and plopped down on the couch.

"Listen," Trey said, "I ran that background check on your friend Owen Menken and, well, let's just say I ran into a couple of interesting things."

This got my attention. I sat up immediately.

"What is it?" I asked. "What'd you find?"

"Too much to discuss over the phone. What are you doing for lunch?"

2

"So, we have some interesting findings here," Trey said.

We were back at Open Sesame, sitting in the patio area, drinking Moroccan iced tea and nibbling on chicken tawook. Trey had a manila folder with him. He pulled out several papers and wiped his mouth with a napkin.

"Let's start with the Owen Menken in Florida," Trey said. "You don't think he's the original owner of the Stingray, do you?"

"No, it didn't seem that way."

"Well, I think that's accurate. He's young, from what I found. Twenty-four. Works as a teaching assistant at a middle school. Pretty much an impossibility. Actually, both of these Owens are too young. Neither could have been the original owner of the car."

"Yeah, I guessed that. But one of them owned the car before the man I bought it from."

"Understood. The Owen Menken who lives in Newport Beach is a different story entirely." Trey flipped through his folder, withdrew a paper. "And there's a few things that simply don't add up."

That comment surprised me. I was about to take a bite of my chicken, but I lowered my fork and looked at my friend. "What do you mean?"

"Well, let's start with Owen's employment history." Trey pointed to one of his printouts. "He only lived in one place before Newport Beach, and that was Portland, Oregon. He has two employers from then. The first is a Fred Meyer. Owen would have been about"—he paused, did the math—"eighteen, give or take. He has another employer a year later. Worked at a donut store. Linda's donuts. Only lasted there a few months."

"Okay. And that's it?"

"Well, here's the thing," Trey said. "He also ran into some problems. Minor problems, I suppose, but problems nonetheless. Right around the same time, age 18-21, he picks up two charges for public intoxication, several misdemeanors for petty theft and resisting arrest, which is a Class A misdemeanor, and one count of trespassing. And all of this right around the time he's bagging groceries or whatever he was doing at the grocery store and dishing out donuts. And then, something strange happens."

"Like what?"

"He goes radio silent."

The waitress returned to our table, refilled our glasses of tea, and hustled off.

"What do you mean, radio silent?" I asked.

"I mean he goes completely off the grid," Trey explained, raising both hands. "No job history. No problems with the law. No places of residence. Nothing. He doesn't make an appearance until about six years ago in Newport Beach. Now he has a residence, some employment data, and so forth."

"Weird," I said, thinking. "So what does that mean? Did he leave the country or something?"

"I don't think so. But I have a feeling I know what happened."

"Okay. What?"

Trey took a bite of his chicken and washed it down with a sip of tea. "I'm willing to bet this Owen Menken isn't the real Owen Menken."

3

"Identity theft?" I asked.

"I'm not an expert on this, but that's what it looks like to me." Trey pointed to the file. "Think about it. You have this young guy who's having problems with the law, probably on drugs, getting into trouble, and then—quite suddenly—he's gone. I'm willing to bet he went homeless. Got deeper into drugs or whatever his vices were and just went off the grid completely. Maybe he died soon after, or maybe it took years, but even though he was dirt poor, he had a couple of things that many people would like."

"And what are those?"

"A name and a Social Security number. There's a whole black market for this kind of stuff. The point is this: I'm willing to bet the Owen Menken in Newport Beach became Owen Menken by using this identity. Maybe he bought it on the black market. At least, that's what it looks like to me."

I had to admit, it made sense.

"And didn't he tell you that his father had owned the car? Had the same name?"

"Yeah."

"I didn't see anything to corroborate that."

All of this might explain why the Owen I had met looked younger. The age didn't quite fit. He had found an identity, perhaps, of someone close enough in age not to raise any serious red flags.

"Interesting," I said.

But a couple of things didn't make sense.

What did any of this have to do with the Stingray?

Since Owen couldn't be the original owner of the Corvette, was he a thief who had stolen the Stingray from the original owner and falsified his identity to cover his tracks? I wasn't sure, but on the surface, I didn't understand how the pieces of the puzzle fit together.

"What about family?" I asked, pointing to Trey's stack of papers. "Did you find out anything about his family?"

"I looked into it a little, but there's not much there, from what I saw. Who knows? He could have grown up in an orphanage or on the wrong side of the tracks with a bunch of deadbeats, but however he grew up, I'm willing to bet there weren't many people around him to pursue him when he went off the grid. It's all speculation, of course, but do you know how many people go missing each day in America? It's shocking. It's, like, well over a thousand. Every day."

"Wow," I said. "This gives me a lot to think about."

The waitress returned with the bill, and I grabbed for it before Trey could make the attempt.

"I can take care of this," Trey insisted, but I wouldn't let him.

"I don't think so. It's on me. Consider it payment for your investigative services."

4

Trey had found a parking spot right behind my car, so we walked back to our vehicles together.

"How's the back pain?" I asked.

"You know, it's kinda been acting up lately—more of the same."

Trey pulled his keys out of his pocket but stopped suddenly and looked at my car. Chuck was inside. It was a cool summer day, so I'd brought him with me and left the windows cracked for good measure. The more miles on the road with Chuck, the better.

Trey laughed and pointed. Chuck had crawled onto the back dash of the Stingray and now sat there, looking at us.

"Is that a cat in your car?"

"Yep," I said. "Name's Chuck. Kind of the neighborhood stray, but I've adopted him."

"But why? Why'd you bring him?"

"Hey, this is California," I said, putting on my sunglasses. "I may even let him drive us back."

Chapter Forty

20.08 Liters of Fuel Remaining

1

The following morning, I woke up too early. 4:53 to be exact.

I heard a car door slam outside my window.

I got out of bed, opened a small crack in the blinds, and looked outside. A gray van with the words ROSE HILLS MORTUARY on the side was parked just in front of Stanley's house. I didn't need to stand there for as long as I did because I already knew what had happened. Still, I spent nearly an hour watching, waiting, and finally—just as I suspected—I saw two men in black suits wheel out the linen-covered body and place it in the back of the vehicle.

When I went back to bed, I wished I was able to fall asleep.

But I couldn't.

2

I was about to make a quick grocery run that afternoon when someone texted. It was Kiki.

The message was brief: *Flight arrives today at 1:15. I will text you when I land.*

I was a little surprised. Our last conversation hadn't been good, and I thought it entirely possible that Kiki would simply get an Uber or a taxi from the airport and call me when she was ready. But apparently not.

And maybe that was a good thing. This needed to be dealt with head-on.

I'd pick her up from the airport, drive her home, tell her exactly what I thought of her, and then I would leave her and her baggage in her beachy apartment so she could go out and fool the next sucker.

When I went out to the garage, Chuck was inside the Stingray, both paws on the glass, and was trying to get my attention.

"I'm sorry, buddy," I said as I approached the car.

I don't think he really accepted my apology.

I opened the door, and he made a dash for the yard. I grabbed his bowls of food and water from the seat along with the litter box.

As I made my way toward the trash to deposit the litter, I couldn't help but think of Tommy and Stanley. I wanted to go talk to them, say something, acknowledge their grief. But what did one say to a kid Tommy's age who had lost his mom? Where would I even begin?

Maybe, I thought, I would pick up some flowers after dropping off Kiki.

Yes, that was what I'd do.

Because grief is a terrible thing. And being alone in it is even worse.

3

It was an awkward drive, to say the least. When I picked up Kiki from the airport, she didn't say much. She put her carry-on in the trunk of my Lexus, climbed into the passenger seat, and we headed straight toward her apartment.

I hadn't driven the Stingray. This was one relationship I didn't want refueled.

"We need to talk," she said as I pulled onto the 405.

It was the first thing she'd said.

"We will."

4

We walked into her apartment.

She sat down her carry-on, put both of her hands on her hips, and for the first time since I'd known her, I saw genuine anger in her face. Her left eye twitched. The storm within her looked quite antithetical to the beautiful portrait of the pier and the waves behind her.

"What is going on?" she demanded.

"I'd like the key to my house back." Her mouth went wide. Her twitching eye filled with tears.

"Charlie, what the hell is going on? I go away, lose the baby, and you act like I've done something wrong. What is going on? Tell me! What happened?"

"Oh, I think you can tell me that." I put both hands in my pockets. "You know very well you were never pregnant. Come on! I know about that, and I know about the other lies."

She stood there, blinking, gaping, out of sorts.

But I could sense she was fishing for something. She knew that I knew, but she didn't know how I knew.

"I know about your bills and your debt. No wonder you lied. I must have seemed like quite the catch for someone like you, desperate to pull yourself out of the hole you'd dug." I watched her lack of response, and I enjoyed it. I'd been fooled. Deceived. I wasn't trying to be cruel; I was merely putting the truth out in the open. "But most importantly, Kiki, I know about Xavier. You don't have to pretend anymore."

"Xavier," she said softly. She wiped away tears.

"Yep, Xavier."

"You know about him?"

"Unfortunately, yes, I do. How many people have you scammed this way, huh? I'm just wondering. Is Xavier like me? A little bit older than you, has some means? Does he think you're pregnant too?"

She started to shake and put fingers to her eyes.

"I need my key, please."

She wailed like a little girl and stormed off into her bedroom.

I sighed. Now that I had said what I wanted to say, I really did want to leave the apartment. This had already gotten intense—maybe my delivery could have been softer—but I wanted that key. I should have taken it off the key ring before giving back her keys. That was my fault. Maybe, subconsciously, I wanted *her* to do it.

I was about to approach her room and ask for the key again when she emerged. She was still wiping away tears, but now there was a look of utter horror on her face. Her eyes were wide, wet headlights.

"You spied on me," she said.

"What do you mean?"

"You went through my computer?"

Then I remembered. When I left her apartment after my unfortunate discovery of her deceit, I'd tossed the MacBook on her bed. She must have seen it and connected the dots.

"Yes, I did. Oh, did I mention your Google search? How to fake a pregnancy? What creative excuse do you have for that one?"

Frantically, she pulled her keys out of the pocket of her jeans, removed my key, and hurled it at me. It was the first time I'd ever been assaulted with a key. It struck me in the chest, bounced off, and landed on the carpet.

"Get out!" she cried.

I bent down and picked it up.

"If you hadn't have lied to me, I wouldn't have—"

"Get out! And don't ever come near me again!"

5

I wish it had ended more cordially. I really do.

When I got back to my Lexus, I thought twice about some of the things I had said and the way I'd handled it, but there was no point dwelling on it.

The final result would have been the same: my driving away from Kiki's apartment with no desire ever to see her again. Nothing would have changed that.

I was halfway home when my phone rang.

I saw the incoming number and recognized it. This 562 number was the Long Beach Police Department. My chest tightened. Was this that detective, Serena Grimm, calling to harass me more about Fergus's death? I was hoping that whole thing would just blow over.

"Hello," I said, answering the call.

"Is this Charlie Phoenix?" It was Detective Grimm's voice. I heard her loud and clear through my car's stereo speakers.

"It is. What can I help you with?"

"I need you to come down to the station immediately."

"You do. Why?"

"Your wife," she said. "I'm afraid there's a situation."

Chapter Forty-one

19.15 Liters of Fuel Remaining

1

"She's dead?" I asked.

The words were strange on my lips. Like a foreign language.

"I'm afraid so, Charlie."

We were back in that small interrogation room, and Detective Grimm had offered me a small Styrofoam cup of terrible-tasting coffee. If this was what they offered to suspects with the hope of keeping them talking, I would think they could offer something better. Too much of this, and I was convinced I'd have to make an unwanted run to the restroom.

"What happened?"

Detective Grimm wore a dark business suit and sat across from me with another file on her desk. "Your wife was found dead inside her Jaguar. In the garage. It appears to be carbon monoxide poisoning. We are waiting, of course, on toxicology reports, but our preliminary investigation suggests this was the cause. However, there are a few challenging aspects with this."

I let that sink in. I wasn't sure I was capable of fully believing it.

"Okay," I said. "Like what?"

"It appears there may have been an altercation of some kind prior to this suicide—if, in fact, it is ruled a suicide."

I had barely digested the fact that Mara was dead. Swallowing the idea that she had been murdered was too much for my brain to handle. I didn't know what to say.

"Did you hear me, Mr. Phoenix?"

"Yes, I did. I'm sorry, I'm just—I don't know—I'm a little shell-shocked right now."

"Well, try to pull it together, because I have some questions to ask you. Can you do that for me?"

"Yeah." I nodded. "I'll try."

2

"When did you last see her?"

"Um, well, the other day she and I went out for a bite to eat, and I dropped her off after. She went into her house, I drove away, and that was that."

"Can you give me the exact day and time?"

I did, and Detective Grimm took note of it.

Replenished: A Novel

"Interesting," she said. "A neighbor said the exact same thing. She was out fixing a sprinkler head, saw someone drop Mara off in a classic Corvette, and, according to her, she never saw Mara leave the house. All of what we have now is preliminary, of course, but that seems to match what we have. Did you talk to her after you dropped her off?"

"No."

"Do you know anyone who did?"

"Maybe her boyfriend."

"That would be a negative," Detective Grimm said. "He tried getting a hold of her, couldn't, and called the police for a welfare check. That's how her body was discovered. According to him, the last time he spoke to her was the morning before you and your ex went out for a bite to eat, and in that conversation, she expressed concern that it wouldn't go well."

"It went fine," I said. "We actually agreed. It was great, for the most part."

"That's not how the neighbor described it."

"What?"

"She described it quite differently." Detective Grimm pulled a paper from her file. "This witness claims that when your wife walked away, you sat in the car for a while and at one point did something to the effect of slamming your fist against the steering wheel. Is that accurate, Mr. Phoenix?"

That was some neighbor. Who needed the Neighborhood Watch when you had a neighbor like that?

"Um," I said. It was terrible lead-in. I was sure every investigator was trained that any answer starting with a long "um" is a red flag. "We had minor disagreement about the property division. Everything went great. She just at the very end said she wanted my Stingray. I was unhappy about that."

"I see."

Detective Grimm just watched me, observing me as if I were under a microscope.

"Look," I pled, "the witness also saw me drive away, right? I went home. That was it. It was the last time I saw her. I'm not a violent man."

Her pencil-thin eyebrows raised.

"Oh really," she said.

She reached for a bundle of papers. I recognized them immediately. They were our divorce papers, which had been filed with the court and were, of course, public record.

3

"So according to this," Detective Grimm said, flipping to one of the pages of Mara's petition, "you do have some violent tendencies, right?"

"No, I don't."

She looked up at me and grinned. "Well, apparently you have episodes of storming through your house in rages and, in one particular episode, hurled something at your son."

"No, I didn't. I hurled it past him. Come on, you know how this stuff works. It's custody stuff. Almost everyone lies and exaggerates."

"Well, is this a lie?" She flipped to several other pages, found what she was looking for. "There are some notes here concerning your mediation appointment. Apparently you were so heated, so enraged, that your wife had to request the presence of a therapy animal."

I felt terrible for doing it, but even after her death, I had to roll my eyes at Mara's ridiculous assertions.

"It's a farce," I said simply. "Yes, she wanted to go pet a puppy or something to make her feel better. I don't know. But it's all a sham, believe me. And listen—none of this even matters. Like I told you and like a witness corroborated, I drove away after I dropped her off. That was it. I went home."

"Well, you could have driven back, right? Formulated a plan and then returned."

"I didn't return, and there must be someone else she talked to after I dropped her off."

"Like who?"

"What about my son?" I asked, and then I felt ill. Despite the differences Mara and I had and despite this ridiculous inquiry, Adam had lost his mother. I sat there, for the first time taking that in.

"Mr. Phoenix?" Detective Grimm asked.

I couldn't respond.

"Charlie, are you alright?"

"Yeah, I think so."

"Your son was spending a few nights at a friend's house. He never spoke to his mom after you saw her that morning."

I remembered then. Mara had told me that.

"Where is he?" I asked.

"He's in another room. You'll get to see him in a few moments, but first, let's finish up here. We're not done."

4

"Let's cut right to the chase." Detective Grimm steepled her fingers, took a deep breath. "What exactly did you do after you left Mara's house that day?"

"I have to think," I said, and I really meant it. What had I done? So much had happened recently that the last several days felt like a total blur. The more I thought about it, I was pretty sure I had gone home, realized Chuck wasn't looking well, concocted my plan to keep him rejuvenated in the Stingray, and went to bed. "I think I just hung out at home that night. Didn't do much."

"Were you with anybody that evening? Make any calls?"

"No, not really. Nothing significant, at least. Mainly just my cat."

"Your cat?"

"Yeah, Chuck."

Detective Grimm sneered. "Well, I doubt Chuck has the ability to vouch for you, now, does he?"

"Listen," I said, trying to take some command of the conversation. "I have no idea what happened to Mara. None whatsoever. And I don't know what happened with Fergus, okay? I get it. I was the last to see both of them—it looks terrible—but I haven't the slightest clue what happened to either of them."

"I'm glad you mentioned that." Detective Grimm withdrew a shiny photograph from a manila folder. "I wanted you to look at this. Some of this has already been made public, but I thought it interesting—interesting enough to bring it to your attention. Do you know whether or not your nephew, Fergus, was right-handed or left-handed?"

I didn't. Simply put, I'd never paid attention—and had never really cared. "Not really."

"Well, Fergus was a lefty." She slid the photograph across the table. It was pretty repulsive to look at. Fergus was facedown on his garage floor in a pool of maroon, a gun a few inches from his right hand. "The problem, as you can see, is that the gun used to commit this terrible suicide was supposedly held in the victim's right hand. Don't you find that a little strange?"

"I guess," I said. I didn't know. But as I thought back to when Fergus had pulled a gun on me, it was true: he had held it with his left hand.

"Do you know the number of victims of suicide who choose to fire the weapon with their non-dominant hand?"

"No, I don't."

"Well, it's small—infinitesimal. Most individuals, when choosing to off themselves, want to get it right."

"I see."

"Which brings me back to the main problem we have here."

"And what is that?" Looking at the picture, I could see beyond the body where some boxes were scattered about the garage.

"The problem is simple," she said. "There are two people dead. One of them was a former worker of yours who was disgruntled. Threatening to sue you. The other was your wife, with whom you were in the middle of a contentious custody battle. You, Charlie Phoenix, are the common denominator."

"I see."

What else was there to say? She was right. It looked really bad.

"So is there anything more you want to tell me?" she asked.

"Nothing," I said. "Nothing but that I assure you I had nothing to do with this. I have no idea what's happening. Literally no idea. Am I under arrest? Is that what you're saying?"

"Not now," Detective Grimm said.

She gathered her papers, stood, and headed to the door.

I knew what she meant by that. She was trying to get her ducks in a row. Waiting on more forensics, I assumed.

"Where's my son? Can I see my son?" I asked.

"Follow me. I'll take you to him."

5

My son was standing by a vending machine, hands in his pockets. He looked tired and fatigued. When I approached him, I put my arms out and embraced him, and when I pulled back and looked at him, I expected him to completely break down.

But he didn't. He just looked down at his shoes.

"Are you okay?" I asked.

"Yeah," he said and wiped his nose.

I realized Adam didn't know how to process this. He was still in the twilight world of pre-acceptance and, like his dad, wasn't a crying man.

"Dad?" he said.

"Yeah, son. What is it?"

"Do you have some money for the machine? I'm thirsty. I want a Coke."

QUARTER OF
A TANK

Chapter Forty-two

18.54 Liters of Fuel Remaining

1

The following two weeks were a blur. Already sleep-deprived, I slept even less. Funeral arrangements were made, legal paperwork dealt with, custody matters dropped, and Adam moved back in with me.

Fortunately, I didn't hear anything else from Detective Grimm or the Long Beach Police Department. The death was ruled a suicide, but I was wary. I knew an investigation could change those kinds of things, and if it did for some reason, I would certainly be the one in the hot seat.

The funeral was held at Long Beach Municipal Cemetery, and it was, at least for me, an awkward situation. I chose to attend, but I was shaken up and out of sorts.

Adam wanted me to, and what kind of message would it send if I hadn't? I hadn't been the greatest father over the years, and if I couldn't suck it up and at least attend his mother's funeral—well, that would have said more about me than her. But it was strange. I stood in the back most of the time, clothed in a black suit, because I knew where the gossip led. At least, I imagined where it led. Mara, so many had proclaimed, was about to embark on a new chapter in life. Her son was nearly grown. She had *everything* to live for. No woman like that would ever take her own life. It made no sense. None.

I agreed with those feelings. I really did. But, then again, when was suicide ever logical?

Still, it unnerved me. I knew Mara well. I never would have imagined her taking her own life, and as I watched her casket lower into the plot of earth adjacent to our deceased son, I wondered if it really had been a murder. Was someone following me? Terrorizing me? But that didn't make sense. Although I wished neither dead, I didn't have a great fondness for Mara or Fergus. I would think that if someone was going after people in my life, he would start with those I dearly loved and cared about.

I made it a point to stay away from Mara's long-term lover during the funeral. What was there to say?

In fact, I made it a point to stay away from nearly everyone. When it was over, I went back to my car and waited for my son.

As I walked across the grass, I tried to ignore the terrible dream from the night before.

There were two voices rising from the soil. One was Seth, and the other was Mara.

"Daddy! Please take Mommy and me for a ride! Please! We'll be good!"

2

Adam grieved his mother's death in a way I wouldn't have imagined. Then again, he was my son, so maybe I shouldn't have been shocked.

I never saw him cry. I never saw him overly despondent. He sat around most of the time, listening to his music or messaging on his phone with friends, and whenever I told him I wanted to sit down and have a talk with him, he found an excuse not to. Most of the time, it was because he wanted to go out with his friends. I supposed this was his difficulty. He was at that strange age in which he was learning to separate himself from his family, and I think that was what he wanted to do with his mourning—he wanted it to be on his own terms and separate from me. Per the landslide of advice people gave me, I enrolled him in counseling. He wasn't happy about it, but he went to the first two sessions, and when I asked him how it went both times, he shrugged and said, "Okay."

There were worse responses, so I chalked that up as a success.

At times, I wished I could drive him around in the Stingray and watch it revive him, but I'd already learned that lesson. It couldn't remedy grief.

One night, while driving him home from his counseling appointment, I noticed he was texting someone. Being the parent of a teenager, I had become quite an adept spy. I glanced down at the phone to make out what he was texting and to who. I noticed the contact's name: KIKI.

"Wow," I said, "you're texting Kiki, huh?"

"Yeah," he said.

"I didn't know you were still talking to her."

I hadn't told him the details of the breakup. He knew nothing. I had simply explained that the relationship didn't work, and considering everything that had happened, Kiki and I had decided to call it quits.

"I don't really talk to her," he said. "I've just texted her a few times. Usually, she doesn't even text back."

"Yeah, she probably doesn't know what to say."

"Nobody does."

We drove on for several minutes without saying much, but it was Adam who broke the silence.

"Dad," he said, and I could tell by the tone of his voice that he was being serious. "There's something I wanted to ask you."

"Okay."

Maybe we'd have a real talk. I was driving the Stingray. It had a way of doing this. I shifted in my seat and prepared to have a real talk about the pain and disillusionment we'd both recently endured.

"Why do you put that cat in this car every night before you go to bed?"

3

That evening, I thought a lot about Kiki.

I went out to the back patio and had a glass of brandy. So much felt unresolved in that end. When we were together, she had been kind to my son. Sure, all of it was a scheme to get at me and my wallet, but they had formed a relationship. I thought about calling her. Maybe it would be the right thing to do to end things properly.

But that was foolish thinking. There was nothing left to say, and she was dangerous. Trey had seen it early on, and I should have too.

I wasn't sure how long I sat outside, but when my phone rang, I was stunned. Of all people, it was Kiki.

"Hello," I said.

"Charlie, it's me, Kiki."

"Yes, I know."

A sigh on the other end of the line.

"Look, your son keeps texting me, and he told me what happened to his mom. I'm really sorry. I can't imagine what it's like to go through all of this—but I don't think I'm the best person for him to talk to."

"He's having a tough time," I said. "We both are."

"Understood. I just think it's probably healthier for him to find someone—I don't know—someone more available."

"I agree." In a way, I appreciated the call. Maybe she did have some fondness for Adam, but I knew in my heart of hearts that it was best to get off the phone quickly before I became entangled in another one of her webs. "I hope you're well, Kiki. I think it's best I get off the—"

"You were wrong," she interrupted. "I've kept quiet because of everything you've been dealing with—God knows you have enough on your plate right now—but you were totally, utterly wrong about me."

I leaned back in my chair. "I don't think so," I said.

"Well, I know so. I have no desire to resume our relationship, but I do have a desire to keep my integrity. I don't know what you've told your son about me, but I'd rather my name not be dragged through the mud."

"Honestly, Kiki, I haven't told him anything. Not a thing."

"Hmm," she said. "Even if that is true, eventually, one day, you'll tell him that I'm a lying whore who lied to you in hopes of living a better life."

"No, I won't say that."

"You need to know the truth," she explained. "I'd like to meet tomorrow at Ubuntu. Remember the place?"

How could I forget? We went there on our first date.

"Kiki, our relationship is over, and I don't know—"

"No disagreement there. Like I said, I'm not trying to rekindle something. I just want you to know the truth and the whole truth and nothing but the truth. That is, if you can handle it."

I thought about it. Had I missed something? Was my radar that far off?

"Fine. Nine o'clock tomorrow morning work for you?"

"Yes, I'll be there."

Chapter Forty-three

16.99 Liters of Fuel Remaining

1

As planned, we met the following morning at Ubuntu. We sat in the corner of the outdoor patio and both ordered omelets. I went for a black coffee, and Kiki, as I assumed she would, asked for a decaf latte. It was a strange, subdued affair, and unlike the last time we visited here in the throes of youthful infatuation, a sour mood settled over the table.

I half-wondered if we would even get through our meal before one of us, upset, would storm off. It was sad too, because Kiki looked beautiful. Usually, her hair was down, but this morning her fiery red hair was pulled into a tight ponytail, and gold seahorse earrings dangled from her ears.

All of it I took to be an illusion, her beauty nothing but an addition to the theatricality that would most likely accompany her lies.

"You know," I said, sipping my coffee, "we didn't have to go through all of this. If you wanted to explain things, you could have just emailed me an explanation. Or texted it. Whatever."

"No," she said, "we're grown-ups. We can look each other in the eye. And I really am sorry, Charlie."

I was stunned that she started with this. It wasn't what I expected. Rarely did someone launch a defense with an apology.

"Well, what are you sorry for?"

She took a deep breath. "I'm sorry that I was not as open and transparent with you as I could have been. That's on me. I really did love you, Charlie, and for whatever reason, I presented myself to you as someone you would have cause to doubt. I'm sorry that you found me to be an untrustworthy person."

I waited and studied her. She was a good actress. She seemed genuinely sincere.

"But you lied to me," I said.

"No, I didn't. But I must have done something somewhere along the line to come across as a liar, and for that, I'm truly sorry. But I never lied to you, Charlie. Not once."

"Wait a minute." I held up a hand. "Let's start with the collection notices. I saw those. Weren't you going to tell me about those?"

She picked up her latte and took a sip. "Those weren't my bills."

2

"Those were Duncan's bills?" I asked.

"Well, they are in my name, but Duncan made the charges," Kiki explained. "I didn't know he was doing it at the time, but he maxed out those cards without my knowledge, and I've been fighting those bills ever since. Usually, fraud is easy to prove, but when it happens with a boyfriend, it's complicated."

"Were you going to tell me?"

"Yes, I was going to tell you. That was what I was talking about when I told you on the phone that I hadn't been entirely honest with you. I felt guilty for keeping that from you, and I was going to tell you when I got back."

I took a second to absorb this, and then I remembered what Trey had told me. Kiki had check fraud on her record. I had to bring it up.

"But what about the check fraud?" I asked. "Was that Duncan too?"

She blinked at me. I think that one caught her off guard because I hadn't found anything on her computer related to check fraud. That all came from Trey's background check.

"Yes, it was," she said. "Like I've told you, he was a terrible influence on me and my life. It took all of my strength to pull away from that."

I wasn't sure if I was convinced yet, so I decided to press further. "And the calendar?"

She looked at me in confusion. "What calendar?"

"You didn't have your OBGYN appointment on your calendar," I said. "Come on, Kiki. You have every event in your life on that calendar, and you happen to leave out the one event that is probably the most important event of your life?"

I saw her studying me, thinking.

"You just explained it," she said.

"What?"

"I wasn't about to forget that appointment because it was, as you said, the most important appointment of my life. I didn't need to put it on my calendar, and just so you know, I don't put every event on my calendar. You're pretty quick to jump to assumptions, Charlie."

"You had hair appointments, meetings with friends, other appointments, all sorts of things."

Sighing, she reached into her purse and pulled out a piece of paper. She unfolded it and placed it on the table beside my coffee. I did a quick scan of it. Johns Hopkins Hospital. A medical bill. *Patient admitted for abdominal cramps and bleeding.* Various notations and medical codes throughout the bill. Most importantly, the date matched perfectly with what Kiki had said. And the patient's name: Kiki Patterson.

That was the first moment I began to feel smaller. As if I were shrinking right there in the chair.

"You really went to the hospital?" I asked.

"Yes, Charlie," she said matter-of-factly. "And, for the record, I really was pregnant."

"But the web search? 'How to fake a pregnancy'?"

"Remember that argument we got into when you implied I might be 'using' you and making all of this up?" she asked.

I nodded.

"Well, did you look at the date on that search?"

I hadn't, and she rolled her eyes again.

"I was so upset that I went home and looked it up. I mean, like, how many women are crazy enough to do that kind of thing? How is it even possible? I just wanted to know if it's a thing."

3

"What about Xavier?" I asked.

I still had to consider some of what Kiki had told me, and I was beginning to feel like an idiot, but what could explain the texts with Xavier? Maybe Kiki really had been pregnant. Maybe there was more to the story with the bills and the check fraud. But I didn't see any other rational explanation for those texts.

"What about him?"

"Your texts," I said. "Come on, Kiki."

"We're friends."

"Friends?" I laughed, slapping my hand on the table. "Come on. This friend just happened to call you sweetie, just happened to ask you to wear a sexy dress, and told you how excited he was to hold you. Will you get real with me for a second? Nobody does that. Nobody normal, at least."

I laughed and took a swig of the ice water stationed beside my coffee.

Now I didn't feel so small. It was a lie, plain and simple.

Kiki leaned over the table and said in a patronizing voice, "He's married, Charlie."

"Married!" Now I pressed the palm of my hand against my forehead. "So not only were you out screwing around, but you were also out doing so while you were pregnant and with a married man."

I laughed again, but Kiki looked at me stone-faced.

She picked up her phone, unlocked it, and began to methodically scroll through several photos. When she found the one she wanted, she turned the phone around so I could see it. There were two well-groomed, good-looking men, cheek-to-cheek on a tropical beach somewhere, smiling wide-eyed for their selfie.

"The one on the left is Xavier," she said. "The one on the right is Gabe. His husband."

4

Now I felt little again. As diminutive as ever.

Our waiter placed both of our omelets on the table before us, but at this point I had completely lost my appetite.

"He's gay?" I asked, trying to accept this fact.

"Yes. Considering he's married to another man, that would make him gay."

"Why didn't you tell me?"

"You never gave me a chance," she said. "It wasn't a big, huge deal. We grew up together in the same neighborhood. A dear friend I visit when in town. Did you expect me to ask for permission? For me to go out with a gay friend?"

"No, I just—"

"We were each other's wingmen when we were young. The whole dress thing—that's just our typical banter. It's harmless. I talk the same way with my girlfriends. And Xavier works in the fashion industry. It's in his blood."

I found it difficult to swallow all of this.

I had been wrong.

I felt absolutely sickened.

Kiki had placed the phone, screen up, in the center of the table. For a moment, I wondered if she was lying to me. Was all this part of her same schtick? But no, I didn't think so. The pieces of the puzzle fit together too perfectly.

How could I be so foolish?

"Kiki," I said, rubbing my forehead. "I don't know what to say. I guess I was—"

Her phone vibrated in the center of the table.

I saw the incoming name: Duncan.

5

She reached quickly for the phone.

"Hello," she said. She listened to whatever Duncan was saying, said "yes" a few times, "okay" a couple of other times. She nibbled on her omelet while she listened, and after saying a quick goodbye, she hung up.

I stared at her, appalled. "You're back with Duncan?"

"Yes."

"What? Are you kidding me?"

"Why would I be kidding?"

"Kiki, are you nuts? Do you know how much you complained about him while we were together? Do you remember what he did to you?"

"Yes, I do." She dabbed her lips with a napkin. "He's changed, Charlie. Duncan is doing much better than before, and he promised to take care of those bills. He's in a much better space than before. A totally new man. People change."

"No," I protested, "people don't change. Men who abuse women don't change."

"Well, I think differently," she said. "We've patched things up, and really, maybe everything was for the best. I hate to say it, but I think you were kind of like a rebound for me. I think Duncan just needed some time to realize what he'd lost, and now he's like a totally different person."

"You're going to regret this," I said. "Big time."

"I'm not going to regret it," she said firmly. "You know, I put in my notice to my landlord when I was going to move in with you. When I realized that wasn't going to pan out, I had to reapply for my own apartment, and because of some legal technicality, it's a new lease. They upped the rent three hundred a month. In the next year, your thinking me a liar will cost me over three thousand dollars."

That one hurt because it was true.

It all hurt.

If I had believed Kiki, this wouldn't have happened. It would have saved her money, for sure, and she wouldn't have run back into the arms of her abuser.

"Listen, I'm sorry about the money. I don't know what—"

"You don't have to be sorry," Kiki said. "What's meant to happen has happened, but I wanted you to know that I'm not a liar. I'm not some wild figment of your imagination."

"I see."

"And I think I've said all I need to say." She got to her feet. She had only eaten a few bites of her omelet. I hadn't touched mine, and it was getting cold. "Tell Adam I hope he's doing well and I think about him often. Best of luck to you, Charlie."

With her purse slung over her shoulder, Kiki walked away.

She left me with the bill, of course, and I couldn't blame her. I owed her far more than that.

In fact, I decided that I was going to write her a check for three thousand dollars and mail it to her. Yes, it was beyond belief that she had gone back to Duncan, but so much of it was my fault. If I had believed her, none of this would have happened.

Our waiter returned and looked at Kiki's abandoned plate of food and my untouched omelet.

"Would you like a to-go box?" he asked.

"No." I pulled my wallet out of my pocket. "I've lost my appetite. And I don't think it's coming back anytime soon."

6

I made good on writing her the check.

I knew I didn't have to, and maybe it was a bit much, but I understood my culpability. Before I went to bed, I wrote the three-thousand-dollar check and added a small note. Only two words: *I'm sorry*. I knew the check wouldn't atone for all of my transgressions, but it would, at least, lighten the load that my decisions had placed on her. I put the check and the note in an envelope, addressed it, found a stamp, and clipped it to my front mailbox for the mailman to take the following morning.

When I went to bed, there was so much to think about.

For some reason, my mind went to Detective Grimm. I pictured her sitting in that little interrogation room with her folders and her documents and her morbid photographs. I imagined her sitting there in the wee hours of the night, flipping through notes, trying to connect the dots and form a constellation of clues that would inevitably point to me.

"You are the common denominator," she had told me.

And she was right.

Two people dead. Both people I was having issues with. And I was the last to see them.

This looked terrible. If it were an episode of *Dateline*, there would be an unflattering picture of me with dreary music and Keith Morrison's voice saying something to the effect of "Charlie Phoenix was a man of many secrets…"

But I didn't do it.

That I knew for sure, and it gave me hope. I knew nothing about those deaths.

I turned off the lights and tried to sleep, but just as I was about to drift off into Neverland, a thought occurred to me. It hit me with such force, I sat up and threw the blanket off me.

"You are the common denominator," I said, parroting Detective Grimm's words.

No, I thought.

I looked out my bedroom window at my garage.

In the cold darkness of the room, I whispered, "She was wrong. I'm not the common denominator. The car is."

Chapter Forty-four

15.25 Liters of Fuel Remaining

1

I let Chuck out of the car, and he was happy about it. A night sleeping in the yard would be a return to old times and probably, for him, a little cozier. He scurried off toward my backyard.

I needed to be alone with the Stingray, so I found a folding chair tucked away in my garage, opened it up, and took a seat right in front of the vehicle so I was looking directly at the hood and front windshield. The engine was on, as it was most nights when I put Chuck to bed. The pop-up headlights were off and in the down position, and as the V8 thunderously idled, the Corvette seemed like some black beast slumbering in its cave.

The garage door was open, but I could smell the rich fumes of exhaust.

"What are you?" I whispered.

The Stingray, of course, didn't respond. The engine loped while in the idle position.

I had always assumed that the Stingray was good. All it did was heal. If this were some horror movie or Stephen King novel, maybe it would have been different. But it never drove itself, never ran over anyone, and the radio never turned on at opportune times to communicate with me. It was just there, doing its thing.

But maybe there was more to it.

2

"The common denominator," I whispered.

The more I thought about it, the more I realized that Mara and Fergus had more in common than just not liking me. Both had wanted the Stingray. Their final acts on this Earth had been attempts to take the Stingray from me. Fergus tried to do it at gunpoint, and Mara wanted to do it through legal tactics.

And both ended up dead.

I considered their fates. Interestingly, both had died in a garage. Maybe that meant something. I wasn't sure. Was that the Stingray's "calling card" when it came to murder? I didn't know, but one thing that struck me as an impossibility was conceiving of any way that this Corvette could possibly murder these two people. How? The Corvette had been with me. And how could it shoot Fergus in the head and then accidentally place the gun in the wrong hand? And how would a Corvette force Mara into her car and force death by carbon monoxide poisoning? In what universe did any of that even begin to make sense?

And then I thought of the obituaries I'd found in Richard Pratt's STINGRAY file. His two friends who had taken their own lives.

"What are you?" I whispered again.

3

I must have sat there for an hour, thinking.

I wasn't entirely sure how everything had happened, but I was utterly convinced that the Stingray was behind both deaths. All things need to be refueled, and even though the car didn't run on gasoline, maybe it ran on people. On their souls. But one thing seemed clear: It was fiercely protective of its current owner, and those who wanted to take it ended up dead.

Strangely, it even fit the name: Stingray.

It had been a while since I'd taken a college class, but a few things stuck with me from the three-unit marine biology course I'd taken.

In the wild, stingrays were considered docile and only attacked in self-defense. They burrowed themselves beneath the sand and wanted to go unnoticed.

But in shallow waters, they were dangerous.

In ancient Greece, venom was extracted from stingray spines to make an anesthetic, a reminder to me that what can be used to cure can also be used to kill. And vice versa.

"So it's been you," I whispered.

The engine loped as I made the accusation. The V8 growled.

I should have seen it earlier.

But it did exactly what it had always done.

As people died and my life fell apart, it had been there all along, a dark shadow gliding through the murky waters.

4

I had to get rid of it.

I made the decision around three o'clock the following afternoon. I would drive to Downtown Long Beach, leave the key in the ignition, catch an Uber, and be on my way.

Somebody would take it. Maybe I'd even leave a FREE sign on the windshield. I'd make it that easy.

I'd spent most of the day in pajamas, so I went inside and threw on a pair of jeans and a T-shirt and headed back to the garage. Chuck's stuff was set up inside the car. I cleared it out, jumped inside, and headed toward Downtown Long Beach.

During my drive, I couldn't help but consider all of the things I would give up for doing this. If the hernia pain ever came back or, God forbid, something worse ailed me, I couldn't jump in the Stingray and go for a road trip to make it better. But maybe that was okay. Maybe it didn't matter. Because where had any of this gotten me? Billy was dead, Stanley's wife was dead, and one day—hopefully long from now—Chuck would kick the bucket too.

And maybe that was okay.

Maybe that was just life.

Whatever the case, I knew something to be deeply true: this Stingray was too much responsibility. The powers of life and death were never meant to be placed in one driver's hands. There were too many roads, too many intersections. It was too much.

I drove several miles into Downtown Long Beach and found a small, worn-down street off Pine Avenue.

I left the key in the ignition, and as I got out, I saw a figure on the other side of the street strolling drunkenly down the sidewalk, a bottle of something in his hand. He was singing, but I couldn't make out the tune. I was pretty sure it was improv.

Looking up and down the block, I decided this looked perfect. Most of the cars here were old and broken down. Anybody strolling down this street and finding a classic '69 Stingray with the key in the ignition would find the event almost providential. How could someone not bite? It was only a matter of time. Once it got dark, I was sure someone would try to take it. Maybe even sooner.

I pulled my phone out of my pocket and opened my Uber app. I requested a ride and noted the wait time. Eight minutes. Okay. I could do that.

Yet, as I waited, I started to sweat. It wasn't hot, but for some reason I found myself wiping my forehead.

I heard a soft, whispery voice behind me: *You can't leave me.*

I spun around, phone in hand.

Nobody was there, and it was no real surprise. There had been a voice, yes, but it seemed to be more inside my head. Yet it was as clear as someone had been behind me, whispering. I tried to understand what—

Walk towards Pine Street, the voice ordered.

This time, I was sure. It was inside my head, and now it could do more than just speak to me. It commandeered my entire body. I found myself unwillingly walking towards the main street. I felt like a marionette, my physical body manipulated by some sadistic puppeteer, and I couldn't turn around or force myself to stop. I was a passenger in my own body, doing nothing more than riding shotgun.

The sensation was so terrifying, I tried to scream—but I couldn't. As if under sedation, I walked towards the main street. For a couple moments, I was briefly able to take control. I staggered back two steps. I flailed one of my arms. But inevitably, it was like trying to take hold of the wheel and rip control from a much stronger driver. I just couldn't do it.

As I neared Pine Avenue, I saw that some restaurants were open. I could hear laughter. Music. A transient dug through a trash can not far from me and, having found an unfinished can of Coke, took several gulps and hurried away.

Cars whizzed by.

Maybe someone would see me and help me?

But I knew that wouldn't happen. How would they know? In their eyes, I was just a pedestrian.

A large blue bus was coming down the street. I saw the digital readout on its frontside: PINE LINE 7.

Now I understood. I was on direct course for that bus. If I couldn't regain control of myself and stop before stepping off the curb, I was going to become a human speed bump. The driver wouldn't even see me before I was splattered on the pavement.

I couldn't even control my own ability to close my own eyes.

My legs carried me off the curb.

Into the street.

I had maybe a second before it plowed into me, and it was over.

Chapter Forty-five

14.98 Liters of Fuel Remaining

1

The bus never hit me, but it was close. At the last moment, whatever force controlled me released its grip. The bus missed me by mere inches.

By the time I got back to the car, I was sweating and shivering.

What had just happened?

I looked down at the glowing gauges on the dashboard, and as the engine rumbled beneath the black hood, I finally understood.

It was the car.

You can't leave me.

This was how Fergus and Mara died. They tried to take it, and in doing so, they had stirred the Stingray. It had controlled them and, in controlling me, it reminded me that I was never really the one in the driver's seat. I think it wanted to demonstrate its power over me, a very real threat to let me know I was not to abandon the Stingray; our relationship was not to be severed.

I got the message. Loud and clear on that one.

And now the deaths made more sense.

That was why there had been signs of a struggle. Grimm had been elusive in her details, but I was sure Fergus had flailed and fought the voices in his head and tried to resist. Maybe he knocked things over, maybe he clawed at something—an old piece of furniture stored in the garage, perhaps—but he had been unable to resist the Stingray's puppeteering. No wonder he shot himself with his right hand. Because it wasn't him. The car had controlled him, and I imagined he had fought like hell to stop it.

The same was true with Mara and explained why Grimm was in my grill. It looked bad—really bad—and I doubted she or anybody else would believe that the car was the one responsible.

I sat there, thinking.

I had to get rid of it, but how?

2

I drove to the Long Beach storage facility I owned.

We had several indoor units that provided garage-like storage, and when I pulled in and asked Zeb, the new relief manager who was preparing to leave for the day, he assured me that two were unoccupied. He got the keys and pointed me toward storage unit E2.

There was only one other pickup unloading some goods. I found unit E2, rolled open the door, and pulled into the tomb-like storage garage.

When I got out of the car, walked out of the garage, and rolled down the door, I felt more at ease.

I needed time to think and figure out what to do with the vehicle.

"You got a nice car there," Zeb said as I walked out toward the street. He was a funny guy. Always a big smile on his face despite his teeth being not the greatest. Whenever he smiled, it reminded me of the BEFORE picture of some teeth-straightening procedure.

"Yeah, it is."

"Well, boss, if you're gonna store it here, I can warm it up anytime you want. Not good for a car to just sit there."

He grinned. His teeth looked like the keys of a busted piano.

"No, it's fine."

"Okey-dokey," he said. "Wouldn't be a problem. Me? I've done a lot of work on cars in my life."

"I appreciate it, Zeb, but I'm good."

He looked toward unit E2, and I should have recognized the wolfish gleam in his eye.

I bade him a good evening and caught my Uber.

Only later did I see my mistake.

3

I felt good having the Stingray away from my home. For the first time, it truly scared me. I had never thought of it as something dangerous. It was always something good. To think that it could extract life just as easily as it replenished it terrified me to the bone and marrow.

I didn't want it near my kid. I didn't want it near Tommy.

But I ran into what seemed like a contradiction of its character. The Stingray didn't want to end our relationship, and I was convinced that if I even tried to sell the car to someone that person would certainly end up dead. If it killed Mara for simply asking for it, I couldn't even imagine trying to sell it.

But that made no sense. Richard had sold the car to me. And Own Menken sold the car to him.

Why had the Stingray allowed it?

There had to be some reason.

I sat at my dining room table for an hour, pondering. At one point I even grabbed a pen and paper. I wrote my name, Charlie, and drew a circle around it; then I wrote the name Richard and drew a circle around it. How were we different? I knew very little about him, but I jotted down everything I could think of that made us different. There had to be some reason he was able to get rid of the Stingray, and I couldn't.

He was taller than me, leaner, older, was a bachelor, no kids…

I wrote down the little I could think of and, rubbing my eyes, decided I needed a break. Plus, I had to make a run to the store to get some food for Chuck. We were low on provisions. I was about to get up from the chair when it hit me all at once.

"Food," I whispered.

I looked back down at my notes.

Many creatures in the wild migrated—even real stingrays—and most of the time it was because of food. They simply needed to eat and went to where the meals were. When I thought of my '69 Stingray, I thought of everything I'd been feeding it. Myself. Mara. Kiki. Adam. Cancer patients. Chuck. I sensed the car wanted—perhaps even needed—to replenish, and it had been an all-night buffet with me as the owner. In the case of Chuck, this was quite literal.

I remembered how Zora had explained her brother as being a loner, and I knew he had no wife or children. Maybe the same was true with the original owner. Whatever the case, I was convinced when the owner didn't bring it enough things to replenish—or ceased driving it all together—it would grow hungry. And if it could convince me not to abandon it and back up its request with the threat of death, I'm sure it was just as capable of persuading me to find a new owner when the time was right.

Maybe I'd be home one night watching Netflix or minding my own business and the Stingray would call to me, threaten me again, and demand I find a new owner. Someone who would drive it and feed it.

I simply hadn't reached that point in the relationship yet with the Stingray.

But I was convinced that when the time came, it wouldn't just kill me. I think it needed me. There was a term for this: a symbiotic relationship. Strangely enough, real Stingrays have this in the wild. I read all about this in prison. They have a "mutualistic, parasitic, predatorial" relationship with blue-head wrasses. They need the wrasses to clean and sustain them, and in doing so, the wrasses live.

But stingrays are purely carnivorous, and, in some cases, they eat the wrasses.

I was convinced. I'd leave the Stingray in my storage facility, let it grow hungry, and prepare for it to call to me. Maybe it would take a week. Or a month? Who knew? And I guessed that when the time came, it would want me to find a new owner for it.

Because if it killed me, it'd just sit there in the garage, and grow hungrier. I guessed it needed me in the same way it needed Owen Menken and Richard Pratt when it needed a new "host."

And when that time came, I'd be ready.

4

It was nearly nine o'clock in the evening. I was in the kitchen and finished eating a piece of toast. I dropped my plate in the sink, and was going to head upstairs when my phone buzzed. It was a text, and it was short and simple: *This is Owen Menken. Call me immediately.*

Owen Menken?

I dialed his number, and he answered without a single ring.

"Charlie?"

"Yeah, it's me. What's going on? It's midnight. And how did you get my phone num—"

"Where's the Stingray?"

"It's, uh…why? What's going on?"

"I didn't tell you everything."

"Yeah, I kinda figured that out on my own."

"Listen," he said, and the tone of his voice was dead serious. "I've made a mistake. Richard made a mistake. We want to make this right."

We? That didn't make sense. Richard was dead.

"What are you—"

"Tomorrow," he said. "I need to see you. Come meet me. And don't drive the car. Can you do that?"

"Yeah, sure, but where?"

"Seal Beach pier. At the very end. High noon."

"Sure, okay. But what—"

The line went dead.

5

I considered this meeting with Owen Menken.

What did he want to talk about? If it was so important, why hadn't he just talked to me when I made the impromptu visit to his coffee shop? And why this whole change of identity?

None of it made any sense.

I poured myself a glass of brandy, but as I reached for it, I thought twice. I'd been drinking too much lately; I didn't need somebody to tell me that. When I thought of the Stingray and looked at the glass in hand, I realized my Corvette wasn't the only thing in this world that appeared to heal but, in the end, took more than it gave.

I thought of Stanley, who I hadn't seen since his wife passed away, and where his grief had driven him.

Just like in the Stingray, I supposed, grief couldn't be artificially remedied.

There were no detours or fast tracks for that one. It had to be driven out—every painful mile.

I pushed my glass away.

"Not tonight," I said and went to bed.

Chapter Forty-six

14.03 Liters of Fuel Remaining

1

I woke up to Adam's voice.

I had been submerged in a dream. I was underwater, disoriented, and a dark creature drifted toward me through the murky waters. Its lantern-like blue eyes cut through the dark ocean like high beams, and there was something else down here too. Corpses. Half-decomposed. Drifting with the current.

One of them was Mara. The other was Fergus. His clothing was frayed. Small underwater crabs scurried over his body, and one was feasting on his rotted eye socket.

And there was a third.

It drifted toward me.

But the face.

Whose face was that?

2

"Dad!"

I sat up in bed, drenched in sweat. Adam was standing over me.

"What?" I asked, flustered. The room spun in circles around me. I still felt underwater, half in the dry land of reality, half in the water world of dreams. "What is it? What's wrong?"

"It's Kiki." He pointed to his phone.

"What?"

"Kiki's boyfriend."

I rubbed the sleep out of my eyes and read the text: *This is Duncan, Kiki's boyfriend. Stop texting my girl! If you text or call her one more time, we're going to need to talk. No more.*

I noted the time. It was about ten at night.

"He's called like ten times," Adam said. "I haven't answered."

"Good. Don't answer. Idiot. He probably thinks you're some guy trying to get with her. Just ignore it."

"Is this the guy you told me about?" Adam asked. "The guy who used to beat her?"

I nodded sorrowfully. "Yep, it sure is."

"Wow."

"Yeah. Sad, huh? Listen, don't answer the phone. Ignore it. He's a bully. He'll go away eventually."

Now my phone went off.

It was on the nightstand beside my bed. I reached for it and, lo and behold, it was also a text from Kiki. Only, when I read it, I realized Duncan was no longer commandeering her phone. This was Kiki herself. It read: *Tell Adam I'm sorry about the calls. Duncan and I got into a fight. Can you come over, please? It was a bad night. We need to talk.*

A moment later Adam's phone buzzed.

The text was brief: *Just texted your dad. Sorry about all that. It was my boyfriend.*

3

Duncan might have gotten physical with her. It wouldn't shock me. And if he had, she probably just needed someone to talk to. Someone to connect with. Since she had control of the phone, I assumed Duncan must have left. I guessed it wouldn't hurt. It was late. I could drive over, listen to her, be a friend, and point her in the right direction. And maybe that was exactly what Kiki needed: help. I'd read that toxic and abusive relationships were as addictive as heroin. They were hard to pull away from.

I left immediately.

On the way out to my Lexus, which was parked in front of my house, I spotted Tommy on the grass, playing with several green army soldiers. He had a little battlefield set up. It was way too late for him to be out here, but I figured Stanley was out of commission.

Chuck was next to him, unconcerned with the military operation.

"Hi, Mr. Phoenix," Tommy said.

"Hey, Tommy." It occurred to me that I hadn't said anything since his mother passed. I had wanted to order some flowers too, and I hadn't done that. What a terrible neighbor I was. I was just utterly submerged in my own problems. "Listen, bud, I never got a chance to tell you— I'm really sorry to hear what happened. You know, that kind of stuff is tough, but I'm just sorry."

"I know," Tommy said. "But it's okay. Mom's in heaven. Dad says no way would she want to come back here."

"Yeah." I smiled. "That's a good point."

"And the car gave us more time with her."

"Yeah, it really did, didn't it?"

I was impressed. This kid was dealing with this better than most adults could.

"Listen," I said, "I'm gonna bring a meal over for you and your dad. Maybe tomorrow I'll stop by and—"

My phone rang. It was Trey.

"One sec," I told Tommy and took the call. "Hey, Trey, what's up?"

"Sorry to bug you this late," he said. "I just got a call from Sentech. You think you could show up before office hours tomorrow, let them in? They're gonna fix those two cameras."

"They broke again?"

"Yep."

"I told you they do shoddy work, but yeah, I can be there. I only have one appointment tomorrow, and it's not until noon."

"Oh yeah?" Trey said. "What for?"

"Owen Menken. He called me."

Chapter Forty-seven

12.42 Liters of Fuel Remaining

1

I arrived at Kiki's apartment at about 10:30 that night. I stood outside her door and made a couple of promises to myself. I wasn't going to make any hasty decisions to get back together with her; I was merely here as a friend and a sounding board. If her altercation with Duncan had been anything like her past, it wasn't good.

I knocked, waited, and listened as footsteps approached the door. There was a delay. I imagined Kiki was eyeing me through the peephole. When the door opened, I saw that she had a black eye and a fat lip, and a blur of eyeliner and mascara ran like wet paint down her face. She had been crying. Her face was slick with tears, and her eyes were red and irritated. It looked like she hadn't slept in weeks.

"Oh my God," I said. "What happened?"

"It's not obvious?" She sniffled and turned around.

I followed her inside. "He did this to you?"

"Yes," she blubbered. "Who else would?"

"You need to do something."

"Like what?"

"I don't know. Call the police. Let's go to urgent care."

"Like that'll help." She went over to the couch and sat down. I took a seat beside her and let her cry it out for several minutes. I wasn't sure what to say. I went to her freezer, found an ice pack, and brought it to her. I didn't have to explain to her, because she knew what to do. She brought it up to her bruised, blackened eye.

"What exactly happened?" I asked.

"Me being stupid," she said. "Once again, Kiki to the rescue. I can't believe I went back to him."

"It's okay. We all make mistakes."

"I know, but I make a lot more of them than most."

"Listen, he's the one who did something wrong here. Not you. When did this happen?"

"Well, that's the thing," she said. "He's been doing meth again. I thought he was done with that—he said he had it under control—but I was wrong. He's been up for a couple of days. And it snowballed from there. It always happens that way. At one point he got my phone and found texts between me and Adam, and he went ballistic. He thinks Adam's some guy I'm hooking up with or something. And then when I told him Adam was your son, he got even more ballistic. Accused me of hooking up with both of you. It was insane."

"Yeah, that is insane. Well, I'm glad you texted me to come over. Why don't we take you to get looked at? That eye looks bad."

She lowered the pack of ice from her swollen eye, and with her one good one glared at me. "What do you mean I texted you?"

"Well, you texted me."

We paused. I noted her confusion.

"I didn't text you," she said. "I couldn't. Duncan stormed off not long ago with my phone."

"He did? But how—"

I hadn't locked the door behind me, and a figure stepped into the room. A big, gnarly guy wearing blue jeans and a leather jacket. He had short, dark, spiky hair, and his face was neanderthal-like, with a square chin and dark, intense eyes.

This was Duncan.

I didn't know what scared me more: his massive physique or the bat in his grip.

2

"So, you must be the kid's dad, huh?" he asked. "You messing around with her too?"

I instantly stood up, raised my hands. "Please, just leave. She's hurt, and I'm not here to fight, okay? Please go."

He closed the door behind him. Then, holding his bat, he took two steps toward us. Kiki had told me about that bat. I noticed his hands were shaking. His eyes were twitching. I wondered, briefly, if this was the meth or if this guy always had the jitters.

"You ain't having her," he pointed. "She's mine or nobody's. Got it?"

"Look, I'm not here for that."

"I knew you'd come running over at a moment's notice," he said, wiping saliva from his lower lip. "No guy I know comes over at a moment's notice like this unless it's for a bootie call. Don't lie to me, ass wipe. After I break your legs, maybe it'll teach you to stay away from her."

"I'm not—"

He lunged at me and swung for my knees, but fortunately I dodged it and fell to the floor. As I got back to my feet, I had one momentary thought: *I can't believe this guy is attacking me with a bat.*

I had barely recalibrated when he swung for my legs again. I dodged.

It was terrible timing.

Terrified, Kiki jumped from the couch, tripped, and as she fell toward the floor, the bat made contact with her head.

I heard the crack.

Blood splattered all over me.

And she crumpled lifelessly to the floor, a halo of blood saturating the carpet around her head.

3

"Now look what you made me do!" Duncan protested.

He looked down at Kiki's body, and I thought I saw a flash of grief across his face, but then it passed. He was back to his enraged self, and his attention was on me, the witness to his crime and, in his mind, the catalyst for it. As he strode toward me and readjusted his sweaty grip on the bloody bat, I was pretty sure he was no longer going to be aiming for the knees.

He was in this to kill.

The best scenario, I thought, would be to run out the front door and call for help, but he was in the way. I ran the other direction and found myself in the apartment's small galley kitchen. Not the worst place to end up, in my situation.

I scanned the counters. There was a toaster. I picked it up, yanked the cord out of its socket, and flung it toward Duncan. He ducked, and the toaster flew through the window. If the neighbors hadn't already known there was an altercation happening in apartment 3, they certainly did now.

Duncan came toward me, a meth-crazed locomotive of human rage. I looked for something else.

I saw my one hope: a butcher block on top of the fridge.

I withdrew the chef knife just as Duncan came toward me.

The bat swung past my head as I ducked, and struck the refrigerator door. Magnetized buttons and photographs went flying like piñata confetti.

I saw my opportunity, and in one upward thrust, I buried the chef knife deep into Duncan's rib cage. I heard cartilage and flesh tear as I drove the blade in to the handle.

Warm blood dripped down my hand, and Duncan let go of the bat and fell onto me.

I lay there on the linoleum floor with all his weight on me, my hands still clutching the knife. With his face only inches from mine, I heard him gargle and breathe his last.

He spasmed twice and then went completely limp.

It was the only time I killed a man.

And to this day, I don't regret it.

4

I pushed Duncan's body off me and got to my feet. I felt wet, and when I looked down at my body, I realized I was covered in blood. It looked like I was the one who had been stabbed. Stepping over Duncan's body, I nearly slipped on the linoleum floor. As I raced toward the living room, I left a trail of bloody shoeprints behind me.

Kneeling beside Kiki, I expected her to be dead.

Before the blow to the head, she had already looked terrible. The swollen eye. The bruised lip. Now I couldn't even make out her face. I wasn't sure exactly where she was hit, but her hair was matted in blood, and her face was covered in it and other bodily gunk.

I felt for a pulse. Brought my ear close to her mouth and listened for any kind of breathing.

And it was there. A faint but discernable pumping of the carotid artery. I removed my hand and wiped her blood on my pants.

There was breathing too. Subtle. Shallow. But it was there.

"You're alive," I said, aghast.

Of course, *alive* might have been a relative term. I hadn't seen the exact angle she had been struck in the head and didn't know what damage had been done, but I had the feeling that when and if she recovered from this, she would not be her former self. A vegetable, maybe. Brain damage. It was bad. I couldn't imagine how anybody could take a blow to the head like that and ever be the same again.

I withdrew my iPhone from my pocket and tried to unlock it with the passcode. But my hand was trembling so badly, I couldn't do it.

I dropped the phone onto the carpet to keep it steady and then, concentrating, punched the EMERGENCY button, which would allow me to make emergency calls. Bloody fingerprints smeared the screen.

"Let's get you to a hospital," I mumbled.

I dialed 9.

I dialed 1.

And then I stopped.

I looked down at her gory, unrecognizable face. This wasn't going to work. It would take the ambulance too long to get here. She would have to be taken to the hospital, they would have to work on her, and I was sure the damage would only be worse by then.

Her brain was swelling. I was sure of it. In minutes, perhaps, her brain would swell so large that gray matter would ooze out of her ears.

They wouldn't be able to heal her. Not fully. So I had no choice.

I scooped up her limp, blood-soaked body and made my way to the front door.

Because I knew what had to be done.

Chapter Forty-eight

10.81 Liters of Fuel Remaining

1

The drive to the storage facility was only fifteen minutes. Not long, but in my situation, it was an eternity. I laid Kiki in the backseat of my Lexus. She was complete deadweight; although, as I laid her down, I thought I heard her cough. It was deep, gurgly kind of cough and definitely didn't sound good, but it told me she was still alive.

And that was a good thing.

If she was alive, she could be replenished.

As I pulled away from Kiki's apartment, I saw two of her neighbors standing outside their front doors. They were watching me, terrified. I was sure they knew something was wrong from the moment that toaster went flying out the window.

One of the neighbors had a phone to her ear.

I didn't have to guess who she was on the phone with.

I hadn't dialed 911, but I was willing to bet that was who she had called.

2

I made it to the storage facility in just under twenty minutes.

I prayed that Kiki was still alive and hadn't slipped away during the drive there.

"Stay with me!" I yelled as I arrived.

Strangely, the gate was open, and the lights were on in the main office. It didn't make sense to me. Zeb should have locked up before he left earlier that night, but I didn't have time to think about it.

It was quiet here. Not a soul stirred.

I parked in front of E2, got out of the car, and realized I didn't have the key. Stupid of me. But maybe I didn't need it.

The door was slightly ajar.

"What?" I mumbled.

I rolled open the door to the unit.

Inside was the Stingray. The LED shop lights reflected off the car's tuxedo-black paint job.

Zeb was there too, on the ground. He was rigid, and his face was purple, and there was a belt around his neck. By the looks of him, there was no question whether he was dead. He had strangled himself with his own belt. No need to check his pulse like I'd done with Kiki.

"Oh my God," I said.

It wasn't difficult to solve this one. Zeb, the car enthusiast, had gone into the unit after I left. I was sure he just wanted to see the car. I didn't think he wanted to take it, and he couldn't have anyway, because I had the key. Maybe he just wanted to sit in the car and admire it.

But somehow, I was sure, the Stingray knew.

It sensed his longing. His desire.

And he paid the price.

As much as I wanted to do something about the body, I simply didn't have time. I had to move quickly.

3

I dragged Zeb's body out of the way and got Kiki into the passenger seat of the Stingray. It was a bloody, terrible episode, but it worked. I had to position her so that she leaned against the closed door.

Another check of her carotid artery suggested she was still there.

Barely, but she was there.

The pulse was shallow and faint, but so long as it was there, I clung to hope.

I climbed into the driver's seat and headed out of the storage facility.

I left the E2 unit behind me along with Zeb's body.

I left my Lexus behind too, the doors open, the engine running.

4

I tried to think this through as reasonably as possible.

More than anything, I needed open road. Fortunately, it was very late in the evening, and that gave me an advantage. My thought was simple. I would head to the 405 South and straight toward San Diego. This was Southern California, and that meant there was almost always traffic, but the 405 South this time of night might give me the chance to pick up some speed, and it would be far better, I thought, than heading toward Los Angeles.

I found the nearest on-ramp, got onto the freeway, and things looked good. Several cars on the road, but not terribly many.

I scanned the road for police officers and, seeing none, pushed the speed to ninety. Getting pulled over for a speeding ticket was never a good thing, but doing so with Kiki in her current condition would be terrible.

A few minutes passed.

I looked at Kiki, who leaned silently against the window without a sound. How long would it take? I thought back to that first drive with Chuck. I hadn't noticed any change in him until the very end of that drive. The same had been true with Jaysa, Stanley's wife. And I had driven her all night.

This took time.

But maybe I could speed things up.

I pushed down on the gas pedal and watched the speedometer hit one hundred.

"Come on," I said, looking down at the car's gauges, "work!"

A moment later, I heard a siren behind me.

I wasn't going to pull over for some speeding ticket. Not now.

But then I heard another siren. And another. And another.

I glanced in my rearview mirror and saw several police cars, flashers on, following me.

And above them, a helicopter.

That was when I knew.

They weren't here to apprehend a speeder. They were here to catch a killer.

Chapter Forty-nine

9.27 Liters of Fuel Remaining

1

This wasn't good.

Although I had open road ahead of me, I counted eight police cars behind me. And now I counted three copters in sky. One of them, I assumed, was a police helicopter, and the others were media. At least, that was my guess. High-speed pursuits sadly made for good entertainment.

Interestingly enough, the police cars kept their distance, and I thought I knew why. The few police pursuits I'd seen on television and the newscasters' commentary had suggested that in certain chases where the driver was not pulling erratic moves and was not endangering the public, the officers stayed back. Why advance on the suspect and prompt the runaway driver to do something reckless? That seemed to be the case here.

I vowed that I would keep my speed at one hundred, nothing faster, and I wouldn't pull any moves that would encourage the authorities to "force" a stop. I didn't know what decisions were made in throwing out spike strips to stop a pursuit, but I didn't want to encourage it.

"Come on," I pounded the steering wheel of the Stingray. I wiped my nose and looked at Kiki. "Work faster! Work faster!"

I thought of what I had to do. Unless I ran into a major traffic jam, I could stay on the 405, get onto the 5, and head straight to the Mexico border. Would they set up a barricade at the border? I didn't know, but I could go for it in a worst-case scenario. I could drive all the way down to Cabo San Lucas if need be.

Hopefully, before then, I would see some change in Kiki. Some kind of replenishing.

I looked back in the rearview mirror. Saw the police cars. Saw the copters. I wondered what they were planning. Were they just following me? Waiting for me to make a mistake? Looking for an opportunity?

Turning on the radio, I spun the dial through several stations. I passed mariachi music, classical music, and sports news in hope of finding a newscast. With those copters in the air, I was sure somebody was talking about me. But I found nothing, and that was no surprise. The normal adrenaline-fueled suspense of a high-speed pursuit didn't translate well to radio.

That gave me an idea.

With one hand on the wheel, I pulled my iPhone out of my pocket. Blood was still smeared on the screen. I unlocked it, opened my CBS Los Angeles app, and waited for the live stream to begin.

When it did, there I was.

On the screen, I saw an aerial view of a '69 Stingray hauling ass down the 405 with a flock of police cars behind it.

It was loud in the car. I held the phone to my ear. A deep newscaster's voice said, "The police are being cautious. They believe the suspect is armed, dangerous, and might have a hostage on board. Details are still surfacing."

2

I drove for nearly an hour with mostly open road ahead of me. Most of the time, my vehicle was blanched in one of the overhead copter's spotlights. Since I didn't push the Stingray past one hundred and didn't make any wild, erratic moves, the police vehicles kept their distance.

The newscasters talked on and on about nothing, speculating about how this was going to end and what would happen. The details they had were vague but roughly true. The suspect, they claimed, had been involved in a deadly assault, taken a hostage, and was trying to make a getaway. The newscaster with the deep voice said, "Pursuits like this never end well. With that many cars behind him and this many copters in the sky, escape is a virtual impossibility."

He was right.

But my plan wasn't to escape. I just needed more time. More mileage.

I was surprised by how fatigued I was. I was gripping the steering wheel so tightly that it exhausted me. I was sweating profusely. Even though I was just sitting in the car, I felt like I'd run a marathon.

As I was driving and glancing down occasionally at the newscast, a notification appeared on my iPhone screen: *Meet Owen 12:00pm tomorrow.*

I swiped it away. That meeting wasn't going to happen.

I took the toll road, CA-73, because it was less congested. Fortunately, there were no toll booths to stop at—this was all done with the help of cameras, credit cards, and home billing. The winding road took me through the Laguna Coast Wilderness Park and Aliso Viejo, then dumped me back onto Interstate 5 right around San Juan Capistrano.

Once again, the coast was pretty clear. There was some traffic, but nothing to slow me to down. And I'd noticed something—most of the cars ahead of me were pulling to the side of the road before I even got close to them. I was sure the squad of flashing lights and copters in their rearview mirrors gave them incentive.

I thought about what was ahead. I-5 would take me through San Clemente, Oceanside, Encinitas, San Diego, Chula Vista, San Ysidro, and on to Mexico. It'd been a while since I'd done a trip down south, but I guesstimated the mileage from San Juan Capistrano to the border to be roughly eighty miles. At the speed I was going, I could get there in about forty-five-minutes.

There were all kinds of variables, of course.

Traffic would change things. A spike strip set out in the middle of I-5 would definitely change things.

And I had no idea how to cross the border. I'd only flown to Mexico. I was sure there would be a stop to show paperwork, a passport, all of those things. Maybe I could circumvent it, or if there was a gate of some kind, I'd just blow right through it.

On the other side, I'd be in Mexico.

And maybe that meant the cop cars would stop pursuit.

That was what happened in the movies. A criminal crossed the border and the United States lost jurisdiction. Of course, there were probably plenty of Federales on the other side of the border to pick up the slack, and I was sure Mexico would extradite.

I tried not to think of these things. My sole goal was to get Kiki back in order. Maybe I wouldn't have to drive all the way to the border.

"You alright?" I asked her. "Kiki, are you with me?"

Nothing.

I pounded my fist on the steering wheel and grunted. "Come on! Work!"

The newscasters continued to speculate. I had placed the iPhone on the center console just to the right of the stick. I picked up again and listened.

"It appears he may be planning to go to San Diego," the deep-voiced newscaster said. "And based on what we see, he has a pretty open freeway ahead of him. At least for now."

"He sure does," a female newscaster chimed in. She was a blonde woman with lots of make-up and, in my assessment, lots of plastic surgery. I thought she usually did the weather. "And don't forget, if he's heading toward San Diego, he could be making a run for the border."

"That's true, Denise," the other newscaster said. "Maybe that is his plan—if, of course, he doesn't run out of gas first."

I laughed.

"That's not happening," I said.

3

My phone rang.

I saw the number and recognized it instantly. This was the police department and the same number Detective Grimm called me from. I'd come to fear that number, and those digits were burned into my memory.

I knew what this was. They wanted to talk. Negotiation.

"Why not?" I muttered. "It could buy me more time."

I answered the phone and held it to my ear. "Hello."

There was a brief pause. Then I heard a voice.

"Charlie, it's me." It was a woman's voice, and I recognized it instantly as Detective Grimm. I was surprised. Maybe they had opted for her to make the call because we already had a relationship, some sense of rapport. But whatever the case, I assumed we weren't on the phone alone. I imagined her in a room with several other people listening, writing down notes, contemplating every moment of this phone call.

"Hello," I said. I wasn't sure what to say. I'd never been on a phone call while in the midst of a high-speed pursuit.

"Charlie," Detective Grimm said, "I want to begin with the woman in your custody. Is she okay? What is her condition? Will you tell me?"

"Kiki is going to be fine," I said.

I assumed they knew her name, but if they didn't, now they did.

"Is she hurt?" Detective Grimm asked.

"Yes, she is. She just needs some time. She's going to be fine. The longer you let me drive, the more you keep the roads clear ahead of me, the better chance she will have. Does that make sense?"

"Charlie, can you please put her on the phone?"

I looked over at Kiki. Her bloodied, tangled hair had smeared the side window.

"She can't talk right now."

"Charlie, can you please hold the phone up to her? We'd like confirmation that she is alive."

"I'm sorry," I said. "I can't."

4

"Charlie," Detective Grimm said, "there are people on the road ahead of you, and the last thing we want is for anybody to get hurt. Understand?"

"Yeah, I understand."

"Good. Now, I've been tasked to talk to you because we've had conversations before, and they've been good talks."

They had? Not really. Not from my perspective.

"So I just want to ask you something very simple," Detective Grimm said. "We don't want anybody hurt, and that includes you. We want you and the woman you are with to come back safely, okay? You have a son. He wants you home safe too. We all want you home safe. What can I do, Charlie? What do you want? I'm putting the ball in your court. Let's talk about this. What do you want?"

I was unable to contain my emotions. It was as if the whole reality hit me at once. My ex-girlfriend, most likely dead, was slumped in the car seat beside me. My clothing was covered in blood. Her blood. Duncan's blood.

This was a colossal disaster.

"I want to keep driving. She needs me to keep driving."

"Who needs you to keep driving?"

"Kiki."

"Why does Kiki need you to keep driving?"

"Because if I don't, she's going to die. Can you just give me open roads ahead? Put out some alert. Let me drive to San Diego, and I'll turn around and drive right back. I just want to drive."

She hesitated, and I was sure it was because of the unusual nature of the request.

"Charlie," she said, "even if we somehow opened up the freeway for you, that car is eventually going to run out of gas."

"No, it won't!"

"Yes, it will, and we need to talk about what happens when it does. Or when you stop. We don't want you getting hurt. We want you to see your son again. You have to do this for him. He loves you, and he needs you."

"You don't understand," I said. "It won't run out of gas. It'll never run out of gas."

"Charlie," Detective Grimm said, "I'm doing this because I care about you. I care about your life. It's time to end this."

"I didn't kill anybody," I said.

That wasn't entirely true, of course. I did kill Duncan—but that wasn't murder. If there was ever a case of self-defense, that was it.

"Let's talk about that after you bring this to an end."

She didn't believe me.

"I'm serious," I said. "I know what you think. I'm not a murderer."

"I understand. Let's talk."

"But I'm not."

Then I looked at Kiki and realized something.

5

I needed Kiki to live. Not just for her, but for me. I hadn't realized it until that moment.

If she died, then the truth died with her. They would paint me as a jealous ex who went over to her house, murdered her boyfriend, and then—in a fit of rage—killed her as well. This was OJ all over again, only now the white Bronco was a '69 Stingray and the victim was riding shotgun instead of A.C.

She had to live.

She alone held the truth.

"Stay with me," I said, looking at her. "Come on, baby, stay with me."

"Charlie?" Detective Grimm asked. "What are you talking about?"

I contemplated.

When this was all over and Kiki explained what had happened, I was sure I'd get in trouble for something like reckless driving or resisting arrest. But if the car brought her back, it wouldn't be murder.

"I need to drive, and I need open road," I explained. "If you try to stop me, I'll kill her."

I ended the call and placed the phone back on the center console.

I had to say something to fend them off. I had to play hardball.

Maybe it would work, and they'd listen, and when it was all over, I'd figure out a way to explain it. Stress. Trauma. I was sure I could weasel my way out of it, but hopefully this would give me the space I needed for the time being. I'd figure out an explanation later.

"Kiki, can you hear me?"

Nothing.

I glanced at the speedometer.

One hundred wasn't doing it, so I pushed it to 110.

Chapter Fifty

8.88 Liters of Fuel Remaining

1

I couldn't avoid the copters' spotlights. They'd lose me for a second, but then, once again, they'd get me in their crosshairs.

Then I had an idea: light. I was too easy a target.

I turned off the pop-up headlights, and the road in front of me went black. I wasn't sure it would help me, but maybe it would give me a slight edge.

Yet there were bigger problems ahead of me. There was a traffic jam on the freeway. I saw the blockade of red taillights waiting for me. Maybe there'd been an accident. Maybe some kind of road construction. But if I stayed this course on I-5, I was going to come to a dead stop in the middle of this pursuit, and that just couldn't happen.

I had to get off.

I wiped sweat from my forehead. My heart pounded like a mad metronome in my chest.

When I buzzed past a freeway overpass, I could see several looky-loos who had seen this high-speed pursuit on the news and made the trip out here to root for me. People were sick like that. I even saw a couple of people holding a giant sign that read: KEEP RUNNING! DOWN WITH THE POLICE!

I snickered. They didn't even know me.

There was one option. I saw an off-ramp before the traffic backup. It would be rough, but I could make it.

I eased off the gas, downshifted to third, and veered toward the off-ramp.

The phone went flying off the center console.

Kiki slid into me, but I pushed her body away.

2

I was off the freeway. On some road near San Diego, and I had a full road ahead of me.

I floored it.

There were stoplights ahead, and I chose to fly through the first red light without stopping. It scared me to death, and it was a gamble. I didn't check the cross traffic at all, but I closed my eyes as I tore right through the red and prayed I didn't hit anything.

It worked. When I opened my eyes, I was on the other side of the intersection, but now there was another problem. I saw police cars ahead of me on both sides of the road. Some kind of roadblock.

My eyes flicked to the rearview mirror. They were behind me too. A swarm of emergency lights and sirens that were gaining on me.

I had to turn around, but I couldn't slow down much. I'd seen how this worked.

If I slowed down too much, they'd perform a pit maneuver on me, intentionally clip the backside of my Stingray with their bullbars, and send me spinning like a teacup.

I had to make the U-turn, but I had to do it while moving as fast as I could.

There was only one solution: a bootleg turn.

3

I slowed down to about thirty miles an hour for the upcoming intersection, and with one hand on the top of the steering wheel, I reached for the emergency brake.

Then I realized how insane this idea was.

I was a forty-five-year-old businessman. Not a racecar driver.

Trying a bootleg turn would probably kill me.

I slowed down, made a U-turn, and avoided a pit maneuver. Now I was traveling in the opposite direction, and I was protected by the concrete median in the street. The police vehicles in pursuit buzzed past me on the other side of the road, and the roadblock was now in my rearview mirror.

But I had another problem.

Another roadblock ahead.

Several cop cars were stopped in the middle of the street.

"No!" I screamed and slammed my hand against the steering wheel.

4

There was only one way to avoid the roadblock.

There was an on-ramp to I-5 South just in front of the stopped cop cars and, having no choice, I drove onto the same freeway I had just exited.

But I knew where this would lead me.

As I merged onto the freeway, I could see the sea of red taillights in front of me. The same taillights I had tried to avoid by getting off the freeway to begin with.

Now the copters were back. White spotlights engulfed my vehicle. Sirens blazed behind me.

I slowed my vehicle and looked toward the "victim" in the passenger seat of my Stingray.

"I'm sorry," I said, reaching for Kiki's cold hand. "I tried."

5

As I slowed the Stingray, I thought of one final choice. I could turn the car around, move to the shoulder, and head in the opposite direction on the freeway. What other chance did I have?

Having slowed my car, I prepared for the U-turn.

And that was when it happened. One of the police cars sped forward and executed a pit maneuver, intentionally clipping the back of my Corvette. Tires squealed, and I lost control of the vehicle.

When I came to a stop, I was sideways on the freeway, and the car that had clipped me was right next to me. Both doors open. Two officers crouched behind the doors, guns drawn. Other cars quickly advanced until there were several police vehicles, all stopped, and officers poised behind more open doors, guns pointed at me.

It all happened so fast.

"Hands out of the car!" a voice blared through a megaphone.

It was over.

I only hoped I had gotten enough miles in.

I rolled down the window and put both of my hands outside where the world could see them. The copters circled overhead like iron vultures.

6

"Keep your hands up! Climb out the window of the vehicle!" I was ordered through the megaphone. "Hands up at all times. Keep near the hood of the car!"

I wasn't sure why they wanted me to pull a Dukes of Hazzard and climb out of the window, but I assumed it was because of some safety procedure. It allowed for my hands to be outside and less opportunity to fire off a weapon. I was preparing to slither out of the window when I heard Kiki.

"Charlie," she said.

Startled, I looked over at her. Her face was still covered in blood, but her one unswollen eye was wide open.

"Kiki," I said. "It worked. You're okay."

"Get out of the vehicle!" the officer blared through his megaphone.

7

With officers swarming the vehicle, I complied. I climbed through the window and obeyed when they asked me to lie flat on the asphalt, belly down, arms and legs spread-eagle.

And then they were on top of me. They yanked my arms behind my back, I was cuffed, and I was ushered toward the back seat of one of the cruisers.

I watched as the officers advanced toward my Stingray in what I imagined was an effort to help Kiki. Maybe she would still need medical attention. I wasn't sure the Stingray had replenished her tank back to full, but she was totally cognizant when she spoke to me, and I knew beyond all doubt that she would be fine when this was all over.

An officer remained in the front seat of the cruiser I was in, watching me. I was sure he attributed my grin to my being some narcissistic killer who was enjoying this, but he didn't know what I knew. He didn't understand that my plan had worked, and Kiki would be fine.

"She's going to be alright," I whispered.

The officer looked at me, stone-faced. He didn't seem to care one way or another.

Chapter Fifty-one

7.72 Liters of Fuel Remaining

1

Everything after the arrest was a blur.

I had hoped things would clear up quickly. With Kiki alive, she would explain things, I'd be let go (at least on the murder and attempted murder charges), but that never happened. Instead, I entered a long and seemingly unending labyrinth of legal proceedings that was as dim and hopeless as the prison cell I found myself in.

I thought a lot about my son, who went to live with my sister. She and her husband assumed the roles of legal guardians. I could only imagine how difficult it was for him. He lost a mother and a father. More than anything, I wanted him to know I would never hurt his mother—no matter how much we grew to dislike each other—but he suspected my guilt. My letters went unanswered, and my sister told me the boy simply needed time to process.

When I inquired, my sister always told me the same three words: "He's not ready."

I was arraigned in Governor George Deukmejian Courthouse on four counts of murder in the first degree, assault with a deadly weapon, and kidnapping. My victims, according to the court, included Fergus, Mara, Zeb, and Duncan, and the counts of assault and kidnapping were in regard to Kiki. The whole thing was a farce, and I found it difficult not to lose my mind. After the indictment, arrest and booking, arraignment, and eventual preliminary hearing, the prosecution made it clear that they would be seeking the death penalty.

My crimes were horrendous, according to prosecution as well as the court of public opinion. My name was all over the news, and I think the media was fascinated by me. I was, according to them, a middle-aged man who had led a quiet, professional life and who had suddenly snapped and gone on a killing spree. These are stories that always make for titillating tabloids and news headlines. Most of the news articles and clips I saw all asked the same questions. What made him do it? Why did he snap? How did someone spend most of his life minding his own business and then suddenly turn into a cruel-hearted serial killer?

I was every psychologist's wet dream.

After I was formally indicted, my attorney, Hasim Rolfe, warned me that things didn't look good.

"They have," Hasim told me during one meeting in prison, "very compelling evidence."

The prosecution's theory was simple. As a jealous lover, I showed up at Kiki's apartment and, during an altercation, killed her boyfriend and beat her to a pulp. In an attempt to cover my tracks, I drove Kiki to my storage facility where I had another car—the Stingray—waiting for her. It had premeditation written all over it. When Zeb, my night manager, got in the way of what I was doing earlier that evening when I planted the getaway car, I strangled him with his own belt.

The time of death matched perfectly, and the two faulty cameras at our facility vanquished any hope of exoneration. If those two cameras on the southern building had been working, they would have shown me driving away and Zeb turning back to the storage unit, rolling away the door, and going inside alone. I was sure he just wanted a closer look at the Stingray, and he must have done it right after I left without even returning to the main office. But instead, the other cameras at the facility made things look terrible. They showed both of us heading toward that storage unit and only me driving out of the parking lot.

I couldn't look more guilty.

This, of course, resonated with the other murders and what the prosecution called my "unbridled rage." I'd done the same thing before. Fergus was harassing me and threatening to sue and had to be eliminated, so I'd killed him and made it look like a suicide. The same was true with Mara. We were embroiled in a contentious custody battle and, unable to resolve our differences, I had taken it upon myself to put an end to her.

All of the same elements were present: a strained relationship, a killing, and in two of the cases, a cover-up to make it look like a suicide.

Hasim suggested we work out a plea deal.

"They are seeking the death penalty," he explained. "I think there's a chance we can plea—ratchet these down to murder without premeditation or something—which would take the death penalty off the table. The prosecution has indicated they'd make a deal. Save everyone time and money. I think it is something to consider. And you have to realize the new DA, Fernandez, ran on the public platform that she is going to come down hard on violent crime—particularly violent crime against women."

Hasim was right.

The media had already elevated my case to an example of everything Fernandez was hired to confront. I think the DA's office was working overtime on my case alone just to assure the public that Fernandez wasn't messing around when she campaigned on the platform that it was time to clean house when it came to bigoted, sexist, violent crime. I was the poster boy for everything she had publicly vowed to go after.

But I declined the plea deal.

I wasn't guilty, and I wasn't going to give anyone—particularly my son—any reason to doubt me.

When it came time for our strategy, Hasim asked for little input. I think because he thought I'd done all of these terrible things. This wasn't going to be a trial filled with Perry Mason moments in which Hasim would pull a rabbit out of his hat. I think Hasim went into it with the sole goal of buffering me from as much damage as he possibly could, because, without a doubt, there was going to be a lot of damage.

Our defense would be simple.

"We'll cast doubt," he said. "All the evidence is circumstantial in regard to Mara, Fergus, and Zeb. We can cast doubt easily there."

I liked that part.

"Duncan and Kiki will be our main problem," he said. "We need a story, and we need to stick to it."

"Okay," I said.

So I told him the truth. Everything except why I took Kiki on that last drive down I-5. How would I ever explain that?

"The drive," I explained, "was because I was panicked. I was scared. I thought Kiki would be fine, but I knew it didn't look good, so I went to get my Stingray—it's way faster—and I thought I'd head to the border. I'd never killed someone before. I was scared. I was operating purely on instinct."

"Understandable," Hasim said, jotting down notes on his legal pad. "We can argue that you were panicked and weren't thinking clearly at the time."

"So you think there's a chance?" I asked. "A chance I'll get off?"

"You never know what those twelve people are going to think."

I didn't like his answer. It was very lawyer-like.

But his eyes conveyed what his words didn't.

Hasim didn't think I had a snowball's chance in hell.

2

The trial was excruciating.

The evidence against me looked terrible. Even the circumstantial evidence.

The forensic pathologist, Dr. Ryder Katz, a rather young and trim man, took the stand and fielded Dillian Flaherty's questions with ease. Flaherty, a tubby guy who always wore bright-colored bow ties in court, was the main prosecutor.

"Can you explain Fergus Hart's entry wound?" Flaherty asked.

Dr. Katz coughed into his hand and nodded. "The entry was in what is called the occipital region of the head."

"Just to make sure we're clear," Flaherty said, "the bullet entered where I'm pointing." Flaherty turned toward the jury and pointed a finger at the right side of his head, just behind his ear.

"Yes, that's accurate."

"And then it exited on the other side?" Flaherty moved to the left side of his own head and pointed a finger. "So the bullet traveled on an even plane, going right to left?"

"Yes."

"The bullet traveled from the right side of the head behind the ear to the front of the opposite side of the head?"

"Yes."

"And you've stated that the bullet traveled evenly and at a slight upward angle?"

"Yes."

"And this seems consistent with two individuals of relatively equal height, both standing next to each other when the shot occurred."

"It is consistent with that."

"And it's consistent with someone who must have been standing next to or slightly behind the victim? Perhaps even engaged in a scuffle?"

"Yes."

"Can you then explain what you have determined to be the manner of death?"

"I believe the manner to be homicide."

Flaherty sauntered back to his table, took two greedy gulps from a bottle of water, and turned his attention back to the witness. With his left hand, he adjusted his bow tie.

"Can you explain why you've reached the conclusion you have and not suicide?"

"The angle of entry seems inconsistent with a self-inflicted gun wound," Dr. Katz explained. He was sweating and dabbed his forehead with a Kleenex. "A self-inflicted gunshot wound would most likely be at the temple, the mouth, the forehead, and in very rare cases the submental or the parietal region."

"What percentage of self-inflected gun wounds occur in this occipital region?"

"Less than one percent," Katz said. "If that."

"Did anything else lead you to conclude homicide as the manner of death in this case?"

"The handedness of the victim."

"Can you explain?"

"Sure." Katz shifted in his seat. "In self-inflicted injuries like this, the dominant hand is usually used alone or as the lead hand. Assuming the victim used his dominant hand, which was the left, the wound should have been reversed. The bullet would have entered behind the left ear and exited the right side of the head."

"I see." Flaherty strolled back to his table. "Can you repeat to the jury what you believe the manner of death to be in this situation?"

Dr. Katz leaned forward into the microphone. "Homicide."

Hasim did his best to cast doubt, but it felt like a reach. He consulted his notes as he approached the stand. "What do you call the position the body is in when you perform an autopsy?"

Dr. Katz seemed confused by the question. "Um," he responded, "it's called the anatomic—otherwise known as supine—position."

"Okay. And this means the body is face up on the table?"

"Yes?"

"And this is the position the body is in when you measure things like bullet entry, bullet path, and exit?"

"Yes."

"And, of course, it is really impossible in this kind of situation to determine exactly what position the shooter and the deceased were in relation to each other?"

"Yes, I suppose that's true."

"All you can say is whether or not a certain set of facts and how people were positioned is consistent with your findings?"

"Yes, true."

"So, in other words, you really don't know exactly what happened and how it happened?"

Dr. Katz wiped more sweat from his forehead. "Well, as I mentioned earlier, we are simply looking for what is consistent with—"

"And it is possible that this was a self-inflicted gunshot wound?"

"Again, a self-inflicted gunshot wound in the occipital region of the head is highly unlikely. Coupled with the other findings, I believe the manner of death to be homicide."

"Can you please repeat your answer to my question again for the jury?"

Dr. Katz looked at the jury, then back at Hasim. "Sure," he said. "Which question?"

"Is it possible? Is less than one percent still in the realm of possibility as a self-inflicted wound?"

Dr. Katz hesitated.

Hasim asked the judge if he could approach the witness, and after he was granted permission, he stood there, consulting his notes. "Can you please answer the question? Is it possible?"

"High unlikely, but yes, I suppose."

Hasim eyed the jury and strode back to his seat.

"Nothing further."

3

It went equally badly in regard to Mara's death.

Her neighbor was called to the stand and claimed she had seen me sitting in my '69 Stingray after Mara had gone inside. I looked upset. I pounded my fists on the steering wheel. Hasim tried a series of objections that attacked her ability to "read the defendant's mind" and to "know what the defendant was thinking," and even though a few of the objections were sustained, I think the jury still got the gist.

Once again, I was the last one to see a murder victim, and we parted on a sour note.

Detective Grimm testified as well.

"So based on your investigation, what do you believe happened with Mara Phoenix?" the prosecutor asked.

"Very similar to Fergus," Grimm explained. "It appears there was some kind of struggle. Several boxes were knocked over in the garage. Several of her nails were broken."

"This time, did you find any fingerprints?"

"Yes, we did."

"Can you tell us if there was a match?"

"There most certainly was. The prints we lifted from some of the tape on those boxes were a match for Charlie Phoenix."

"I see."

Later, in cross-examination, Hasim didn't challenge this fact, but he did shed some light. I had helped pack, tape, and carry out those boxes when Mara left. Of course my fingerprints were on them. But I didn't think the jury was listening at that point.

My only hope, of course, was that Kiki's testimony would set me free.

But that dissolved the moment she took the stand.

Chapter Fifty-two

6.18 Liters of Fuel Remaining

1

"Can you please tell us what happened the day the defendant came to your apartment?" Flaherty asked. On this day he was wearing his typical dark suit but had opted for an orange bow tie. Totally obnoxious.

"From the beginning?" Kiki asked.

I hadn't seen her in a long time, and she had avoided eye contact with me when she was sworn in. She held a wad of tissues in her right hand. Her hair was shorter now, and she had bangs. Still youthful and beautiful.

"Yes," Flaherty said, "from the beginning."

"Okay." She swallowed. This appeared difficult for her. "I was at my apartment, and my boyfriend at the time, Duncan, came over in the evening. We got into an argument. It was a stupid argument, really. He thought Charlie's son, Adam, and I were having a fling or something. Adam and I still occasionally texted. So he got very upset and sent some messages to Adam, if I remember correctly. It took me a while to calm Duncan down."

"Okay," Flaherty said, "and then what?"

"Well, it was fine. I was really upset that it had turned into such a big deal, so I texted Charlie and asked him to come over. I wanted to talk to him, and I thought Duncan should talk to him too. I thought the three of us should just sit down and talk and work through all of these things like civilized people."

I had been doodling on a yellow notepad alongside my attorney. Now I looked up.

What was she talking about? This wasn't true. Duncan had taken her cell phone, impersonated her through a text, and lured me to the apartment.

"And then?" Flaherty prompted her.

"I'm sorry," Kiki said, wiping her wet eyes with the wad of tissue in her hands. Her voice trembled. "That's when Charlie came over and the attack happened."

2

"Can you walk us through everything step by step?" Flaherty asked.

"I'll try." Kiki paused, took a breath. "Charlie came over quickly. As I mentioned, Duncan thought it might be good if all three of us just had an adult discussion. The three of us had to talk."

Flaherty nodded.

"We invited him in and thought we could talk through this. Charlie was very, very jealous of me. Couldn't let me go. He was totally obsessed. And Duncan had his own issues. He wanted to apologize in person for contacting Charlie's son. But you have to understand that Charlie was really the jealous one."

"So Charlie was jealous?"

"Yes."

"Can you think of why?"

"Well, I think he had this delusion that I was pregnant. He insisted on it. Truthfully, I've never understood it."

"Objection!" Hasim rose from his desk. "The witness cannot read the defendant's thoughts."

"Overruled."

Flaherty continued. "Can you think of why he had this delusion?"

Kiki paused, seeming to genuinely contemplate. "No, sir. I can't."

"And you never were pregnant, correct?"

"Not that I know of."

"Very well, let's proceed with what happened."

Whenever I'd watched courtroom scenes in the past, I'd always seen the defendant sitting beside his attorney, taking notes. I always wondered what those people were writing. I knew that in my case I was writing down lots of expletives. All directed toward Kiki.

She had conned me. I should have known that medical bill she produced at Ubuntu was forged. It wasn't like I closely examined it. And that picture of her friend, Xavier, and his husband? Probably a Google search. I was sure of it.

And to think, she had lured me there to make amends, and I went home and wrote her a fat check.

Now, in all caps, I scrawled IDIOT on my yellow notepad.

That one wasn't directed toward Kiki.

That was for me.

3

"So, let's get back to that evening," Flaherty said. "What happened after Charlie arrived?"

"We all sat down in the living room and talked," Kiki explained. "Charlie corroborated my explanation that I wasn't messing around with Adam, Charlie's son, so that was cleared up quickly. Although by then Duncan knew he'd been paranoid to even suspect that. But again, Charlie was really the jealous one. He wanted me back, and he made it very clear. Charlie didn't think Duncan was good enough for me. It got very loud and escalated very quickly. Duncan tried to be reasonable, and after it was clear that nothing was going to be resolved, Charlie agreed to leave. He just asked if he could use the bathroom first. We said yes, of course, but instead of going into the bathroom, Charlie ducked into the bedroom. Maybe on his way to the bathroom he saw the bat lying next to the bed—I'm not entirely sure—but he picked it up and came into the living room."

"And why was there a bat in the bedroom?" Flaherty asked.

"Duncan could be a little paranoid at times. He always carried a bat in his car and always took it out when he stayed the night and put it near the bed." She paused and for the first time looked at me. "And he was worried about him—about Charlie. He thought he might try something rash, so he wanted protection."

"Objection! Hearsay!"

"Sustained."

"Fine," Flaherty said, "let me ask a different way. Did you want the bat in the room? Why was it important for you?"

"Because I was worried too. Charlie got really weird and paranoid in the end. I thought he might do something rash. I slept better at night, knowing Duncan was there next to me and the bat was there too."

4

"What happened when he came out of your room with a bat?" Flaherty asked.

"So much is a blur," Kiki said. "I remember he rushed at me and swung the bat. I ducked the first time, but the second time he hit me in the head. And honestly, I don't remember much after that. I was totally unconscious."

"Do you remember an altercation between Duncan and Charlie?" Flaherty asked.

"Like I said, I was pretty unconscious," Kiki explained. "I think I faintly remember hearing some kind of struggle going on the kitchen, but it's very drowned out."

"When do you remember waking up?"

"I started waking up when Charlie was taking me out of his Lexus and putting me in his Stingray. We were at his storage facility, I think. That's the first memories I have."

"What do you remember of it?"

"Not much," she said, "except that he said something about a guy named Zeb. He had gotten in the way earlier. Had to kill him. Said he was a lazy worker anyway, and he didn't need any witnesses. I wasn't doing well at that point, in and out of consciousness, but I was very scared."

"Did he say why he was putting you in another car?"

"Yes, he said we could get away faster. Get to Mexico faster. Start a new life. That kind of stuff."

"And during the drive down I-5, is that what he kept telling you?"

"Pretty much," Kiki explained. "Again, I was still slipping between consciousness and unconsciousness, but yeah, that's what he kept telling me. He was going to take me to Mexico, we could start a new life together, and if I didn't agree, then…"

She dabbed her eyes with those tissues.

"Can you finish your statement?"

"He said if I didn't agree, he'd put a knife in me the same way he put a knife in Duncan. She broke down in a fit of sobs. Gasping for air, she fanned herself and turned to the judge. "I'm sorry. Can I have a moment?"

5

The little hope that I had of being found innocent evaporated the moment Flaherty played the recording of my phone call with Detective Grimm.

I noticed several jury members leaning forward with interest as the audio played. Not a good sign. I knew that when a jury took notes, it wasn't good for the defendant.

At first, there was nothing but road noise.

And then my voice: "If you try to stop me, I'll kill her."

Flaherty played the recording three times. When he was done, he simply walked back to his table and took a seat.

A moment later, coughing, Hasim got halfway to his feet and asked, "Your Honor, I'd like to request a brief recess."

When it was granted, he sat back down and rubbed his temples.

6

Hasim did everything he could for cross-examination.

Kiki hadn't actually seen me murder Duncan, so it was impossible to know what really happened. It was possible, he asserted, that I attempted to leave the apartment, and Duncan pulled me back into the apartment to enact vengeance. If that were true, one could argue I was simply acting in self-defense. In the eyes of the law, perhaps I was guilty of attacking Kiki, but the evidence was simply inconclusive as to what happened with Duncan and where the responsibility fell.

"There is serious doubt here," Hasim said. "Plus, the toxicology report indicated Duncan had meth in his system."

The jury seemed unconvinced.

He also opened the door to the skeletons in Kiki's closet.

"You have check fraud on your record," he said while consulting one of the many documents on his table.

"Yes," she admitted. "That was a long time ago, and—"

"And you also have had some issues with credit," he explained, flipping to another page. "It seems that you have a problem with telling the truth and being honest, don't you?"

"Objection! Argumentative!" Flaherty called out while adjusting his bow tie.

"Sustained."

"Nothing further."

7

I was already prepared when the verdict was read. Hasim had instructed me that even if I was found guilty on any counts, there were many resources at his disposal. He would immediately file an appeal; in fact, he informed me, in a capital punishment case like this, an appeal was automatic.

I stood stoically as the verdicts were read.

Guilty of four counts of first-degree murder, attempted murder, and assault with a deadly weapon.

As the foreman read the verdicts, each *guilty* echoed through the room like a death knell.

A second, mini-trial was conducted for the penalty phase, using the same jury to determine whether or not I should be put to death.

My sister and my son were present at the sentencing. Trey never came to any of the court dates, and I hadn't spoken to any of them since I was arrested because I thought they believed I did it. During the sentencing phase, families of the victims were given a chance to speak and victim-impact statements were read, and almost all of them harangued me for being a cruel, cold monster who had needlessly taken the lives of their loved ones. Almost every one of them implored the justice system to evoke the death penalty.

Shockingly, it was only Shane Miller, Mara's long-time lover, who displayed any semblance of mercy.

"I do hope the court gives you leniency," he said as he read from his statement. "I think what you did to Mara—what you did to all of these others—is a terrible thing. I don't know if I'm capable of forgiving it, but I know that God is. We all make mistakes. Adam has one father, and that's you, and he's already lost his mother. It won't benefit anyone to go forward with this execution. So I plead with the court to give you mercy."

No wonder Mara fell for him. He had a depth of compassion that I didn't.

But there was no mercy.

I was sentenced to death.

8

The civil trial was stayed until after my conviction.

My hopes of overcoming that verdict were as fruitless as the criminal trial, and Kiki was awarded a massive sum for the emotional and physical trauma she had endured during my attack and my reckless drive down I-5. The money would help compensate her for the tragedy and the debilitating migraines the blow to the head had left her with.

During the civil trial, I learned that Kiki's last name had changed. She'd married some guy named Xavier and relocated to Baltimore.

No surprise there.

As I was informed in my prison cell that nearly everything I had worked for was being handed over to her, I couldn't help but think of Trey.

He had been right about her all along. Kiki was a master manipulator and a shrewd opportunist.

If only I had heeded his advice.

Chapter Fifty-three

4.63 Liters of Fuel Remaining

1

One day before my execution, two visitors came to see me.

I was informed that the first was my son, Adam, whom I hadn't talked to in nearly eight years. The second was a cousin, Herman. That one confused me. Herman? I didn't know any Herman, and I certainly didn't think I had a cousin by that name, but getting out of my cell and talking to another human being sounded far better than moping in the shadows and dreading what was going to occur later.

In handcuffs, I was led to the visitation room. I took a seat at the small booth with the plexiglass partition that separated me from the other side.

I waited, and then I saw Adam take a seat on the other side of the glass.

With both cuffed hands, I reached for the phone on my side of the wall. He did the same.

"Adam?"

"Yeah, Dad. It's me."

2

Adam looked like a young man now. The gangly, acne-pocked face of my teenage son was gone. It had been eight years.

"Wow," I said into the phone. "You look great."

He smiled but looked nervous. This was difficult for him. I hadn't seen him since my sentencing.

"So, your aunt wrote me. She says you're graduating Cal Poly this year?"

"Yeah."

"That's great, son! Music theory, huh?"

"Yeah, that's what I chose."

I wished I could have supported him more. Back when he was a teenager, I had dissuaded him from that major. I guessed the joke was on me.

"I'm glad you came to see me," I said. I hated that he had to see me sitting here, handcuffed and in this jumpsuit. But it was better than nothing. "You doing okay in your apartment up there? I hear it's right by campus."

"Yeah, me and Chuck are good."

"Chuck?"

He grinned and pressed a photograph against the glass. There was Chuck, sitting on a couch, and my son sitting next to him. No phones were allowed in the visitation room, so I assumed that was why he'd brought the photograph. This was clearly a recent picture. Adam looked his current age. But Chuck didn't look a day older than when I'd last seen him.

"You took Chuck with you to college?"

"Yeah," Adam said, "he kinda got attached to me."

"That's amazing." I was stunned. "He doesn't look a day older than when I left him."

"You must have fed him some good vitamins."

I laughed, but not at what my son thought I was laughing at.

It wasn't the vitamins.

All those nights in the car and those long drives really had supercharged the cat. And all the drives I'd taken with Kiki and that high-speed pursuit must have done the same to her—no wonder she didn't look a day older when I saw her in the courtroom.

3

"Where's the Stingray?" I asked.

I had never told him my theory about the Stingray, but I had told my sister, Donna, whom I appointed co-trustee of what was left of my estate after the civil trial. Long before I was accused of any crimes, I had set up my living trust so that, in the event of my death, Adam wouldn't get anything until he was twenty-five years old. I didn't want him to be a trust fund baby. I wanted him to get an education, finish college, and find some direction before he could reach into the coffers. Now that I was looking at him, I realized how young a kid is in his mid-twenties. I should have pushed that date back to thirty. Thirty-five, even.

Adam rolled his eyes. My sister had definitely conveyed to him what I believed about the Stingray.

"She put it away, right?" I asked. "I gave her explicit directions as co-trustee to put it away after the police got whatever evidence they needed out of it. Lock it up somewhere and throw away the key."

"I don't know, Dad. It's in some storage facility. She wanted to come see you today too, but—she just couldn't. I'm not sure what she plans to do with the car."

But he did. I could hear it in his voice.

"She's not giving it to you, is she?"

"I don't know," he said. "Considering what happened in it, I'm not sure I want it. But I have some debt, Dad— college loans. And I don't want to mooch off of Aunt Donna. That car is worth something. It's almost all that's left."

"Son, listen to me," I pleaded, leaning toward the glass. "Stay away from that car. Do you hear me?"

Adam sighed. "I came here because I thought maybe in your final hours you would be honest with me. I want to forgive you, Dad, I really do, but how can I forgive someone who wants to blame a car for what he did?"

"But," I said, faltering, "it's the truth."

Adam stuffed his photograph into his pocket, looked at me one last time, and nodded.

"Good luck, Dad," he said.

He got up, and an officer standing in the corner escorted him out of the room.

Chapter Fifty-four

3.09 Liters of Fuel Remaining

1

The next visitor was my supposed cousin, Herman.

The man who strolled into the visitation room was tall, strong, and wearing a pair of khaki pants and a red T-shirt. He took a seat across from me and picked up the phone. He had short, dirty-blond hair, a chiseled jaw, and a deep tan that conveyed he was a man who liked to spend time in the sun. I guesstimated his age to be somewhere in his mid-thirties.

"Hello, Charlie," he said.

The voice was familiar, and now I recognized him. The short hair had thrown me.

"Owen?" I asked. "Owen Menken?"

2

"No," he said. "It's me, your cousin. Herman."

Herman?

Impossible. This was definitely Owen Menken. He didn't have the Sammy Hagar locks and hadn't strolled in wearing flip-flops, Bermuda shorts, and smelling of salt and sea, but I knew that face. I couldn't imagine why he was here and what he wanted, but this was most positively him.

"Herman?" I questioned.

"Yep," he said. "I came to tell you the rest of my story."

"Your story?"

"Yes," he said. "You know, the story I wrote in college. The one you liked and always wanted to know the ending to. The one with the car that has the ability to heal people. It always frustrated you that I never told you the ending, so I thought there's no better time than now."

I sat back in the uncomfortable plastic chair I was anchored in.

He winked at me.

It was subtle, and I found myself nodding. I glanced at the officer in the corner. He was looking our way but seemed utterly uninterested in our conversation. Owen Menken—or whatever his name really was—was talking in code. It made sense. I had always assumed these conversations were recorded. If we were talking about an old story he wrote in college, who would care?

Actually, the more I thought about it, even if we talked about what had really happened, who would care? I was going to die tomorrow. They would chalk up whatever conversation we had to pure nonsense. Who would believe it?

So I played along.

"Oh yeah," I said. "I think I remember. Can you remind me of the story?"

"Sure thing," Herman said. "Good to see you, cousin. Let me start from the beginning."

3

"So, if you remember, in the story a guy named Tom Willow bought a '69 Stingray right off the lot," he said. "He was a young guy, thirty-four, and this was his dream car. He'd wanted one for so long and had finally saved enough money to buy one. And everything was great until he realized there was more to this vehicle than met the eye. The car was normal at first. It wasn't until it hit about 111,000 miles that it changed."

"111,268?" I still remembered that number like it was yesterday.

"Yep. You remember what it could do?"

"Yeah, it healed things. Made them better. Replenished."

"Bingo," he said, smiling. "See, you remember the story. Well, Tom Willow drove around in that vehicle for years and years and years, and he noticed something. Tom never aged. Not a day. The car was like a fountain of youth fueled by its V8 engine. So Tom realized he had to do something, because he wasn't looking any older, and it didn't fit. People were starting to ask questions. Do you remember what he had to do?"

"Change his identity," I said. "You—I mean, Tom—was the original owner."

"Bingo again," Herman said. "He had to change his identity several times to be consistent with his age. Plus, there was a problem with the car. It healed and replenished—but it did other things too. Things that weren't so pleasant. Do you remember that?"

"Oh yes," I said.

We didn't need to say what those unpleasant things were.

We just looked at each other.

Because we knew.

4

"So eventually," Herman continued, "Tom Willow realized this wasn't good. The car was a problem. He needed to get rid of it, but it was difficult to get rid of because to get rid of it was to let go of what it could do. So, if you remember the story, Tom Willow—who went by the name Owen at this point—eventually sold it to a guy named Richard."

"Yeah, that I remember too."

"Well, Richard got tired of it really quickly and felt guilty because of some of the things the Stingray did, so he sold it to another guy. Remember him?"

"A total sucker," I said.

Herman smiled. "You said it, not me. Anyway, afterward, Richard felt extremely guilty because he had passed on the burden to someone else. If there was more blood, it would be on his hands. So one night he tried to kill himself."

"Jumped off a bridge?"

"Yep. But miraculously he lived. And that was when he realized he must have lived for a reason. He even thought of going back to the man he'd sold the car to in hopes of warning him, but he worried that if he was near the Stingray—and if the Stingray felt threatened—he would be another of its victims. And Richard liked being dead on paper. He wanted to start a new life. So Richard went back to the original owner to ask him what to do."

"Tom Willow?"

"Well, yes, but it was Owen at that point."

"Gotcha."

"Owen actually felt bad too. You see, a day before Richard came to Owen, the third owner of the car, the sucker, found him in his coffee shop and wanted to talk to him about the car. Owen was scared. He didn't want to get involved. He wanted to be done with the car. But a day later, as Owen listened to Richard, he felt the same guilt overtake him. He had denied it before, pushed it away, but now he realized he had to do something. They both had to do something. So after taking a little time to think about it, they vowed to meet with the third owner, the sucker, and talk to him. To formulate a plan."

"That sounds right," I said. "They were going to meet on the end of a pier."

"Yep, they were," Herman said. "But the sucker never showed up. Unfortunately, he was a bit preoccupied."

5

It was a lot to digest.

I sat there, the phone in my hand, staring through the plexiglass, unable to say much of anything.

"In the story," I finally asked, "does the reader ever find out why the car became what it is?"

"Ah," Herman said, "good question. Well, I did a little research—uh, brainstorming—and I think we have one possible explanation. Based on a real-life situation, actually. You see, if you do some research, you'll discover there was a terrible accident at the Corvette production facility in St. Louis, Missouri. This was before Corvette officially moved its operations to the Bowling Green Assembly Plant in Kentucky in 1981. Anyway, this accident happened on November Twelfth, 1968. You can read about it in the papers yourself."

I pondered that date. "November Twelfth," I mused. Then it occurred to me: "Wait. The mileage. Eleven. Twelve. Sixty-eight. That matches the mileage."

Herman grinned. "I know. Maybe that's why the car's abilities started then. Maybe those numbers were important. And maybe *accident* isn't the right word—*suicide* is a better term. John Eads, a maintenance supervisor, allegedly killed himself. Took a bunch of pills and climbed into the front seat of one of the finished Stingrays one night."

"Really?"

"Yep. I guess there was no mess, so they decided to sell the car, but if you look into John's history, it's quite interesting."

"Okay. What was his history?"

"He did a couple of years in med school, got disillusioned, and went into manufacturing. He liked working more on machines, I guess, than people. Kinda interesting, isn't it? You have death and healing right there at the same time. It's a possibility that that's when it began." Herman looked over his shoulder at the officer in the corner of the room. "And there's more. During that same time, there was a string of murders. All up and down that area. You can read about them in the paper too. After John's suicide, they stopped. He was never convicted—never even suspected—but it kinda fits."

"Interesting," I said. "If what you're saying is true—or, at least, if that's how you write the story, then we basically have a classic ghost story. John, a failed med student and secret serial killer, inhabited the car with his spirt or something when he killed himself."

"Maybe." Owen shrugged.

"That could work," I said, "but maybe that's not how it began."

"What do you mean?"

"What if it started before that? What if John was the Stingray's first victim?"

6

"So why did you come today?"

"Everybody needs closure, cousin," he said. "I didn't want you to pass away without being reminded of the story. It's a good story, Charlie. I wanted to make sure you knew it and you knew the ending."

"I see," I said. "I'd rather be having this conversation at your coffee shop."

"Not sure what you mean. I don't own a coffee shop."

Of course not. That was his other alias, Owen Menken. I had no idea what Herman's occupation was.

"What do you do these days, Ow—Herman?"

"Me? Just a custodian. Nothing glamorous."

"Okay."

"But I have a great gig. It took me years to get where I wanted. Very reputable institution."

Funny. I had never thought of the job of custodian as being competitive in this way. Weren't all toilets, windows, and floors the same?

"Thanks for coming," I said, "but you never did tell me the ending. So what happens?"

"Oh, there's more to the story. You see, at this point, Tom Willow has had the opportunity to live a long time and to see a lot, and with that comes wisdom. More than anything, he feels terrible for the sucker, the third owner of the car. He'd do anything to help him and to find atonement. Really, Tom feels that everything that happened to the sucker was Tom's own fault."

"Interesting." I shrugged. "But I don't think Tom Willow is able to help the sucker at the end of the story. The third owner dies at the end."

Herman leaned toward the glass. He grinned knowingly.

"That's the thing, Charlie. What if that's not the end? What if there's more?"

Chapter Fifty-five

1.5 Liters of fuel remaining

I was given my special meal that evening, the night before the execution.

Everyone thinks the last meal is the big, special meal on death row, but that isn't true. Mine, like everyone else's I knew of, occurred the evening before.

I requested In N' Out and was brought a double-double animal style, an order of fries, a strawberry shake, and a large Coca-Cola. I remembered going to Laguna Beach with friends one day back in high school. We were in the sun all day, goofing around, and one of my buddies went and bought us some In N' Out.

I had sat on the beach in my trunks, with sand in my hair and in between my toes, eating that same meal. It was one of the best days of my life, and when I thought about what it was like to be young and free and careless, I always thought of that day and those tastes.

That was how I wanted to feel.

Young and free.

Prison had taken a lot from me. But it couldn't take my memories.

2

My state-appointed attorney met with me one last time.

He told me he was doing everything possible for a last-minute stay of execution. We had already been granted one stay several months ago, so the chances weren't great, but there was always a possibility that it could be granted. In many cases, he explained, such stays were granted hours and even minutes before the time of execution.

Ultimately, I think he wanted to give me hope. Even if it was very little.

"I have a question," I said.

"Sure." He looked fatigued. I was sure my case weighed on him. A man's life was at stake.

"What happens to my body, you know, after everything's done?"

"Uh," he said, rubbing the back of his neck. "Well—assuming we aren't granted a stay of execution—your body will be taken to the State Forensics Lab. From there, it will be released to family, which in your case"—he consulted one of his documents—"is your sister. It will be up to her to determine exactly how to proceed, but all of this, as we have already discussed, has been made known in your will."

"Yes, I understand."

"Is there anything else I can do for you?" Nelson asked.

"I don't think so," I said. "But I take back all the bad lawyer jokes I've made over the years. You've been helpful. I can see that. I repent of all my obnoxious one-line lawyer jokes."

He laughed, and it felt good to see a flash of light in such a well of darkness.

Billy was right. If you didn't see the humor in things, if you didn't pull toward the light, the world—and this prison—would break you down.

I wanted to be brave like him.

When I died and felt myself moving toward the light at the end of the tunnel, I wanted to be as brave as Billy.

3

I was taken to the Death House last night.

This was the place of execution, but the inmates referred to it as just that: the Death House.

I spent my last night under constant surveillance. They didn't want me to kill myself. They wanted to do it their way, and they wanted to do it right.

I didn't sleep a wink last night, and at 4:30 a.m. this morning I was informed that no stay of execution had been granted. No surprise there. I was given the opportunity to make any last phone calls that I wanted, but I declined the offer. I had nothing left to say.

I met with the chaplain, who sat across from me. He had large brown eyes that would have been easy to look into and repent of just about anything, but I didn't feel I had much to repent of. At least, not what the State thought I should repent of.

"Is there anything I can pray about for you?" the chaplain asked. "Anything you are seeking forgiveness for but do not yet feel at peace about?"

"Yes."

"Okay."

I folded my cuffed hands in front of me, looked at him. "I should have been more honest with myself about the death of my young son," I said. "I never grieved. My ex-wife never grieved. We ran in opposite directions. It was the worst thing I ever did."

"I understand."

"You know, I should be nervous, but I'm not. I don't know why, but I'm not. I can't wait to see my son again. I can't wait to see his face."

4

I was asked to take a shower and change into a new prison uniform before the execution.

I wasn't sure why, exactly.

I supposed the State wanted its victims freshly showered and nicely groomed. That's probably why they had me put on an adult-sized diaper once I was clean and smelling fresh. Less mess to clean up later on.

5

I am now strapped to a gurney.

Because of previous conversations with my attorney, I know what to expect.

Three drugs are going to be given to me, and an IV has already been placed in both of my arms, with one serving as a backup in case the other fails.

The first drug will sedate me.

The second will be a paralytic, vecuronium, which will paralyze the muscles in my body, including my diaphragm, which will make me unable to breathe.

The last drug, potassium chloride, will induce cardiac arrest.

I wait patiently. All is silent. I can't see through the one-way mirror on the wall, but I know that witnesses are watching me.

And then I feel it.

Slowly, I am pulled into dark, warm waters, and the world slips away.

I am down there, floating, waiting.

An anvil strikes the center of my chest.

This isn't supposed to be painful—but down here, it is—and as I dissolve and break apart into a thousand tiny pieces in the salty waters, a dark creature drifts over the sandy bottom.

EMPTY TANK

Chapter Fifty-six

0 Liters of Fuel Remaining

I wake up.

The last thing I can remember was being underwater, an agonizing pain in my chest, and I remember crumbling apart.

There was something in the waters below me. Something dark.

I don't know where I am.

I don't know where I've been.

I only know that I am here, and when I open my eyes, it is pitch black because something has been draped over me. I sit up and pull it off. It is a white sheet.

I am naked, lying on a steel gurney.

There is a tag tied to the toe of my left foot, and in black Sharpie, someone has written on it: PHOENIX, C. 10312.

"Where am I?" I mumble, and I climb off the gurney.

2

The floor is cold on my bare feet.

I stumble around in the darkness. There is only one small window built into the door of this room, and the only light in here is coming in through that window—fluorescent light emanating from the corridor beyond.

This is a small room, and there are other gurneys in here as well. I can see white sheets draped over the bodies. On a shelf, I see several tools. Scalpels. Scissors. Forceps.

Above the tools, on the wall, I see a large emblem for the OFFICE OF THE CHIEF MEDICAL EXAMINER. Two snakes surround a staff below the wings of Hermes, and the scales of justice hang from each wing.

"Justice," I mumble, and that's when I remember.

I was on another gurney. IVs were in my arm.

They were draining me, siphoning the life out of me.

But how can I be here? Driving around in the car so much must have done something permanent to me. It must have supercharged me in the same way that it supercharged Chuck.

Maybe there was a reason Richard Pratt survived that fall.

Maybe he couldn't die.

Suddenly, I hear the jingling of keys outside the door.

Somebody is trying to get in.

3

There is nowhere to run.

I stand there, naked, defenseless, until the door swings open and a man steps into the room with me.

He is wearing a blue custodian's uniform, a blue ball cap, and he's looking down.

He walks toward me, a massive set of keys dangling from his left hand.

"Who are you?" I ask, but before he looks up, I can read the name embroidered on the chest of his jumpsuit: HERMAN.

"Owen?" I gasp.

He looks up for the first time. It's him.

"Let's get you out of here," he says. He has come prepared. In his right hand, he has another folded uniform. Frantically, I get into it. I'm still barefoot and have a tag on my toe, but at least I'm clothed.

"Follow me," he says, and he races ahead of me down a long corridor with a light at the end.

I follow, my bare feet slapping against the marble floors.

Running down this corridor toward a light reminds me of what it was like to die. It was more painful than I thought it would be, and equally frightening.

They tried to take my life.

They took me below E.

But now I am here, replenished.

FULL TANK

75.70 Liters of Fuel Remaining

Special Thanks

I had lots of help with this one. No book is written in total isolation, and this was no exception.

Thanks again to the two "dads" in my life who understand cars, engines, and Corvettes far more than I do. My father-in-law often jokes with me that I'm not the most "handy" of guys, but my comeback is always the same: *You can fix cars, yes, but can you write poetry?*

Thanks also to my brother-in-law, Jon, whose love and understanding of Vettes helped with this; if it weren't for that night at the firepit with you talking about this story, the ending here would have been totally different (and not nearly as good, I think). Cheers!

Thanks to Steve Tomory for your thoughtful reading, automotive expertise, and advice.

Thanks also to Richard Ramirez for helping me get some of the investigative and courtroom elements right. If I got anything wrong—automotive or legal—blame me.

Thanks to my wife and my parents, my first readers, along with my editor, Jessica Barnes.

And lastly, thanks to Marcos Mercado, for reading the final version of this manuscript to make sure the chrome was the polished and everything was waxed to a shine.